W9-AVL-707

Fishing for Trouble

Fishing for Trouble

Elizabeth Logan

THORNDIKE PRESS
A part of Gale, a Cengage Company

An Alaskan Diner Mystery #2.
Thorndike Press, a part of Gale, a Cengage Company.

Thorndike Press® Large Print Clean Reads.
The text of this Large Print edition is unabridged.
Other aspects of the book may vary from the original edition.
Set in 16 pt. Plantin.

LIBRARY OF CONGRESS CIP DATA ON FILE.
CATALOGUING IN PUBLICATION FOR THIS BOOK
IS AVAILABLE FROM THE LIBRARY OF CONGRESS.

ISBN-13: 978-1-4328-8844-2 (hardcover alk. paper)

Published in 2021 by arrangement with Berkley, an imprint of Penguin Publishing Group, a division of Penguin Random House LLC.

Printed in Mexico
Print Number: 01 Print Year: 2021

For Dick

ONE

When an ambulance pulls up to the doors of a diner, it's never a good sign.

Such an occasion is bad for the person headed for the gurney and bad for the diner's owner. The owner would be me, Charlotte Cooke, aka Charlie, on the wrong side of thirty and owner of the Bear Claw, the finest and only diner in Elkview, Alaska.

I was proud of our new entrées and the constant refrain of "Best mooseloaf I've ever had," from natives and tourists alike. And our new "snack pack" for diners on their way to Fairbanks to immerse themselves in the northern lights was a big hit, especially since we'd added our new spicy elk jerky to the mix.

But it was our supine customer, not our tasty menu, that was in the spotlight this cloudy summer afternoon with its rare threat of rain. Some of my lunch patrons had poured into the parking lot, joined by passersby, attracted by the dizzying strobe effect of spinning lights on the Matanuska-Susitna Borough ambulance.

The paramedics had moved the patient to the back of the diner, where there was a small hallway with more elbow room than there was between the booths and stools.

I stood in the doorway leading from the hallway to the back parking lot and surveyed the scene. Had it really been necessary for the enormous fire truck to pull up across the street? Was there even a building in Elkview tall enough to require the polished white ladder stretched along the engine's body? Maybe the truck had simply been in the neighborhood? Similarly for the patrol car of the Alaska State Troopers, the cartoonish bear on its door giving the lie to the seriousness of the situation.

It occurred to me that my close connection to Trooper Cody Graham, simply "Trooper" to his friends, had expedited the response to the nine-one-one calls my diners made when a young man had toppled over onto the table in his booth.

I was close enough to hear the chatter among the diners crowded in the aisle.

"Such a shame," repeated more than once.

"He's just a boy," from anyone with a touch of gray.

"I saw him come in with that group of fishermen."

"They were too young to be fishermen."

"Maybe he had an allergic reaction."

"I think they worked in that fish processing plant across the river."

"J and M?"

"Did he choke on something?"

"J and M. That's the one. A small local company."

"They didn't even have food yet in that booth, so he couldn't have choked."

"What did he order?" A popular question, asked by a number of diners who clutched their stomachs waiting for a response.

"What does it matter? It hadn't come yet."

"Even so."

I winced at that and other snippets — mercifully few — that included the dreaded suggestions of food poisoning as the cause of the man's misfortune.

The comment "I think he said, 'I'll take the special' " had me drawing in my breath every time I heard it.

Sighs of relief followed from those who did not order the special of the day — grilled king salmon with mustard sauce and a choice of rice or a mixed greens salad — and groans from those who did. I wrapped my arms around my body to hold a shudder at bay as I waited for another victim to fall over, grateful for every minute that passed free of new drama.

No amount of questioning or supposition was acknowledged by the EMTs. Their carefully choreographed, coded movements inspired confidence as they stripped away layers of clothing and worked on the man's torso. The patient was perfectly still, his countenance almost serene, his dark hair neatly in place, as if he'd brushed it when he'd heard cries of "Nine-one-one?" and "Hurry" all around him.

All I knew for sure was that the poor young man was not responding to their efforts, and I was left wondering what part, if any, the Bear Claw kitchen had played in the man's distress. I listened for signs that a simple antacid would be the solution to this disruption. Instead I was pushed aside by a hefty woman in a uniform and purple rubber gloves as the medical group loaded the young man onto a gurney and wheeled him out to the ambulance. It didn't help that it was now pouring rain.

"What happened to him?" and "Will he be okay?" from me and others drew no response from the professionals.

The Bear Claw had been at capacity, fifty-plus patrons seated in our retro red vinyl booths and on stools. Many of the diners wore name tags, marking them as members of a bus tour that had originated in Anchorage, about a hundred miles to the south. The crowd was on its way to Denali National Park, where, June or no June, the mountains would be covered in snow. It had been a coup for the Bear Claw to earn a spot as one of the tour's regular stops.

At least until today.

What to do now? Mentally crossing my fingers was my only recourse to hope for the patient's quick recovery.

I was amazed at how many onlookers held their cell phones high, taking pictures of the action. I cringed as the patient's right to privacy was being violated. The EMTs were situated around him. Whether it was deliberate on their part or not, their positioning ensured that no one could catch an image of the young man's face.

I noticed an additional group of onlookers across the street, in the doorways of stores and hanging out of second-floor windows. Usually the sound of loud sirens indicated that a grizzly bear had been sighted wandering the neighborhood. The sirens would be accompanied by a police or volunteer car with lights flashing and someone on a mic bellowing, "Bear sighted. Everyone stay indoors."

Though it was clear that no bear was visiting, the crowd hung around. Was it otherwise that boring in Elkview? I had to admit the answer was *yes,* compared to my former life in San Francisco, where I'd been a chef at a four-star restaurant before returning home to Alaska. I wasn't thrilled at the idea that the Bear Claw was providing the best entertainment in town on a Wednesday afternoon. Or, worse, that someone's video would end up on social media for all the world to see. Not the kind of publicity I wanted.

Of all times for the previous owner of the Bear Claw, Evelyn Cooke, my mom, to be away. She'd have known what to do to get all the diners safely back to their seats. It took all my courage to resist texting her. But what could she do from San Diego, California, more than three thousand miles away? And didn't she deserve a vacation, given that her Danube River cruise in the spring had been cut short? She and my dad were now taking a shorter do-over trip, though he'd stayed to finish the business part of the first trip at European ports, as evidenced by postcards from Amsterdam, Cologne, Würzburg, Nuremberg. I doubted he'd immersed himself in the thermal baths of Budapest, since that card said simply, "Wish you were here." Right now I wished both he and Mom were here in Elkview.

Earlier in the afternoon, I'd taken a leisurely stroll through my kitchen, admiring the smooth workings of my staff, led by my chef, Victor Fiore. Since taking over three months ago, he'd made significant changes to the Bear Claw's menu. Even some of our regulars took delight in Victor's "culinary experiments," as he called them. Like a special grilled cheese sandwich with an added layer of shepherd's pie. Or his spaghetti made of arugula and served with cheese, a kids' delight as long as no one revealed the healthy ingredients.

A dessert fan myself, I'd been snacking on a strawberry dipped in white chocolate when I heard the loud calls for nine-one-one.

I made my way now to the diners who'd waited outside, huddling under the overhang, the better to see the ambulance screech its way to the nearest medical center. Smells from our menu wafted out of the Bear Claw's open doors, clashing with that of petroleum jelly and other persistent odors from the ambulance. I'd done my best to assure my diners that all was well, that the emergency was being handled by experts, and that my staff and I were still available to meet their needs. And, by the way, coffee, tea, and all desserts — pies and cakes alike — were on the house.

Today's tour guide, a middle-aged brunette whose name tag read JO DAVIDSON, had stepped up and made sure her charges were calmed down and even offered to warm up or replace meals that had become less appetizing for the wait.

Jo and I had a somewhat cool relationship, since she'd made it clear when we first met that she'd have preferred what she called a "real restaurant" for her tourists. I was pleased when she admitted that not one of her clients had ever complained about the food or service at the Bear Claw. Rather, we had both heard the opposite: that classic American diner food and ambience were a treat on any tour.

My mom had tried to place our diner fare somewhere between the stale coffee and kitschy posters of old and the haute cuisine that marked some modern restaurants. I hoped today's upset wouldn't change that, any more than Victor's experiments in diverse special recipes had.

The glow from the bright bars and strobes that had brightened up the area around the

Bear Claw was slowly abating. If I never saw that vehicle or one like it again, it would be fine with me.

Nina Fiore, Victor's sister and my treasured waitress, pulled me back inside the diner and steered me toward the people our patient had been sitting with. My flitting back and forth inside and outside the diner and the hallway in between had made me dizzy, the perfect word for my mental state also.

"The guy in the ambulance? His name is Ethan Johnson," Nina told me, adjusting an apron around her tiny waist. It didn't escape my notice that she always folded it to hide the silly Bear Claw logo. I didn't blame her. Mom had suffered a lapse in judgment when she ordered the aprons, pot holders, and other supplies adorned with the grinning bear. I didn't have the nerve to get rid of them until she was truly retired or the linens were stained and torn beyond repair, whichever came first.

"Ethan was a college student working in fish processing for the summer," Nina continued. "I guess you can earn an awful lot. Like, up to fifty thousand dollars just in the three summer months." She stopped for a deep sigh, no doubt doing a little arithmetic comparison with her Bear Claw wages.

If Nina was angling for a raise, she'd have to wait. Right now I was anxious to learn more about how Ethan's emergency had come about.

We walked toward the booth where Ethan's companions were assembled. "Did you serve his booth?" I asked Nina.

She nodded *yes.* "They were saying how they were looking forward to getting away from dormitory food. Not college dorms, but the dorms out at the processing plant."

"Had they been in the diner long?"

"No, they didn't even get served yet. They went outside until the ambulance left and now they're back. His friends are Garrett and Kevin. Garrett's the one with his hand all bandaged up. They're all juniors or seniors at some small college in Oregon, but they didn't know each other until they got the jobs here. They work at the processing plant, as I mentioned. It's just a small one up near Talkeetna, but it's a branch of a big plant with headquarters in San Francisco."

"You know a lot about this company?"

Nina sucked in her breath, as if to say, *Busted.* Instead she mumbled, "I might have looked into them at one point."

"How about the young woman in the

booth with the guys?"

"I don't know her name, but she's in the worst shape, so I'm guessing she knew Ethan before." Nina took a breath. Then, "Can you imagine fifty thousand dollars on summer vacation?"

I smiled. "Certainly not," I said, figuring the message got through.

"Of course, that's probably for the rougher jobs, like working on the boats hauling the catch, and not some of the less skilled jobs in the plants, like all the sorting, cutting, and cleaning up. But still."

"The booth, Nina?" With a customer in an ambulance, I needed to move on from salary talk. Nina deserved a raise and would soon receive one, though not at the scale she coveted.

Despite a slight frown, Nina remained the ever-gracious hostess and introduced me to Ethan's friends as I joined them in their booth.

"Ethan was here for the summer, working, like us," said the teary young woman in a long denim skirt. A girlfriend? Or just a sensitive companion? She looked frail to me, but that might have been due to her hunched-over posture and the helpless expression on her face, as well as an oversize parka.

I learned that even before their meals arrived, Ethan had let out a loud croak (said Garrett), then grabbed hold of his throat (said Kevin, who demonstrated the movement). The two young men, each sporting contemporary stubble, seemed more surprised than upset at the incident.

"Then he just crumpled," the woman said, turning to me. "Do you think it's a bad sign that they took him away?"

I wished I knew. I settled for a lame "He's in good hands."

"I wouldn't say 'crumpled.' More like 'jerked,' " Garrett said. A quick jerk of his own head sent long blond hair whipping around his neck. "In fact, he had a kind of spasm and fell on Zoe. Right, Zoe?"

Zoe squinted, as if blocking her eyes from a bad memory. "I was so scared. He hugged me. It was like he didn't want to let go of me." Each word got softer than the one before, and I hesitated to ask her anything more.

I noticed the bandage Nina had mentioned during our walk-and-talk briefing, a significant one on Garrett's left hand, as if he'd also used the neighborhood's medical services, though short of needing an ambulance.

"After that, he fell with his head on the

table," Kevin said, slumping, then throwing his well-built shoulders back, for all to see.

Since Ethan hadn't received any Bear Claw food, I was satisfied that his distress had been brought on by something other than today's special. "Did he say anything?" I asked.

"I think I heard 'harbor,' " Garrett said. "Like it had to do with fishing, which makes sense, considering where we are this summer."

"I thought I heard 'archer,' " Kevin said. "Like bow-and-arrow stuff. Or it could have been 'arcing.' Like an electric arc. I sort of remember something like that in physics, but I couldn't tell you what it means right now."

"How about you, Zoe? What do you think he said?" Garrett asked. "You were the closest to him."

Zoe shook her head and shrugged, signaling she hadn't heard what Ethan said — or didn't want to remember. She busied her hands trying to find a dry spot on a well-used tissue. When I pulled out a small packet of tissues and handed it to her, she gave me a look as grateful as if it were concert tickets to the hottest band of her generation. I had no idea who that might be. Did ten or twelve years make a generation these days?

Zoe stood up suddenly, zipping up her parka. "Why are we sitting here? I want to go to wherever they took Ethan."

"There's nothing we can do," Kevin said.

"Kevin's right," Garrett added. "We'll find out when they know something. And don't forget that's my parka you're wearing."

Both men laughed. I chose to interpret it as nervous laughter rather than thoughtlessness over the misfortune of their coworker.

"Who dry-cleans a parka?" Kevin asked.

Both men answered: "A girl," from Garrett; and "Zoe Michaels," from Kevin, who added, "Probably the only pink one in the state."

Zoe fell back on the seat, not the least bit amused, though I suspected the guys were trying to lift her spirits as well as ease their own nervous tension. Her tears started again, though she held back any sounds.

I put my hand on her shoulder. "I'll drive you," I said. "Let's go see Ethan."

Two

Victor and the staff gave me their assurance — "Hey, no prob," to be exact — that they'd be fine taking over and would make sure the tour group had snacks for the bus ride to their next stop. The insulated container — with our logo, of course — held Victor's special elk jerky, hard-boiled eggs, a host of nuts and seeds, and a dash of chocolate. I was especially solicitous of these tourists since they'd been guests at the inn down the road, which belonged to my BFF, Annie Jensen. Like me, Annie had inherited her family's business and counted on tourism for success. Now that I was back in town, we'd renewed old customs that we'd had as schoolgirl friends, like black-and-white movie night.

I figured Ethan was not a guest at Jensen's Elkview Inn, since most of the summer help for the fishing industry stayed at dorms operated by the company. They dined at the

Bear Claw rarely, sticking instead to the food provided by their employers, in keeping with saving as much money as possible. I knew that at some point, depending on Ethan's diagnosis, I'd have to address any role our kitchen might have played in his attack. I told Victor as much.

"Be ready for a briefing when I get back," I said, earning a salute and a smile from him. As my mom had commented when she met Victor the first time, he was at the fun age, somewhere in the not-yet-thirty range.

I stepped into the shadows of my diner hallway and allowed myself a quick visit via my smartphone with my tabby, Benny, short for Eggs Benedict. Benny came with the diner, in a way, although he'd never stepped a paw into it. He was my mom's until she retired — though she was still on call, more exactly — and handed the diner over to me.

"You're going to need someone to come home to after long workdays," she'd said, only the vaguest of references to my failed engagement to a San Francisco lawyer.

Which was why she wasn't thrilled when I set up a remote care and feeding system for Benny.

"What's the point of having this beautiful cat?" she asked, with understandable reservations about petting via a phone app.

I didn't use the app all the time, of course, and it worked for Benny and me. Benny didn't have the opportunity to bring me presents, like the chipmunks and other tasty creatures outdoor cats could deliver, but we were tuned in to each other all the same. We were in sync enough for me to know Benny was okay with the automatic feeder I'd bought him, which guaranteed he'd have plenty of food even if I had to work late, and the exercise he needed, through our laser dot program and other games.

I checked on him now, hoping he'd be in camera range, and would also hear the sound of my voice. He was there, purring his understanding of my predicament. Actually, Ethan's predicament, but I felt responsible to help in any way I could. The most immediate help I knew of was to take Zoe to see him.

I met her in the parking lot, the rain down to only a trickle. She seemed to feel better now that she was on her way to check on her friend.

"Thanks so much for doing this, Ms. . . . ?" she said, reminding me of my age, relative to that of a college girl.

"It's just 'Charlie,' " I said, at the same time resolving to do something with my too-long hair — something more than simply keeping it out of my eyes.

Zoe pulled an obviously hand-knit cap over long brown hair. The hat, blue and gold striped, was probably pure comfort clothing, since the temperature hovered around the mid-sixties, warm for Alaskans.

"They wouldn't let me go with him in the ambulance," she said in a soft voice.

"I'm sure it's some kind of regulation."

"Still. He's all alone there."

"It won't take long before we'll be with him."

I hoped I sounded reassuringly cool.

I hesitated to pry into the relationship between Zoe and Ethan, but I didn't need to. Zoe was forthcoming on her own, becoming energetic and talkative as soon as we buckled into my car.

"We just met a month ago, but it was like we've known each other forever, if you know what I mean?" she said.

I did, but I chose not to tell Zoe how badly that scenario had ended for me. I'd been engaged to a lawyer, a man I'd also felt I'd known forever, but apparently didn't know at all. I couldn't have predicted that Ryan would drop me when one of his young paralegals caught his eye. Since then, I'd managed to protect myself from falling for that again.

I knew by now that people deal with grief in different ways, some withdrawing into silence, others pouring out nervous chatter. For now, Zoe chose the latter.

"This is my first summer in Alaska, but Ethan took a year off. He's from Boston and has this accent that's so funny. He works on the boats, plus in the processing plants, so he taught me a lot, and he even works in the office sometimes. He says he wants to learn all aspects of the fishing industry." She paused and I could tell she was trying to hold back tears. "He's very smart."

"What's your job this summer, Zoe?" A diversion that seemed to work.

"Oh, just entry level. I do whatever they tell me, like hosing down the production line. Sometimes I'm in the freezer." Zoe shivered and pulled her parka tighter around her, as best she could through the seat belt. "Sometimes I'm on the dock, moving pallets around." She grimaced as if she were doing heavy lifting on the spot in my car. "Next year I'd like to do more and learn more about actually fishing." She laughed lightly. "I didn't even know what seining was, and that's so important. I thought you just dropped a net into the water and scooped up the fish, but the whole thing is so much more complicated."

"I've never done it," I admitted. "But I've watched them prepare that netting, with the anchors and all."

"And lay it out geometrically, in a circle, and be sure there's no way for the fish to slip under. It's amazing."

Once we'd exhausted the intricacies of seining, Zoe let loose with a bevy of statistics about the fishing industry in Alaska. Statewide annual harvests of more than one hundred million salmon. More than a trillion pounds if you counted all salmon species. Similar numbers for herring, halibut, octopus, and scallops.

"J and M taught us a lot about what goes on up here," Zoe said. "In the orientation they give everyone."

I assumed she meant Alaska by "up here," a general term used by many in the lower forty-eight. Zoe translated the data into monetary value and employment profiles, revealing how closely she'd read the *Fishing in Alaska* pamphlets around town. I was happy to hear these figures, though few were news to me, thanks to my summer break stints working at visitors' centers for the area's parks. Anything to keep Zoe from imagining what might be going on with

Ethan was a plus.

It was too bad Zoe couldn't have simply enjoyed the breathtaking landscape as we drove north from Elkview toward Talkeetna and Denali. I never tired of the drive, with the mountains' majestic peaks and thick woods following us all the way. I hoped the drive back would be less stressful, celebrating Ethan's recovery.

At the sight of the medical building, Zoe let out a groan. She'd gathered her hair into a ponytail, making her look even younger than a typical college sophomore.

"That's pretty small," she said, close to a wail. "It's not even a hospital."

I could see how Zoe might be disappointed in the rambling two-story clapboard building that looked more like a temporary first-aid setup. I wished Ethan had been taken a few more miles to the new emergency medical facility in Talkeetna.

But I knew that the staff on the outskirts of Elkview was as competent and as dedicated as any at whatever more imposing facility Zoe was used to elsewhere. So what if there would be many fewer attendants?

I pulled into a parking space just before two o'clock in the afternoon. But I felt the fatigue of a full day's work, as well as sympathy for Zoe, or I might have been tempted to defend our borough's medical resources. Instead I decided we'd simply enter the building and she could see the professionals for herself.

As we prepared to exit my Outback, a car pulled into the slot next to mine. A tall, handsome man got out. Too bad he was old enough to be my father. Too bad he was State Trooper Cody Graham. Not that I didn't love the man, one of my parents' oldest friends, the honorary uncle who'd helped me with my homework all through grade school. But he and I had a different take on my tendency to get involved in problems that (he claimed) belonged in the realm of law enforcement. Sometimes I had to remind the trooper that I'd had a whole year of law school.

"Imagine seeing you here," he said, a familiar grin overtaking his face.

I was about to answer when Zoe stepped forward.

"My friend Ethan is here," she said, "and Ms. — and Charlie offered to bring me to see him."

"Did she, now?"

I wondered how Zoe knew that I'd need a defense to justify being here. Apparently our expressions, Trooper's and mine, were all too revealing. Trooper was bound to be wary of my presence at the medical center and what could seem like meddling.

"Let's all go in, then, shall we?" Trooper said.

But I knew it wouldn't be that easy.

In fact, even though he held the door for Zoe and me, he managed to get to the nurse's desk before we did. He also made a gracious gesture that sent us to a row of seats against the wall. Disappointingly old, weather-beaten seats of an indeterminate color, I noted, suddenly aware of the inadequacies of the facility.

It was a busy time, and Zoe and I were lucky to find two seats next to each other. Several of those waiting wore braces or casts. I felt sorry for a child on the smallest crutches I'd ever seen. She smiled at me and I smiled back, wishing I had a lollipop to give her. At least she sported a fantastic, colorful array of cartoon characters on her leg cast.

Trooper made sure his body was between the reception desk and us, and that his voice would be heard only by the woman I recognized as a regular Bear Claw patron on weekends. I strained to read her nameplate — NANCY SAMPSON — for future reference. Meaning for when Trooper wasn't patrolling.

After a few minutes, Trooper headed for the double EMPLOYEES ONLY doors leading to the patient area, without so much as a word or a nod to us. Zoe and I rose to approach the desk and the nurse gave us an oh-so-subtle but immediate shake of her head. I took Zoe's hand and sat us down again.

The time passed slowly. Zoe got up often, paced, stared at the photos and signs on the dingy walls. NO SMOKING. NO PETS. QUIET PLEASE. When she stood before a set of photos that depicted the original facility construction, I was sure it wasn't due to intense interest in the history of the center, but rather because she needed a spot to space out.

I stepped into the small vending machine area and took a call from tour group leader Jo Davidson. She asked after Ethan and wanted to check with me before she took her charges back on the road.

"I convinced most of them that splattering pictures all over social media wasn't the appropriate response to a fellow diner's misfortune," she said. "Not that I threatened them, but they realize it's never a good idea to annoy your tour guide."

"Thanks for that. And for pitching in. I know it was tense there for a while."

"No problem. It's not my first rodeo," she assured me, laughing as if it were the first time either of us had heard the line.

I was starting to like her. It wasn't everyone who could control amateur paparazzi when surrounded by emergency vehicles. I was sorry we'd gotten off to a bad start last year and resolved to turn that around when she and her busload from the lower forty-eight stopped at the Bear Claw on their return.

I kept myself busy on and off reading a paperback mystery I'd stuffed in my tote, an Agatha Christie my mom had given me in an attempt to draw me into her crime fiction addiction. I had trouble focusing, however, distracted by those coming and going in front of us and by the sounds of chatter and of people body-slamming the unruly vending machines.

Our seatmates on the waiting side of the lobby were in various states of sleep or stress. I couldn't imagine a resting posture that involved leaning my head against the wall behind me, but one man in work clothes and an elaborate hand brace did just that, the occasional barking snore coming from his respiratory system.

Although I was counting on Victor or Nina to text me if there was more trouble at the Bear Claw, I held my breath each time the ambulance squawked and howled its way to the entrance here at the medical center until I was sure it wasn't another of my dining patrons on the gurney.

When Trooper finally came out of the patient area, he was accompanied by a middle-aged man in a white coat.

I stood and took Zoe's arm as the men walked toward us.

Their faces gave us the news.

I caught Zoe as she slumped, nearly missing the chair she'd been sitting on.

THREE

Medical center rules forbade any nonrelative to visit Ethan in the basement morgue. I knew he'd be there only a short while before being transported to the nearest full hospital in Anchorage for a complete evaluation. I was lucky that my pleas to Nancy at the desk paid off. I pointed out that Zoe could be a shortcut for contact with Ethan's parents in Boston and other information that might be needed for his admittedly thin file. The result was a declaration of an extenuating circumstance, and Zoe was allowed five minutes with her deceased friend.

Trooper got to accompany her. While I waited on the other side of the double doors, the press arrived, in the form of the one and only reporter from the *Elkview Bugle:* Chris Doucette, tall, rugged looking, and cosmetically bald.

Chris and I had known each other casually in high school and more recently as coinvestigators on a murder case. Some days there was a spark between us, other days just a friendly "Hey, how's it going?" My mom was rooting for more sparks, and an outright flame, but I'd experienced that with Ryan. I was wary — once burned, I shied away from flames.

Today's greeting was in the casual category, since Chris was at the medical center for news, not for me personally. I figured I was his best, closest source, after Zoe. Therefore, I felt it my duty to protect Zoe from him. She needed comforting now, not grilling. The news-hungry *Bugle* readers could wait at least twenty-four hours.

"What's up?" Chris asked, taking what was formerly Zoe's seat. I'd moved her parka — more correctly, Ethan's friend Garrett's parka — and held it on my lap. Chris pointed to the vending machine area, where, besides candy and crackers, there was also a coffee machine. Two tables and their accompanying chairs earned it a "cafeteria" designation. "Can I buy you a cup of coffee?"

I made a face. Chris knew what I thought of institutional coffee. "We can chat here," I said. Read: *Don't think of this as a private interview, where secrets will be revealed and a reporter will get a scoop.* Situations like this were always awkward because of our poorly defined relationship. Colleagues? Friends? Potential dating material? There was a good deal of overlap.

I couldn't be sure if Chris knew that Ethan had died, but decided he probably did. He wouldn't be here to say *hey* to me or to ask after the well-being of a diner patron if he thought said patron had simply suffered an allergic reaction to our spicy mustard.

The doors to the patient area opened, and this time it was Trooper and Zoe who appeared, having come from the morgue that housed Ethan's body.

I jumped up. "Zoe," I said, loudly and forcefully. "Finally. We're going to be very late." I threw the parka around her tiny shoulders and marched her toward the exit and my car. Fortunately, as I'd predicted, Zoe was too overcome by what she'd seen in the morgue to question me.

As we pushed through the doors to the parking lot, I turned slightly and caught Trooper's knowing grin and Chris's look of defeat.

"Of course," my mom said when I asked if Zoe could stay at my parents' home.

I wasn't ready to give her the particulars,

and she didn't question me. Instead she regaled me with details of her trip. The museum with its collection of Spanish devotional art for her, and the more than nine-hundred-foot-long aircraft carrier USS *Midway* for my dad. I promised to call her later with a full explanation of the reason for her houseguest.

I tried to sound casual when I added that of course she didn't need to come home. Everything was being handled. I simply wanted to offer their home as comfort to a young woman who needed it.

"Just for the night," I said.

"I get it. At least it won't be the first place everyone will look for her."

Mom had always been a quick study.

I'd considered asking Annie for a room for Zoe at her inn, but I knew she had another tour group moving in. Plus, she'd intimated that there might be a special problem with a guest who'd be arriving tomorrow. The guest's son had called her and left a troubling message. Like Ethan and his friends, her son was a college student working in the fishing industry for the summer. The guest called the plant supervisor, who claimed the young man had not returned from lunch, wasn't sick in the dorms, and hadn't given notice.

Annie didn't know the content of the son's message, but there was no way to stop my brain from thinking that there was something fishy going on in the industry, specifically at the processing plant where Ethan and his friends worked. But I had enough to worry about without developing conspiracy theories around people I'd never met. On the other hand, a parent from the lower forty-eight didn't just jump on a plane to Alaska over a simple "I'll be going camping and will be out of touch for a couple of days, Mom."

Thinking of fish and fishiness brought me back to Benny, among whose favorite foods were salmon and tuna. I'd had only one contact with him since this terrible drama began at the diner. Once I got Zoe settled, I told myself, I'd spend some quality time with my cat. For me more than for him. I needed to hold him, listen to his purring, to calm my nerves. Then maybe a little playtime with him.

I'd bought Benny a new *thing,* part toy, part treat container. The vendor's pitch called it "an interactive box to stimulate your cat's mind." Various sizes of toys and treats could be put into compartments carved out of the box. Benny would then have to sniff out the box and locate the rewards. I was eager to try it out, though in truth, Benny would probably have more fun playing with and lying on top of the container the product was delivered in. I realized that buying a box for a cat seemed silly in the extreme, since any old box would do when they needed one. But this was Benny — nothing but a new box, with his name on it, would do.

I'd texted Victor that I'd be back to the diner around six this evening. I asked that he gather whatever part-time staff he could for a briefing at that time, though it was doubtful I'd have more information by then as to what killed Ethan Johnson. I needed to keep my employees fully aware of the status of any investigation, lest they be drawn into rumors that were sure to circulate and alarm them. I planned to close the diner until tomorrow morning, then open it in time to have breakfast ready for Annie's new touring guests.

I let Zoe and myself into my parents' home — my home for the first eighteen years of my life. This four-bedroom house of my childhood was only a short distance from where I lived now, though in between I'd gone to college, then law school, which I'd quit to attend culinary school. Six years as a chef in a four-star restaurant in San

Francisco, then back here. Yes, it had taken me a while to find where I belonged — back where I started, in Elkview, running the diner I'd grown up in. If this made me an unadventurous, boring person, I'd have to live with it.

"This is so nice of you, Charlie," Zoe said, looking over my parents' very neat guest room. "You should see how cluttered my place is in the dorm. And your mom wasn't even expecting company." Zoe paused for a breath. "I don't think I could go back to the dorms right now. Maybe never. Not to the school dorms, either." She gave me a wistful look. "I might just drop out of school altogether. What does it get you anyway? Maybe I'll get a job in a diner, like yours."

Uh-oh. "Let's take it just take it one step at a time," I said. "Tomorrow I'll take you to talk to Trooper Graham. I wanted you to have some time to yourself first."

She nodded, her eyebrows raised, her cheeks wet with tears. "Will he know what happened to Ethan?"

"He probably won't have a complete report. He'll want to find out what you know, too. Maybe between the two of you, and me, and all the lab people, et cetera, we'll be able to figure out what went wrong."

I bit my tongue. *Way to phrase it, Charlie.*

I wished I could take it back. "What went wrong" sounded like a blown fuse or a leaky roof, not a young man's life cut short. I was grateful that Zoe didn't seem to notice. She'd flung herself on the bed, parka and all, hardly moving. She reminded me of a toddler who'd run around all day in Mommy's clothes and, exhausted, checked out for the night.

I waited until I was certain Zoe was asleep, then headed for the grocery store and picked up only enough items to fit in my tote so I wouldn't be seen with a suspiciously large amount of supplies. I made an exception for Benny, adding a fresh package of tuna treats. There might have been a bit of guilt associated with that purchase, but it certainly wasn't the first time I had brought him treats. In fact, he was so accustomed to what used to be called "treats" that it was hard to think of something special to bring home to him.

I had time to drop off milk, a packaged salad, and other perishables at my mom's before I was due at the diner for the staff briefing. I'd peeked in on Zoe, seen the heap of parka on the bed unmoving, and decided not to bother her. I left a note in the kitchen inviting her to help herself to anything in the fridge and cupboards, along with my cell phone number in case she needed anything — including just someone to talk to.

Poor Benny, undeservedly without attention.

I'd read a book about cats owned by famous people. One story about a writer's cat had me feeling sorry for Benny, who was stuck in the house all day, unable to roam around a bucolic farm, for instance, mingling with other animals, maybe hunting. Benny hated getting into his carrier and leaving the house, but that might have had more to do with always ending up at the vet's when the carrier came out. On the whole, it seemed cats had different personalities, like humans.

I decided to pay Benny a quick visit. At home, I stocked the new treats toy box. As I predicted, he curled on top of the packaging, which was in the corner of the room on its way to the trash.

I picked him up, cradled him around my neck, and rubbed his back. "Sorry, Benny. Just one more meeting this evening, and I'll be back for the night." I got a rewarding purr in response.

In my car on the way to the Bear Claw, I called Trooper. Hands-free, of course. I could imagine my luck if Trooper's deputy, Josh Peters, happened to be patrolling and caught me with my phone at my ear. Somehow, we'd gotten off to a bad start when I arrived home to Elkview last year, and we hadn't been able to resolve the unspoken issues. For some reason, Josh thought I was meddling whenever I tried to help out our local law enforcement office, which, everyone was aware, was severely understaffed.

Trooper finally came on the line. "We have nothing definite, Charlie."

"How about indefinite?" I was only half joking, as Trooper well knew.

"Doc Sherman says he put a rush on it."

"Okay. But surely if it were something simple, like a heart attack, he'd be able to tell right away?" I was winging it here, medicine being one of the few careers I had not pursued.

"I'll let you know when I hear anything. How about I meet you in the morning at your mom's house to talk to Zoe?"

"Sure, I'll be —" I paused. "Wait, how did you know Zoe is there?"

"I do now."

I groaned. "Guess I'm not great at clandestine detective work."

"You're good enough." He chuckled. "But I'm better."

Somehow, I found that comforting.

I was a few minutes late to my staff meeting, and when I arrived, I found my employees a little too cheerful to suit me.

"Maybe your new barbecue sauce did him in, Victor," I heard Bert, a college student who worked late nights in the Bear Claw, say.

"Don't even joke about that," Victor said. I watched from the doorway as he made little slits of his eyes and gave Bert his version of an evil look, focusing on the seafood salad balanced on Bert's lap. "But maybe you should toss that salad in the garbage and eat somewhere else, just in case."

"Sorry, sorry. I know this is serious."

"Yes, very," I said. "A young man, not much older than you, is dead," I told Bert. *And don't bother coming in tomorrow, or ever again* was on the tip of my tongue. But I'd learned the hard way what I'd advised Zoe about earlier this evening — not to make decisions when overly depressed, tired, angry, or otherwise operating in the heat of battle.

"Boss, we didn't know Ethan died," Victor said. "Not that it's an excuse. But that changes everything."

"Yeah, and I'm so sorry," Bert said, as did

Nina and everyone else squeezed into the back room.

"Does the doc think it could have been food poisoning?" Nina asked, when no one else would.

"How could it be?" Victor chided his sister. "He didn't eat anything, right?"

"Maybe he snuck something when no one was looking."

Victor looked around for who said that. No one owned up to it.

The staff went through all the possible ways our kitchen could have played a part in the death of a customer. Was the hot water hot enough to wash our hands thoroughly? Was the cold water cold enough for careful rinsing of the lettuce? How about the fridge? The freezer? The pantry? The dishwasher? My head was spinning.

Tammy, who shared the late shift with Bert, had an opinion. "You know, he didn't even eat here, did he? He just ordered, is what I heard." The others nodded *yes*. "And even if he did, just because someone eats, then gets sick, some people will blame the food," she said. "But if he fell over in the parking lot on the way to his meal, would they have blamed a car? A Mercedes, perhaps?"

It was hard to follow Tammy's logic,

especially since her voice had reached an abnormal pitch. She seemed quite unnerved by the death, and no one questioned her.

"Shouldn't we talk about salmonella?" Rachel, a new waitress and Victor's girlfriend, asked.

"You mean from our salmon?" Hank asked.

Victor allowed himself a smile. "It has nothing to do with salmon, the fish. It was named after the scientist who discovered the bacteria."

"For real?" Hank asked.

"For real. Google it. And really, salmonella can be in almost everything else. Chicken, eggs, fruit, veggies. It makes people get sick to their stomach eventually, not fall right over on the table the way Ethan did."

I was tempted to add what I knew of Daniel Salmon, the veterinary pathologist from a century ago, but thought instead I'd let Victor keep the stage.

After a few more questions for my staff, I ended up satisfied that everything on tonight's menu had been tasted by at least one of us, and none of us had fallen over. Nina reiterated that although Ethan had ordered the special of the day, which his table companions had also ordered, none of them had been served.

I reminded everyone of the regulations we were responsible for, from OSHA's anti-fatigue floor mats to the FDA's nutritional information and overall transparency requirements.

Since I had nothing more to offer by way of information on the cause of Ethan's death, the meeting wound down.

Victor was happy about our closing shop until tomorrow morning, when we'd be ready to serve breakfast to our regular weekday patrons and to Annie's tour group guests. Victor, young as he was, had turned out to be a valuable asset to the Bear Claw. He stepped up now.

"I'm on it," he said. "You take care of this other thing and keep us informed."

"Deal," I said, neither of us needing to spell out the "other thing."

Wouldn't it be nice, I thought, if none of this mattered because what killed Ethan was a diseased gnat that had come in on a boat far from Elkview? No more investigation would be necessary.

I headed for my car in the parking lot and was cut off by Chris Doucette. *Touché.*

Chris was enamored of the heated steering wheel in my Outback, but it was summer, and I knew that wasn't the reason for his pulling up beside me.

"Need a lift?" he asked, with my car a few feet away, forcing me to laugh.

"No thanks. I'll grab a cab," I said.

Chris got out of his old pickup, a vehicle without heated a steering wheel, or heated anything as far as I knew, and walked with me to my car.

"Trooper thinks Zoe is at your mom's, but there's no sign of activity there."

"I guess you were just in the neighborhood?"

He nodded. "Driving by and I happened to notice."

"What kind of activity were you looking for? Lights on?" A joke since it was June and the sun wouldn't set for several more hours. "Why don't we leave Zoe alone until tomorrow? She was fast asleep last I checked."

"So you're not on your way there now?"

Not that it was any of his business. "No, I am not. I'm heading home."

"How about —" Chris's cell phone rang to a tune I recognized from my high school days. "Excuse me?" he asked.

He turned away to answer his phone, thus sparing me from having to make a choice between him and Benny.

Four

I suspected Benny's day had been better than mine, what with a loaded feeder and a new toy and not having to worry about paying bills, keeping track of inventory, and handling the occasional emergency situation.

I had a quick dinner of leftover shepherd's pie, thanks to my crew, and sat on my rocker with Benny on my lap. Mom had known what she was doing when she bestowed her gifts on me — a demanding job with Bear Claw management, offset by a calming companion at home. It occurred to me that it might have been better if I'd brought Zoe here, so she could have shared the comfort Benny offered. But interested parties would be more likely to look for her here.

In any case, it was too late now. I wasn't about to leave my house and Benny again, especially since the rain had started up once more. Nor did I want to risk pulling Zoe from what I hoped was a restful evening and night.

I had the nagging feeling things would get worse for her tomorrow, with Trooper and Chris both seeking her out. And probably Garrett and Kevin and others she and Ethan worked with would want a report from Zoe, assuming, as they might, that she'd learned something at the medical center. I knew Trooper had his own professional methods of contacting Ethan's parents in Boston. As for Chris — well, he was a reporter. Enough said.

I made a note to ask Zoe who her boss was so I could maybe assist in getting her some time off.

As I gently worked my fingers along Benny's back, listening to and feeling the vibration of his purrs, I asked myself — or maybe Benny was asking me — why I was so concerned about a young woman I'd just met and hardly knew. Was it because she seemed so frail? A sophomore in the fall, Zoe might not be out of her teens. "Would I have put myself out if she were my height?" I asked Benny, and I was fairly sure I heard him laugh. Technically — legally — Zoe was an adult. Would I have treated another adult woman as if she were a vulnerable child?

I didn't have a good answer, but I didn't

need one, either. Didn't I have my parents' examples of helping where and when needed? That should be motivation for the little-enough assistance I was giving to a grieving person, one who'd been sitting next to a friend when he'd toppled to his death.

These heavy questions, as well as a few light ones, such as *Does my mom's pantry have enough flour for me to make pancakes for me and Zoe in the morning?,* followed me to the shower and into bed, where Benny curled beside me, with the sleep-inducing rain washing my windows.

Thursday morning, seven o'clock was much too early for me to give up my bed and my grandmother's quilt. I'd just turned off the blast from my clock radio, a relic from my grandmother, passed down to me when I moved home, which Benny counted among his toys. Even as little more than a kitten, he would hit the buttons until some loud sound — a cereal commercial, upbeat music, or a raving talk show host — blew through the house.

This time the sound was followed quickly by my doorbell. Who'd be so rude as to ring it at this hour?

I trudged out of my bedroom in my fleece robe, leaving Benny in the warm spot I'd left behind. I tried not to think the worst when I looked through the front curtains to see Trooper on my porch.

I heard "Where's Zoe?" before he was all the way through my doorway.

"Coffee?" I asked, leading him toward my kitchen, my eyes at half-mast. Since he didn't have his handcuffs out, I decided Trooper's mission was not so urgent that we couldn't have a civil conversation, with coffee and the cinnamon muffins I happened to have handy.

Fortunately, my coffee maker is always on standby, and I hit its GO button. I took a seat while Trooper helped himself to a tour through my house. The question *Would you like to do my laundry while you're back there?* came to mind. He managed to rouse Benny, who scooted out of my bedroom and wrapped himself around my ankles. Claiming his territory? I'd stopped being amazed at how Benny sensed the slightest change in the emotional field around me. Though he'd been around Trooper often enough, and liked him, he knew a confrontation when he smelled one.

Trooper let out a major sigh as he sat, accepting a mug of coffee and reaching for a muffin. Things couldn't be all that bad.

I ventured a question. "Why are you asking where Zoe is? I thought you knew yesterday, before I could tell you. I took her to my mom's. She stayed there overnight. That's where she is now." For emphasis, I flicked my thumb toward the south.

"Not anymore she isn't."

It was too late to stop the cream I was pouring into Trooper's mug from splashing onto the table.

The trip to my mom's superseded the rest of breakfast, and I had no idea where I might be going next. Thus the mini convoy as I followed Trooper's patrol car in my vehicle. The rain had cleared the air — one of Mom's expressions — and I would have preferred a leisurely walk to this caravan of vehicles.

Trooper arrived first, of course, and opened the front door for me as I climbed the steps. He'd had a key to my parents' house for as long as I'd known him. And, for all I knew, to every home in Elkview. Trooper wandered the house, peering into every room, presumably for the second time this morning, while I headed straight for my mom's guest room. I stared at Garrett's army green parka and realized this time that it was all that was on the bed. The parka. Nobody under it. I mentally slammed my forehead. Zoe might even have already left when I looked in late yesterday afternoon, before my staff briefing at the Bear Claw.

How embarrassing. How could I have been so naive? I remembered the time Trooper had unofficially deputized me, along with Chris, Annie, and my mom, to help him when he was overloaded with cases this past spring. I still thought of myself in that capacity. If I was, I'd sure blown it yesterday.

It took only a few minutes for Trooper to believe me that I had mistaken an extra-large downy parka for a slight college girl. That I wasn't trying to put one over on him by hiding Zoe somewhere else.

I was mad at Zoe, but mostly at myself. I should have stashed her in my house, or stayed with her in this one. I should have done a lot of things differently, but here we were.

I noted that the coffee I'd set up for Zoe hadn't been used. Trooper and I had our second mugs in my mom's kitchen, brainstorming where Zoe might have gone, how she might have gotten there, and, of course, why, why, why?

"Maybe she's taking a long walk and will be back soon?" The idea sounded lame even to me.

"Without that parka? I doubt it."

I didn't have the heart to tell Trooper that the *why* of Zoe's leaving might have something to do with the thought of being questioned by an Alaska State Trooper.

A thought hit me. "What if she was kidnapped?"

"Not likely. No sign of any kind of struggle. The parka was obviously staged. Why would a kidnapper do that?"

"To slow us down. Which is just what happened. He's had a head start. Zoe could be in a lot of danger."

Trooper bolted up, clearly hit by a thought of his own.

I followed him to the laundry area and the door leading to the garage. "How did your parents get to the airport?" he asked on the way.

"One of Dad's clients gave them a ride."

By now I was looking over Trooper's shoulder with enough of a view to see that my mom's Honda was gone. Dad's Chevy, his vintage Camaro, was present and accounted for, which was one vote against Mom's habit of keeping the Honda key hanging in plain sight on the garage wall.

Trooper sprang into action. Elkview did not have an abundance of police coverage, but Trooper had a volunteer force that was at his disposal. Sometimes I thought they were like the ride-hailing companies, but where cars and drivers patrolled the area waiting for a call from Trooper or Josh Peters, his one official, badged deputy.

"License plate?" Trooper asked.

"I'll have to look it up."

"Never mind, I got it," he said, tapping on his cell phone.

A little disconcerting. Should I be grateful that Trooper could track an Elkview citizen that quickly? Or a little worried?

"Where do you think she might have gone?"

I shrugged. My first thought was that'd she'd fled to the airport and then home to Portland or wherever she lived. Or to her dorm at school in Oregon.

We were back to our mugs at the kitchen table. When Trooper had finished his phone commands, I gave him my most serious almost-deputy look. "Is all this concern about where Zoe is because there was something suspicious about Ethan's death? Did you get a call from the lab? Is that why you came here to find Zoe? Is that why you woke me up?" I took a breath, deliberately avoiding the term "suspect."

"Yes to all of those."

Great. Now I had to remember what I had

asked. I knew what I hadn't asked, besides whether she was a "suspect" — did it have to do with food at all? It was time to face that possibility. "Poison?" I asked.

Trooper nodded. "A form of mercury, which is, I guess, one of the easier poisons to detect. This form was used in the past to cure various diseases but was eventually determined to be toxic. Apparently, Johnson had been exposed to the compound gradually, over a period of time. A big question now is why."

I let out a long breath. Ethan didn't die from sniffing the Bear Claw air. Was I so selfish that I cared more about the involvement of my establishment than the death of a young man? At the moment, I had to admit I was.

My mom had run the Bear Claw for twenty-five years. Had she ever had to deal with an incident like this? Had she kept such disasters from me? Is that why she gave me Benny? Because she knew I'd need someone extraordinary to help me deal with these events that were anything but routine?

I thought back to all the happy times in the diner: When I was very young, sitting on a red stool trimmed with shiny chrome that Mom showed me how to polish. Looking out the window and waving to passersby when I was supposed to be doing my homework. François, a now-retired chef, teaching me how to hold my arms and where to put my fingers so I could carry three plates of food at once. All that time, was Mom dealing with mayhem and murder, as I'd been doing since this year started?

Trooper's cell phone ringing brought me back to the unresolved issues of the present. His side of the conversation was not enlightening, consisting as it did of long pauses and mostly negative phrases like "Again?" and "I'll get to it as soon as I can."

I kept myself busy checking my emails and phone messages. One from Victor and one from Annie. Victor first, I decided, and clicked on his number. *The sooner the better that I know,* I thought, *if something — something else, that is — is wrong at the Bear Claw.*

"Hey, boss." The way Victor always started a conversation, or "convo," as he would say.

"Everything okay there?" Holding my breath.

"Yeah, just this guy came around asking for you. Said he was an old friend from San Francisco. He wanted to know where you were, how he could get hold of you. I told him I'd give you the message and you could call him if you wanted. I hope that was okay. I was polite and all, even though he seemed a little creepy."

"Thanks, Victor. That was the right thing to do. Did you get his name?"

"Yeah, Ryan. Ryan James or something like that. Tall. Not dressed like a fisherman."

It was a good thing I didn't have a pitcher of cream in my hand this time.

Trooper finished his calls and turned to me. "I'll be off now," he said. "You okay here?"

I assured him I was fine, hoping for a self-fulfilling prophecy.

Ryan? *Really?*

Could there be a Ryan James, a stranger I didn't know, as well as a Ryan Jamison, whom I did know, and had been engaged to? I wished it could have been so. Then my stomach wouldn't have cramped up from the memory.

I thought I was done with Ryan James or Something Like That. What was he doing in Elkview, which he'd visited only once, to meet my parents, during our brief engagement? I wouldn't have put it past him to have come all this way to ask me to be his best man at his wedding to an even younger paralegal than the first one whose charms he'd succumbed to. In any case, I was glad Victor hadn't provided him with information for contacting me directly. It would slow him down, and possibly discourage him from pursuing me further.

Back to important matters.

Now that Trooper was gone, I took another turn around Mom's house. I checked the coat closet to see if Zoe might have taken one of Mom's coats, since she'd had to leave Garrett's parka as part of her getaway scheme. I pictured her in the seat at the overheated medical center. She'd removed the parka to reveal a simple cropped sweater over a tank top. Not enough to keep her comfortable in June in Alaska.

But what had Garrett's comment been about a girl needing a clean parka?

I headed out the door. I knew what my next stop should be.

FIVE

Millie's dry cleaning was on Main Street, between our general store and our hair salon. Elkview's bustling downtown. I needed the hair salon more than any other establishment in town, but at the moment I had a different mission to accomplish: to find Zoe.

Millie Crockett had been a fixture on Main for years, offering careful and fast service for your wardrobe, just as the *Bugle* ad claimed. I knew she'd help me if she could. I answered her questions about how my mom and dad were and how I liked managing the Bear Claw.

"Things seem to be going well there every time I come in," she said, leaving me to feel some guilt that I hardly patronized her shop anymore, though she patronized mine. I couldn't remember the last time I'd had an item dry-cleaned, but it might have been the poufy bridesmaid dress for my friend

Heidi's wedding. I never wore it a second time, but it was ready, wrapped in protective plastic, in the unlikely case of emergency nuptials.

It was finally my turn to talk, and I launched into my story. "I'm trying to find out if my friend picked up her parka. We got our signals crossed, and I'm not sure if I'm supposed to do it or if she already did. It's a pink parka, a small size."

Should I have worried, even a bit, about how easily the lie — a small fib, really — came from my mouth? I told myself that law enforcement and their helpers sometimes had to twist the truth to get much-needed information. Something to run by Benny this evening.

"Oh, we get a lot of parkas, as you can imagine," Millie said. "But that young woman's was a pretty one, down filled, with a nice fur ruff."

"That's the one," I said, as if I'd seen it often. Or ever.

"She was in just before we closed last night, but it wasn't ready. I told her it would be ready midmorning. So either one of you can pick it up then."

I waved my hand. "I'll just let her come and get it, then. Thanks."

It was nine eighteen, according to my cell

phone. Ten would be mid-morning, considering the shop opened at eight. How handy that there was a coffee shop across the street from Millie's. Perfect for a stakeout — and it would serve double duty as a place to have breakfast.

I left my car in front of Millie's, assuming Zoe wouldn't recognize the black Outback, a model and color ubiquitous in Elkview. I walked over to Jan's Coffee, Tea, and More, a new place I'd been wanting to try. I knew from the *Bugle* that the owner planned to host musicians and other arts happenings in the venue on weekends. I ordered a coffee and picked up a flyer with the schedule of musical events, poetry readings, and visiting author signings. When things settled down, I told myself, an interesting educational and social life was waiting. Meanwhile, the flyer served as cover for my lookout spot.

My window seat faced Millie's shop. I didn't dare take out my mystery novel, lest Zoe slip in and out while I was engaged in trying to figure out who killed the butler in the library. I sipped a cappuccino and tried to imagine Zoe walking or driving around in my mom's car, hanging around Elkview just to claim her parka, when she had her pick of my mom's clothes. Evelyn Cooke was heavier than Zoe, but not much taller.

Any number of styles and weights of outerwear clothing, of which Alaskans, including my mom, had an abundance, would have worked. Why wait for her parka unless it had some kind of sentimental value? But who gets attached to a parka?

I tried to look meditative rather than like I was lurking or downright creepy. A copy of the *Bugle* left at an empty table helped further my disguise. I scanned stories of a fire at a glass-blowing shop and the acquisition of new wolves at a wildlife conservation center outside town. An article about an unexplained drop in the caribou population made a headline. The Bear Claw played no part in the decline at the moment. Mom once served caribou meat, but it was very lean and therefore hard to prepare, drying out unless it was served with a labor-intensive marinade.

Several articles were by Chris Doucette, who had the police beat when there was enough to report. I wondered why he wasn't here now, since he often followed me when there was potential sleuthing afoot. I didn't see his battered pickup in the vicinity.

I allowed myself to turn away from the window in short spurts to check my email. I clicked on one that had come in from my mom earlier in the day with an attached photo of a clouded leopard from the San Diego Zoo. With nothing to help with scale, the animal looked for all the world like an overgrown adult cat. Long whiskers; uneven, dark markings; short ears; nonthreatening expression. I decided I could spare a couple of minutes to read the email again and respond to show my interest.

This is a genus of cat, Mom's email explained. *They're larger than small cats, but smaller than large cats.*

I had to reread that line, as convoluted as some of Annie's, but I finally got it. Mom went on a bit about the "clouded" part of their name, how they didn't have traditional more or less round spots, but extended spots, like clouds. She was excited that she got to see the leopard up close, since the animals were exercised by strolls on the grounds.

On a leash, with a trainer, she'd written.

You're not going to adopt one, are you? I wrote in response now. *To replace Benny in your house?*

I added a smiley face and quit my email app.

It crossed my mind that I should inform Trooper of where I was and why, but I was able to talk myself out of it. Why waste the valuable time of an Alaska State Trooper when I couldn't be sure Zoe would show up? Maybe the parka Millie described wasn't Zoe's. And thirdly, though I'd lost count, surely there were other pink parkas in Elkview and the borough, in spite of Kevin's claim that they were rare, if non-existent. The one in Millie's shop could belong to anyone.

My only purpose in coming here was to take Zoe back to the safety of my home or my mom's and have her available to Trooper for as long as he needed her to answer his questions.

My phone beeped me at ten o'clock. I looked up and down the street. Zoe was right on time. I watched as she turned off the ignition of my mom's Honda, undid the seat belt, and headed for Millie's Dry Cleaners.

I exited Jan's, leaving behind the better part of a delicious blueberry scone. I'd almost reached the curb on my way to cross the street when the *whoop, whoop, whoop* of a police siren stopped me short. In a flash, there were two Alaska State Troopers and their patrol car between me and Zoe.

No, no, no. Trooper stood with his hands behind his back, his domed blue hat squarely on his head, while Deputy Peters slapped handcuffs on Zoe. I raced across the street.

Of all the reasons I didn't have to tell Trooper where I was staked out, I'd forgotten the most important one: he could keep the BOLO on Mom's license plate.

"What is this, Trooper?"

"Not in your job description, Charlie."

"I have one? I have a job description that might cover this?" I chuckled, hoping Trooper would join me in the lame joke, but he maintained a serious expression. As for Deputy Peters, he was always serious, and I had the opinion that he relished using those cuffs no matter whose wrists he clicked them on. I wished he'd be called away. Maybe to rescue someone who was stuck in a tree after being chased up its trunk by a runaway moose.

A small crowd had gathered. What else was there to do on a Thursday morning on Main Street? Out of the corner of my eye, I saw a bald man hurry out of the general store, headed for the action. I removed my sunglasses for a better look.

Chris Doucette. Not bald, technically, but with a shaved head.

Of course. He must have followed me. Or Trooper. I pushed back the memory of how I'd misjudged him another time, with embarrassing consequences. But Chris had no other connection to the Pink Parka Case, as I now called it. I cringed as I foresaw tomorrow's headline about a college girl arrested on Main Street trying to retrieve a bloody parka. It wouldn't matter that there was no blood; that wouldn't stop Chris's boss at the *Bugle.* Editor in chief old Wally Bean had shown his willingness to adopt questionable ethics more than once. Chris, an army vet and a good guy, claimed he was stuck with his boss until he could earn his Pulitzer.

"And you think following me is going to get that prize for you?" I asked him once.

"As good a shot as any," he'd said, causing me to blush.

I waffled back and forth on thinking of Chris as a dating partner or not. Which reminded me that Ryan was looking for me — the dating partner turned fiancé turned cheater. With any luck, he'd give up and go home to San Francisco.

This week was turning into a mind bender.

That I might have led Trooper here, straight to Zoe, added to my dismay.

"Zoe is driving a stolen car, for one thing," Deputy Peters said, with all the smugness one man could muster.

I was tempted to congratulate him on besting a ninety-eight-pound girl.

Instead, I asked, "What if the owner of the car doesn't care? I know the owner." Another chuckle with no takers.

I wanted to push law enforcement aside and wrap my arms around Zoe, who now stood with her head down, in a simple sweater, shaking as if it were the dead of a winter morning. But I was helpless as Deputy Peters escorted her to the back seat of the patrol car. The car left with Peters in the driver's seat, sans sirens, thankfully.

Chris came up to me. "Time for another visit to the station house?"

I managed a reluctant nod. Our last experience at police headquarters, where Trooper and Peters were probably headed, had left me with unpleasant memories. But I wasn't about to leave Zoe in the hands of the two troopers and the sturdy gatekeeper woman whose job it was to block access to residents of the building.

"I'll meet you there," I told Chris. "First, I have a parka to retrieve."

"Was I just part of a sting operation?" Millie asked, as if she'd been waiting all her life for such a moment.

I laughed. "Unwittingly. But yes."

She snapped her fingers. "Wait until I tell Gill, my hubby. All those TV shows we watch coming to life. Thank you, Charlie."

"Glad I could help." *At least someone feels helped,* I added to myself.

She handed Zoe's parka, on a hanger and nicely draped in clear plastic, over the counter to me.

I reached for my purse.

"No, no, Charlie. This one's on me."

Complimentary dry cleaning. Another first for me this week.

On the way to the station house, my phone rang through the car's speakers. Annie's voice filled the car.

"I'm so sorry I've been MIA. It's been crazy today, and it's not even noon," I said.

"I heard some of the craziness. It's on the local channel."

"That's too bad. I was hoping to prevent that. I'm on the way to police headquarters."

"I hate to do this to you, but one of my guests needs help. You wouldn't remember, but I told you she was coming in this morning. She came in on a red-eye and has already looked for her boy over at the plant."

I supposed it was too much to hope that she simply wanted our mooseloaf or elk jerky recipe. Unfortunately I was right. Annie continued, "She came here because she got a message she hasn't told me about yet, and she hasn't been able to find him. She's being given the ring around by his friends in the fishing dorms. That's what I call them. You know what I mean."

I did know what Annie meant, even when her sentences or vocabulary weren't what we might call standard. And this time, "ring around" and "runaround" were so close.

Or maybe I was tuned in to Annie because of all our shared memories. Our friendship went back to our days of walking to school together singing "North to Alaska."

Maybe because I couldn't handle another crisis, I allowed myself calming memories. I thought of how our classmates cherished Johnny Horton's contribution to musical history, especially given the absence of Alaskan references in the songs of the lower forty-eight. Johnny's lyrics lent stature to a team of huskies, the northern lights, the Yukon River, and cherished phrases like "the land of the midnight sun."

I couldn't count the number of copies of Johnny's single we sold in the visitors' centers of the national parks. As far as I could remember, I liked that job, routine though it was. In decent weather I could take groups outdoors. And I always enjoyed the retail part, genuinely pleased when we got a new design for our T-shirts or, more than once, a new stuffed bear with the particular park's logo. Plus, there was the discount on all snacks and trinkets.

"Hello? Charlie, are you there? This is important." I heard Annie's voice and a tapping that indicated she was hitting the screen of her phone, as if that were the problem.

That's why I'm not here, I wanted to say. A glimpse back to what seemed like a carefree time — never mind those zits that erupted at the worst moments — had me wishing that Annie and I could carry out the promise we had made when we both returned to our childhood homes. That we'd go to dinner and a movie once a week, take long walks, hike into the Talkeetna wilderness. Instead, it seemed we were dealing with one crisis after another.

I accepted Annie's summons and heard more about the woman who thought her son was missing when he was probably enjoying the equivalent of a frat party somewhere. I managed to convince myself, if only temporarily, that it was better to be helping someone than to be sitting, feet up, with Benny and a bowl of popcorn sharing my lap. I wondered if Benny would agree. Another question to ask him. The sooner the better.

Six

The police station was distinguished from other fixer-upper buildings in Elkview only by a small sign over the door and an enormous dish on its roof. I knew that what awaited me inside was peeling paint and worn and stained furniture. Plus a burly receptionist and a barely post-adolescent deputy with a chip on his shoulder, or some as-yet-to-be-determined grudge against me personally.

I couldn't help comparing the low-lying building with the majestic multistory police headquarters in San Francisco, an imposing structure of concrete and glass that I had passed on my way to work every day. I seemed to keep jettisoning my mind backward these last few hours, maybe because I sensed Ryan Jamison's presence encroaching on my territory, or maybe because I felt I was responsible not only for a dead customer but also for his girlfriend, now in police custody. The hectic days as head chef supervising a large staff at one of San Francisco's sprawling, highly rated restaurants now seemed idyllic in comparison.

I wasn't surprised that I beat Chris to the troopers' headquarters. I found it amazing that his old pickup had made it this long. Apparently Chris needed that Pulitzer Prize money as much as he needed the status of the award. Fifteen thousand dollars would go a long way toward financing a new truck.

"Are you ready?" he asked. He pulled up the collar of his leather jacket, mostly as a cool fashion statement, I guessed, since there was hardly a breeze on this mild day. It could also have been the sight of the ever-present caps of snow on the mountains around us that reminded him of Alaska's harsh winters and gave him a chill.

"I'm wondering if I should call Willow," I said, expecting that Chris would remember the name of the Anchorage lawyer who had helped us out with a friend in the spring. Willow Yazzie was one of the few people in my law school class whom I kept in touch with, and one of even fewer I knew who welcomed pro bono work.

When we entered the police building, we were met by a much younger greeter than the woman who'd admitted us last time we'd had occasion to appear. The woman who ushered us into the same old room today seemed not much older than Zoe. I noted that the nameplate on her desk read, ADMINISTRATIVE ASSISTANT, as if she had no personal name and the desk was ready for whoever might occupy it tomorrow or the next day. We thanked her but declined the surprising offer of "something to drink."

"We're here for Zoe Michaels," I said, pulling myself to my full five-ten. "Can you please take us to her?"

It was a long shot, but the only one worth taking. *Might as well, since she's new,* I thought.

Ms. Assistant, sporting ankle boots and a swing vest, tapped a pen on the palm of her hand, as if I'd asked a difficult question.

Chris was ready to take a seat. He cleared his throat, about to speak. I interrupted him before he could say anything that indicated that we were amenable to a long wait.

"Trooper Graham said we'd find Ms. Michaels here," I said, my best and most confident smile showing.

"Oh," said Ms. Assistant. "Come this way, then."

Chris completed his unspoken thought with a second clearing of his throat. I managed not to laugh.

We three walked down a narrow hallway past black-and-white photos that depicted the evolutionary structure of law enforcement in Alaska, from its early days under the management of the US military, then the US Marshals, and further into a complicated history. The last photos showed the establishment of the Alaska State Troopers in 1967.

Ms. Assistant left us alone with Zoe in a dull gray room, the kind with handcuffs welded to the table. The fact that Zoe's hands were free was on Trooper's orders, I was sure.

Zoe jumped up when she saw us. "Charlie!" she said, as she made a soft landing around my waist. She choked back tears that I could tell were on the edge of overflowing. "I'm really sorry about taking your mom's car."

Zoe broke away and continued. I had a feeling — a hope, really — that she hadn't talked much since she arrived at the station, especially not to anyone official. "I figured the Camaro was your dad's and he'd be madder if I took that. But I was going to leave a note on your mom's car when I got to the airport, honest."

Chris, who'd stood back while Zoe spilled

out her story, now stepped forward. "Not that we're not grateful that you're here, but why didn't you go straight home to Manteca?"

Had Chris said "Manteca"? Across a bridge, about eighty miles east of San Francisco, and the pumpkin capital of the world? I realized I had no idea where home was for Zoe. Chris must have looked it up in his all-knowing database. For all our conversing in the car between the Bear Claw and my mom's house, for all the statistics on the billions of pounds of fish processed through Alaska's fisheries, we never got to where Zoe was from, where her parents lived, or all the data that identifies us on a daily basis. I'd have been willing to bet that Chris knew all that, plus what her favorite color was.

Zoe responded to Chris's question. "I wanted to go home. My aunt in Manteca raised me and I wanted to go back there, but I couldn't afford a last-minute flight. It's like almost a thousand dollars by the time you make all the connections, so I had to wait until she could send the money to me and then I can take a flight this afternoon." She surveyed her surroundings, and her already hopeless look intensified. "I thought I could, anyway. I didn't want to hang around an airport up here. I figured that's where everybody would be looking for me. So now here I am and I'm going to miss the flight and my aunt will lose her money and —"

"We know the rest," Chris said. His voice was soft, his tone delicate.

I liked that Chris seemed sensitive to Zoe's plight, even though we weren't sure yet what that was. He wasn't taking notes, which I also appreciated. I'd compliment him later, I thought. Right now, I was conscious that we might not have much more time before someone above the pay grade of Ms. Assistant realized what was going on. Not my fault, I rationalized, if they couldn't keep better track of who came and went and where in their building.

"Zoe, I'm so glad you're holding up well while we sort this out." I wished I'd thought to bring a couple of snack packs. Who knew how long she'd be in this room?

"Thanks." A whisper.

"Why didn't you simply stay around to answer some questions from the trooper?"

No answer, so I forged ahead. "You'd have been able to stay at your job here or go home whenever you had originally planned to."

"I was upset. I just didn't want to deal

with it."

"I understand that. But you realize that makes you look like you have something to hide?"

Silence.

"Is there something you want to tell us?" Chris asked.

She looked around the sad little room. "Do you think this room is bugged?"

I wasn't sure how to answer that, except to say that I wouldn't have been surprised, but before I could respond at all, our meeting was cut short.

I heard a loud throat-clearing, and Trooper walked in.

I turned my face away from his stern look. In my long experience with him, he never lost control, no matter how angry he might be, and today was no exception.

"Charlie," he said. He nodded to me and repeated the gesture to Chris. "I guess you were just leaving," he said to both of us.

As was usual in these situations, I would have preferred a loud scolding so I could claim an affront.

He held the door and we slinked out. My only consolation was that he surely knew Zoe had no part in the charade that had gotten me and my reporter friend an early, if aborted, interview. I hoped Ms. Assistant would be able to go home with a simple "lesson learned" and keep her job at her nameless desk.

"So can I just junk my pickup and ride back to town with you?" Chris asked.

"It's not cold enough for a heated steering wheel."

"That wouldn't be the reason."

And we were back to "awkward," the word that described most times when we worked together.

The most recent project we'd colluded on had ended during the last days of March. It was now mid-June. That left two and a half months during which we had interacted only in the Bear Claw, where he ate breakfast most mornings, sometimes with Trooper (working the police beat, as he put it), sometimes without. In all that time, there were a few coffee meetings, so to speak, when he would run article ideas by me, or chat for a while in the Bear Claw, but there was no *Are you free for dinner?* or *How about a drive down to Eklutna Lake, where we stopped that time on the way back from an interview in Anchorage?*

Nothing like that. Yet when we were together like this, back on a job, so to speak, there was an abundance of mild flirting.

All of which told me I was right to simply forget about dating, or anything else that might lead to another failed engagement.

This afternoon, I pretended to Chris that I didn't hear his last comment and suggested we meet at Aly's in downtown Elkview to debrief our briefing. No other dining establishment we knew of could boast perfect coffee and excellent pizza, newly added to the menu, under the same roof. Moreover, the clean, brightly lit room would be a welcome contrast to the so-called interview room we'd just left. I wished we could have brought Zoe with us, but Trooper wouldn't grace us with even an estimate of when she'd be ready to leave his custody.

To be on the safe side, I called Willow through the car's Bluetooth. I explained how little we knew about Zoe's status.

"I can find that out," she said. "And we'll take it from there. Since I'm a lawyer and all."

"And all what?" And we both laughed.

If I had stayed in law school after the first year, it would have been because of Willow, my best friend at the time. It had taken a homicide, the murder of my chef, for Willow and me to reconnect in the spring. She was a pleasant reminder of the good aspects of being in law school.

I beat Chris to the best parking spot in front of Aly's. Not that I was competing. Of course not. I heard my mom laughing all the way from San Diego.

I was glad for the time to spare for a virtual visit to Benny and a check-in with Victor at the Bear Claw, in that order.

Benny was curled up, snoozing in a cone of sunlight directly in front of the camera, as if he were posing. I tried to divine his mood. Was he showing me he was fine, warm, and napping? Did he mean to emphasize that he was by himself, waiting for the promised playtime with me? I wished he'd stand up and signal me, preferably with his tail high in the air, meaning he was happy and was looking forward to when I got home. But he lay still, and I had to be content with waiting another couple of hours.

Victor, being verbal, was quick to tell me not to worry, everything was going fine. He even had a new idea about a piece of equipment he wanted to buy. I thanked him for his creativity and referred him to our June budget, already strained.

"We'll talk," he said.

I realized I should have left Benny for last so there'd have been no residual anxiety.

■ ■ ■ ■

We were past the lunch rush, so there was no delay for a waitress with menus. I gave her my order on the way to our table, for pizza with mushrooms and extra cheese. Chris said he needed a menu, then ended up saying, "Same here, please."

"Did you believe Zoe?" Chris asked me, once our waters and paper straws arrived.

"That she's innocent of anything to do with Ethan's death? Yes."

"But?"

"Was she holding something back? Also yes," I said.

"Do you think maybe she was afraid of someone or something?"

"Like whoever or whatever caused Ethan's death?"

"The 'whatever' was mercury; that much is easy," Chris said. "Well, not easy. We have to find it, and figure out who slipped it to him."

I heard the tinkle of a bell and looked up, over Chris's right shoulder.

It couldn't be.

But it was.

Ryan Jamison. I felt my eyes burn as if he really had sprouted the flaming, smoky horns I pictured on him.

Was he here to claim the gifts he'd bought me over the course of our engagement? Items I finally saw as guilt presents for every time he cheated on me with the CLP, as my friends and allies called her. *Cute Little Paralegal.*

He approached our table. "Charlie," he said, with no pretense of claiming this encounter was one happy coincidence.

"You found me," I said, with the same lack of pretense that I was surprised to see him. Or happy. I was definitely happy he didn't look as good as I remembered him. He'd shaved off his fancy beard. His eyes were at half-mast, the way they got when he'd lost sleep.

"Small town. Even though your employees dutifully played dumb. You should give them a raise."

"Thanks for the advice," I said. I introduced him to Chris, but not vice versa. With any luck, Ryan would never be in our presence again.

"Do you have some time this evening?" Ryan asked me. "I'd like to talk to you."

I gave Chris a slight kick under the table, hoping he understood my language.

I looked at my watch; had no idea what it read. "Sorry, not tonight, Ryan. Chris and I are meeting some friends."

Chris checked his watch and confirmed. "We'd better get going, in fact," he said.

He signaled our waitress to pick up his credit card and asked for the order to go. We both got up, turned our backs to Ryan, and walked to the register to claim our order.

"I'll be around for a few days," Ryan said, calling out after us. "Maybe I'll catch you another time."

"Maybe," I said. *Or maybe I'll think of another excuse,* I added to myself.

Outside, I waited until I saw Ryan drive away in a rental car. An ordinary sedan. I was sure he missed the bright orange sports car he drove in San Francisco. I remembered it, if not its make and model. I wondered where he was staying. Surely Annie would have texted me immediately if he'd booked a room in her inn. On the other hand, I didn't care at all where he was staying.

"Thanks for playing along, Chris," I said as we approached our vehicles.

"No problem. I don't even have to know." He made a show of rubbing his ankle. "But next time, maybe you could just give my hand a squeeze?"

I obliged. I gave his hand a squeeze and told him he could keep both pizzas. I'd lost my appetite and knew where to find food if I needed it. I got in my car and drove to Benny's.

Seven

Only when I pulled into my driveway did I turn and see Zoe's freshly cleaned pink parka, lying flat and down low in the rear bed of my car. I tried to remember the weather inside the police building. Not too cold, I thought. With any luck, I'd get a call to pick her up before the temperature dropped. A girl can dream.

What was obvious to me now, with Zoe's pink parka front side down, was a view of a plastic bag taped to the outer plastic covering. Millie had done her due diligence in clearing out the pockets of the garment. I could see a few coins that must have been Zoe's loose change, a packet of tissues, and a small bottle of hand sanitizer. I noticed a couple of stray mints that I doubted Zoe would want and a few slips of paper that looked like receipts. There might have been a dollar bill or two, also, but I wasn't about to take the assembly apart to look more closely or to secure a small amount of money. The assortment closely resembled my standby clutter in the days when I was forced to wear business suits, as a law student heading for a court gig. Zoe's collection probably came about because of the many pockets in a typical parka, on both the inside and the outside of the garment.

I was willing to bet that Millie enjoyed the surprises that came with many of the pieces of clothing entrusted to her, though I imagine some of the odors, like ones from a fish processing plant, canceled out the pleasure. I could also imagine someone who was as fastidious as Zoe seemed to be not willing to abide the odor or any stains for very long.

I picked up the hanger and brought it inside. Whatever was in the bag, even if there was more cash, both it and the parka were safer in my house, I decided, on the off chance that some would-be thieves would patrol my street looking for loot. Another dream scene, this time uglier than the first, but equally unlikely. I hung the garment in my coat closet, the overly long plastic covering dragging on the floor. I hoped to return it to Zoe soon. I placed my confidence in Willow and tried to relax as I went searching for my cat.

My cell phone rang as I stomped around, selfishly wanting to find Benny even if it meant waking him. Lately, he'd keyed in to his sometime habit of hiding — in a closet, under a bed, in a shoebox.

For now, I switched my attention to the call from my go-to attorney.

"They haven't charged her," Willow said. "It hasn't been twenty-four hours, so we can't pull her out yet. Let's hope Zoe is fully cooperative so we can take her home."

"I'm sure she will be."

"I plan to drive up tomorrow. That's Friday, right?"

I laughed. There was normal-busy and then there was Willow-busy, when days ran into each other. We planned to meet during her Friday trip. The only times we had managed to visit were during crises for someone I needed her to take legal care of. Anchorage, where Willow lived, was at least a two-hour drive from Elkview — hardly close enough to have coffee together on the spur of the moment.

Benny had come out from wherever he'd been hiding and was at my ankles by now, ready to hear me out. I'd been quick to assure Willow that Zoe would cooperate with the authorities, but I remembered my unease when Chris and I had the brief meeting with her at the station house. We'd both thought she'd been holding something back. The slight meows I heard from Benny confirmed my misgivings. I declined sharing this with Willow, who might not appreciate my instincts or Benny's wisdom. She'd figure out whether or not Zoe was telling the truth on her own, one way or another.

Spending quality time with Benny was long past due, and as luck would have it, another package had arrived for him. I believed my mom when she said Benny didn't need more toys — didn't he have an entire condo-shaped multistory tree house in my guest bedroom? No matter. I loved finding new toys or games we could play.

I opened today's package literally under Benny's nose, having to gently nudge his head to the side to get to the sealing tape. Inside was a white ball about four inches in diameter that purported to light up and spin automatically, or at the touch of a cat's paw. For the toy to move on its own, the paperwork read, its interior battery needed two hours of charging. In the meantime, Benny seemed okay just chasing it around on the floor without electronic peripherals.

I cooked an omelet for myself, enjoying the activity of adding a variety of fillings. Ham, spinach, mushrooms, and chopped olives, along with thyme, parsley, and tarragon and, of course, three different shredded cheeses. What my mom would call "Cooke's kitchen sink."

Much more satisfying than pizza under the eye of Ryan, I thought as I sat down to call my parents in San Diego. Benny jumped onto my lap. He probably still remembered when the rocker belonged to Mom. I rubbed his back, my fingers running through his beautiful orange and white stripes. Someday I was going to test him and leave it to him to punch the keys, but for now I performed the task. I didn't relish calling with bad news, but I figured sooner or later my mom and dad would hear about Ethan, either from an Elkview friend or from a television broadcast. It might as well be from me.

"Charlie, I'm so sorry," Mom said, before either of us said hello.

"How did you hear?"

"Oh, you know your dad's friends, the Russells, are here, and they're tuned in to social media twenty-four-seven, I think."

"I didn't know the Russells were with you."

"Yes. They have a place here, a very nice condo in a new development right on the water. We toured the city yesterday. I thought I told you we're staying with them."

"Well, I'm glad I don't have to find a way to break the news about a death in the diner."

"I want to hear your version, Charlie. And are you all okay at the diner?"

I filled my mom in on the details as I understood them. I knew she'd be as distressed at a young man's death as she was relieved that our diner didn't participate in his downfall.

I kept Benny on my lap and put my phone on speaker. Benny's ears twitched the whole time; he was clearly enjoying the sound of Mom's voice, even if she did sound concerned and not overjoyed at our subject matter. Now and then Mom would stop to say hi to him and tell him she'd be dropping by soon.

"I know J and M, of course," Mom said. "We bought our salmon and halibut from them at one time."

"How come you stopped?"

"There was some funny business with them a few years ago. I don't remember now. But we decided to switch to a smaller company."

"I thought J and M was small."

"They are small in Elkview, compared to the big companies in Anchorage and Juneau and along the panhandle, but their main plant in San Francisco is quite large." I heard a gulp of liquid being downed. Diet soda, if I knew my mom. "How's Benny?" she asked. "Any new toys?"

"As a matter of fact —" I began.

"Of course he has a new one. Probably with bells and whistles and that artificial intelligence that's so popular. I thought I spoiled that tabby, but you take the prize."

I took that as a compliment. And so did Benny, as he stretched and purred.

I tended to overdo it with my omelet meals, often putting myself in an overeating fog as I added toast and fruit to the mix. At least I'd left one slice of toast. Victor didn't expect me until later this afternoon, since I planned to keep the Bear Claw open all night. All those factors together meant it was okay for me to nap. Benny agreed, and we settled in.

Only to be startled into action by the doorbell. We resisted — and were startled again.

I groaned and, after a consultation with Benny, decided to look out the window to identify the persistent caller. Benny trailed me as I pushed aside the curtains in the living room, next to the front door.

Ryan. Again.

I did not need the extra anxiety from the memories the man stirred up in me.

But he signaled with a wave that he'd seen the curtains move, so I was trapped into opening the door to him. He entered, taking in the rooms in front of him, judging as always. Which was it? I wondered. Too modern or not modern enough? The colors wrong? The fabric unappealing? It didn't matter that he wasn't trained in interior decorating; he was judge and jury for anything and everything.

"Charlie," he said.

Benny hissed.

Ryan still had that annoying way of saying my name, as if he were prosecuting me for some misdemeanor. *Charlie. Your car is crooked in the driveway. Charlie. You left the mayo out again. Charlie . . .* I shook away the unpleasant memories and glared at him as I awaited today's scolding.

Benny stared, daring him to ruin the air around him.

Ryan didn't disappoint. Today it was, "Your Outback's out front. Your passenger side window is pretty grimy, by the way. You might want to give it wipe. So I figured either you'd left in someone else's vehicle, or more likely you were avoiding me."

A bevy of snide remarks, like *Avoiding you*

doesn't seem to be working, came to my lips, then faded as I offered him a seat. Why give him the satisfaction? Why waste one of my sarcastic jewels on him? Benny sat at my feet and continued to growl, either because he didn't like Ryan, whom he'd never met, or because he knew I didn't.

Without planning to, I looked around the environment I'd created in my house, hoping there was nothing that harkened back to my days in law school, or even in California. I was fairly certain that I'd wiped that slate clean when I left the Bay Area more than a year ago. I relaxed when I spotted nothing Ryan could interpret as a souvenir of my days with him.

"What brings you to the Last Frontier?" I cringed as I heard myself utter that ridiculous question. To his credit, Ryan didn't laugh.

"I had a little business in the area and thought I'd look you up."

Ryan's more sophisticated version of "I was in the neighborhood."

I wondered what little business a big San Francisco law firm might have in Elkview, Alaska, or nearby, but I wasn't about to reveal my curiosity. Since he hadn't asked a question, I gave him only the slightest of nods. He started up again.

"How are things going with your diner? Has it been a good move for you?"

"Absolutely. I have a great staff, and of course my mom had already built a firm base of loyal and satisfied customers in the area." I felt I was talking like a politician. It was a good thing to remember how Ryan brought out the traits I disliked most about myself.

Benny slinked under my chair, his hair raised along the back of his spine.

"I heard around town that there was some kind of a disruption yesterday?" Ryan asked. "Someone got sick in the diner?"

Bummer. Who could have told him that? It was understandable that my mom would hear, but Ryan? An attorney from a big firm in a big city, far removed from the Elkview gossip hotline? "Everything's okay there," I said, neither confirming nor denying.

"Really?"

A suspicious tone. The lingering smell of the omelet, so appealing when I cooked it, now left my stomach feeling queasy.

I had no desire to share misfortune, or even good fortune, with Ryan Jamison. I pointed to the clock on the mantel, an antique from my grandmother's days and notoriously unable to keep even remotely accurate time.

"That late already?" I said. "You know, Ryan, I'd love to catch up, but I need to get to work. I have some deliveries and other things I'm a little behind on. By the way, how is that little paralegal of yours?"

It happened again. The words were out before I knew it, like most of my words with Ryan today. Did I really care about his paralegal girlfriend, or did I just want to make a point, that by "little" I meant "too young for you"?

"Brandi and I aren't together at the moment."

At the moment, or at all? Another unspoken question. "Huh," was all I said. I stood up, then he did. I walked to the door and held it open for him.

"I hope to catch you again before I leave," Ryan said, taking the hint, one foot out the door.

"Maybe," I said.

"I've missed you."

What? Since it wasn't a question, I felt no compulsion to respond.

What exactly was going on? Was I supposed to be flattered that he bothered to look me up? Did it matter that he and Britany or Brandi or whoever had broken up? Was that what he came to tell me — that he was single again? That he wanted me to take back his ring?

"I'll call you. We can have coffee."

"I'm pretty busy, Ryan. Have a safe trip back."

I closed the door in his startled face.

Nothing can ruin the mood for a nap more than the appearance of an ex. I figured I might as well make myself useful and go early to the Bear Claw. I was about to head out the door when the bell sounded again.

Benny and I looked at each other. *Not again* passed between us, but we opened the door to Chris. At least with Chris there was a chance I might learn something. He did have a direct line to Troop, for example, and for some reason — probably misogynistic — Deputy Peters was civil to him. Also, I didn't recall any unsolicited criticism coming from Chris in all the time we'd traveled together.

"I need a minute," Chris said, squatting to rub Benny between his ears. The way to my heart, if it mattered.

If I had about ten minutes for Ryan, I should allow triple that for Chris, I reasoned.

"Do you have some news?" I asked.

"Maybe, maybe not. I noticed Ryan Jamison was here."

I gave him a quizzical look. "You did?"

"I recognized the rental car from when he appeared at Aly's."

"He was in the neighborhood on business and wanted to catch up."

"Right."

"What kind of 'right' is that?"

We'd taken seats by now in the family room, which held many of Benny's toys. Rubber mice, squeezable fish, and too many balls to count, spread everywhere. Chris picked his way through them without comment, which I appreciated.

"Do you know where he works? Your ex?"

"He's an associate at Smithern and Dodd in San Francisco, last I heard."

"Do you know who they represent?"

I could play guessing games for just so long. "I give up. Where is this going, Chris?"

"J and M Fish Processing."

I sat back, doing some processing myself. "Where Ethan Johnson worked."

Chris nodded. Together we said, "And Zoe."

"I'd better tell Victor I'll be late."

EIGHT

I put on a pot of coffee and dug out an apple pie from the freezer, one with Nina's special Dutch crunch top. It was all done rather swiftly, since I could hardly wait to work out the significance of this news: My ex-fiancé, Ryan Jamison, was an attorney for the company that employed my deceased diner, Ethan Johnson, and his girlfriend, or maybe just girl friend, Zoe Michaels, now in police custody.

It was enough to wake me up.

"What made you look him up?" I asked Chris. "I would never have guessed this. The last case Ryan was working when I left had to do with a labor dispute at one of San Francisco's large financial institutions."

Chris sighed, as if trying to decide whether to tell me the truth about his motivation. "I got a vibe, I guess."

"It wouldn't be from all those stories I told you about him?"

"Okay. The truth? I knew he was a scuzzball who caused you a lot of grief. I didn't want that to happen again, is all."

I was touched. If I were keeping score, I'd have to say that Chris was ahead in the good-guy column.

"And you did a search."

"Uh-huh. Checked to see if he was married, if he had a social media profile, that kind of thing." Chris tilted his head down toward his newly warmed pie, during what must have been an embarrassing confession.

"But this means he wasn't trying to hide anything, like where he worked. If it was on social media," I said.

"He probably figured that if he caught you off guard, you wouldn't have time to search."

"But why didn't he just tell me, instead of slinking around wanting to, quote, 'catch up,' as if — ?"

"As if he wanted to get back together," Chris said. "That's what I was concerned about. What if he was some fickle joe and would keep showing up, leaving, showing up? Have you on a seesaw."

I meant it when I said, "Thanks, Chris."

"Man, this pie is good. You said Nina made it? My compliments to her."

In other words, *Let's not get too touchy-*

feely here. That was okay with me.

"I feel I owe it to you since I whisked you away from Aly's before dessert and also left you with the check."

Chris nodded, smiled, and pointed his fork at me. "Yeah, you owe me."

With my omelet still occupying a significant spot in my stomach, I passed on the pie for once.

"Here's my theory," Chris said, after more than half of his hefty slice of pie was gone. "He was going to find out all you knew, what the buzz was on the whole thing, the sudden death of one his client's employees, the scoop on Zoe, et cetera, all before he told you what he was doing here. If at all."

"I think you're right, though it's unclear why he'd play that hand. I'm glad now that I didn't tell him anything. Not that I know a lot."

"If he didn't get information from you, he's going to want to see you again." He paused. "Charlie, if he really does want to get together with you, I hope you don't think that I don't think that you're worth . . ." A big sigh that seemed torturous.

"Don't even go there. He's not worth my time. And I would never go back to him, for all the reasons you laid out, and more that you don't know about. I don't trust him." I took a breath, thinking. "He wants to meet for coffee. I'm definitely going to do it now."

Chris's eyebrows went up. "What? Why?"

"To see how long it takes him to tell me his real mission. See if I can get something useful out of him about Ethan, Zoe, whatever he might know."

"Turn the tables on him."

"Exactly. He doesn't know I know and so on. There's got to be something related to Ethan's death — something the company is afraid of, that they're liable for or think they're liable for."

"Like bad fish?" he asked.

"Could be. Or worse." I shrugged. "Who knows?"

"Ryan," we both said.

"Where's Troop when we need him to deputize us?"

"Who says there was an expiration date to the last time he did?" I asked.

"Let's go for it," he said. "You have to tell me when you're going to meet Ryan."

"It never occurred to me not to."

Once I promised to keep him apprised of any date I made with Ryan, Chris left. "To sketch out a plan," he said.

I was finally able to text Victor and Nina

that I'd be on my way back to the Bear Claw soon. Right after I checked the batteries on Benny's new treat box. It was the least I could do for the world's most patient cat. Orange tabbies have a reputation for being smart, loving, and devoted. Benny was the poster cat for that claim.

Nina texted me back.

No rush. Not busy here but Annie is waiting for you.

Annie! I kept forgetting about Annie. If she weren't so mellow and easy to please, she'd have a better chance of getting her needs met by neglectful friends like me.

Leaving in ten!

I pulled around the back of the Bear Claw as usual and on reflex looked for Ryan's rental car. Not present. Good, because I wasn't ready with a script and a plan to get him to talk while I held back — another reason I missed my mom. She was a master at being able to extract information from unwitting and unwilling parties. I was the victim of this almost daily through my teenage years. She could stand calmly, arms folded, not speaking, while I poured out answers to unasked questions about where I'd been, with whom I'd been, and whether I'd finished my homework.

Annie was in a back booth with the woman I presumed was the guest she'd mentioned, the one looking for her son. I waved to them, holding up five fingers to signal I needed a few minutes with Victor.

"Hey, boss, you've been busy, but we've got you covered," Victor said.

A couple of months ago, Victor had been thrilled to be promoted to head chef. His eagerness was impressive, his dedication to the Bear Claw's reputation admirable. I could only hope he'd maintain the enthusiasm. I'd done my best to keep him happy — by accepting his desired changes to our menu; by hiring his girlfriend, Rachel, who'd just moved from L.A., while she looked for employment as a teacher; and, of course with well-deserved raises all around. His sister, Nina, was an equally good worker but was sticking it out at college and I guessed would be moving on once she graduated. All in all, I was lucky, even with my graveyard shift of two other college students, Tammy and Bert.

I signed a few checks Victor had prepared in my absence and went over the needs for breakfast tomorrow, at which time there would be a new tour group staying at Annie's inn. I also asked Victor to please change the upbeat pop music to something that would suit an older woman who was stressed out over her missing son.

I made my way back to the booth Annie was sharing with a woman I could tell was in distress. Her eyes were puffy, her eyebrows arranged in a questioning pattern, as if to ask why this was happening to her. The two women shifted in the booth to make room for me, each moving toward the wide window. I chose to sit next to Annie for a better view of the stranger and of the Bear Claw front door. My mom, whose obsession with crime fiction had intensified now that she was retired, had taught me that trick.

"Cops always try to sit with their backs against a wall or in the corner of a room so they have a view of the whole place. No surprises," she'd told me.

"Even at a wedding?" I asked, teasing.

"Especially at a wedding." Teasing back.

I'd been making that choice ever since.

Annie was ready with introductions in her special ad hoc manner. "This is Irene Bloom from Wisconsin," she said to me, then gestured that we should shake hands. "And this is Charlie Cooke," she told Irene.

For once Annie didn't point out the coincidence of a Cooke running a cooking establishment. "Irene's son is Noah, and he's a sophomore in college, the same one as the boy and his friends who were in here yesterday. Noah has a girlfriend, Hannah, and Hannah hasn't heard anything, either."

I noticed that Irene had Annie's unmistakable bright green parka over her shoulders and wondered if I should adjust the heat in the diner. I also noticed Annie's avoidance of the word that described Ethan's current state as *dead,* as well as her shunning even more euphemistic phrases like "has passed away" or "is no longer with us."

"Can you fill her in, Annie?" Irene said, and she left for the restroom in tears.

Annie gave a loud sigh. "She can hardly talk without breaking up. You have to help her, Charlie. Noah has always lived at home with her, in Milwaukee. And then suddenly he wanted to go somewhere, you know, different, just to see. So he transferred to the same college in Oregon as those other guys, the ones who are friends of the other one, and he found out about jobs in Alaska just for the summer."

"How long ago did he come to Alaska, Annie?" I asked, interrupting, only so that my friend would slow down before her syntax became permanently entangled.

Annie looked over her shoulder toward the back of the diner where the restrooms were. "What about Ryan?" she asked. A complete change of topic, but that wasn't unusual for Annie. "Did he find you?"

I gave only a slight nod, in case anyone was tuning in, and whispered, "Yes, but let's keep to Noah, okay?"

"Sure," Annie whispered back. "He came about four weeks ago, I think, and he wrote her every day and then he didn't and now he hasn't for a long time."

I did the math. First, an entering sophomore might be only nineteen, like Zoe. Writing home to Mom every day for the first week seemed reasonable, but eventually wouldn't a teenager be making friends, have less time to write, or even want to break away and write only once a week, and then become more socialized, and then . . .

Irene came back, looking no better. She seemed much older than the mother of a college student would be. She'd made no attempt to cover her gray hair, and her clothing looked as though she'd slept in it, which was probably true, given the flights she must have taken to get here. My mom would have called her pleasantly plump, but today she looked simply heavy in all ways, from her torso to her spirits.

"I'm so sorry you've had to go through this," I said. "It must be very stressful." I paused before drilling down. "How long has it been since you've heard from Noah?"

"Ten days. I know it doesn't sound like a long time, but he knows I love to get regular mail and he would always drop even a card, or if he was too busy working overtime or something, he'd send a text even though he knows I have a hard time with texting." She showed me her texting fingers as if they were visibly inferior in some way.

"Tell her what you did, Irene. With the stamped envelopes." Annie, prodding.

"Oh, it's sort of embarrassing, but before he left I gave him a stack of cards and stationery and stuck stamps on and addressed them to me, so he could just write a few lines and drop them in the mail. This way I could keep track of him, and it made it very easy for him."

"And she left some blank, with just a stamp and no address, so he could send them to his buddies back home." Annie put her chubby hand on Irene's fleshy wrist. "That was so thoughtful, Irene."

"It certainly was. Did he call you regularly?" I asked.

She pointed to ears that housed serious

hardware. "A few times, but I don't hear too well, and phones are getting to be impossible to hear, so we stuck mostly to writing. At first I wasn't too worried. I figured he'd made a lot of new friends and was putting in a lot of hours, and maybe was sightseeing, and you know kids like to party. But he wasn't answering my calls, either. Coming here was all I could think of to do."

Nina, thoughtful as ever, refilled Annie's and Irene's coffees and brought me a fresh mug. The Bear Claw was in its lull between lunch and dinner, a time when the staff could slow down and do some prep for the dinner rush. Or, in Nina's case, make extra desserts. She came back with a plate of cookies and gave Irene a sympathetic smile. "These are just out of the oven."

I knew what Nina's chocolate chip cookies tasted like and I wanted one badly, in spite of my recent meal. I resisted, however, deciding Irene should take one first. Annie felt no such compunction, though, and immediately reached for a cookie with chips melting on top and a piece of macadamia nut sticking up.

"Noah is all I have," Irene said, ignoring the treat in front of her. "He was a very late baby. We thought we would never have a child, so when Noah came along . . ." She opened her palms, as if welcoming her infant son again. "Then his father died when Noah was only ten, and it's been just the two of us."

I felt it was important for Irene to go through all of this, but, if I was supposed to help in any way, I needed more concrete and current details.

"What have you done since you arrived in Elkview?" I asked.

"She's been out to the plant already, but Noah's supervisor . . . Tell Charlie what he said, Irene."

Irene started to choke up. "He was not very nice at all. Treated me like I was some kind of crazy mother blaming him for the fact that my son had skipped town without telling me. I just wanted to know when the last time he reported for work was."

"He implied that Noah went off in some drug-induced stupor," Annie said. "He would never do that."

She was simply trying to be supportive, but she spoke as if she'd known Noah and Irene all her life, could vouch for Noah's clean-cut behavior, and was there when the mean boss dissed Noah's mother. My law school training, minimal though it was, kicked in and I almost yelled, *Objection!*

Hearsay!

"Did Noah's boss answer your question about when he was at work last?"

"No, he did not."

"Don't you think that's strange?" Annie asked

It certainly was strange, but I didn't want to make too much of it and upset Irene further. I wondered if Garrett and Kevin would be any help in figuring out where Noah might be. Or maybe Zoe would. Which reminded me to worry about Zoe. I snuck a look at my phone to see if there might be a message from Willow, her newly acquired lawyer. None.

I had no idea what the summer dorm arrangements were at J and M Fish Processing. All the guys in one building and the girls in another? Was it all coed? Did all the employees stay there or did some find a motel more suitable? I did remember that fisheries offered a substantial discount on their housing. It was to their advantage to keep the kids, which many of them were, close by, available for long shifts and as substitute workers when needed.

My head was spinning, thinking about Ryan, about Ethan and Zoe, and now about Noah, and all the issues and possible outcomes. *One at a time,* I told myself, and settled on Noah for now, since his mother was right in front of me.

Then Alaska State Trooper Cody Graham came into my field of view, through the Bear Claw front door, in his full working blues.

"Troop!" Annie said, so excited she neglected to announce the presence of Chris also, who was right behind him. She turned to Irene. "Troop is our chief law enforcement officer, as you can tell by that cool uniform. He's come riding in to save the day."

Everyone laughed, even the kitchen crew, except Irene, who slunk down even farther in the booth. It didn't seem to take much to overwhelm her, and I worried that she might slip to the floor.

"I'll bet Troop can help us," Annie continued.

"Help with what?" Troop asked.

"Take your pick," I said.

Nine

It occurred to me that maybe troop and Chris just came in for a cup of coffee and a cookie, but the chances of that were pretty slim, given all the disruption in town. In my life, as a matter of fact. You'd think that as the owner of the diner where we'd convened, I'd have the privilege of stating my concerns first, but Troop took over and set the agenda.

He started by looking directly at Irene, as if he knew her, and not in a positive way. If he had looked at me that way, I'd have run for cover.

"Mrs. Bloom," he said, bringing out his most soothing voice. "If you don't mind, I'm going to ask you to step outside, where one of my aides is waiting in our patrol car. He's going to take you back to Annie's inn, where he'll interview you in the comfort of one of her little parlors. I'll follow soon after. Is that acceptable to you, Annie?"

No one was more surprised at this turn than Annie, who barely managed, "Of course, but —"

"Thank you, Annie," Troop said.

"But, Officer, if you have news of my son —" Irene seemed afraid to address Trooper, and I didn't blame her, given his so-to-speak request to her.

"I'm sorry to say we don't, Mrs. Bloom. Could that be because you haven't reported him missing? Unless I'm mistaken?"

Irene drew in her breath.

"Am I? Mistaken? Have you reported him missing?"

Irene's shoulders sagged as she let out a puffy sigh. "No, I have not."

"You arrived in town on Monday evening. Is that correct?"

"No," Annie said. "She just came in on a red-eye . . ." Her voice fell off as she glanced at Irene. Then, as light dawned, "Oh," she said.

"I wanted to try to find him myself," Irene said.

"Any particular reason?"

I'd never heard Troop approach a Q and A of any kind with such waffling.

"I just thought I'd go directly to his boss at J and M."

"And what did you learn from Mr. . . .

what was his name?"

"Preston something. Or something Preston. Louis Preston, that was it. The sign on his desk said he's the human resources manager. He admitted he was in charge of the summer program and the dorms the students sleep in. But that's all he'd say."

"Do you see now that it might have been better to come directly to us?"

Without answering Troop's question, Irene made her way out of the booth and retrieved her long coat from the hook attached to the seat. Troop helped with her coat, and Irene headed for the door.

"Thank you, everyone," she said to the booth, now in a hurry.

I watched out the window as Irene approached and entered the patrol car, Troop close behind, waiting in the parking lot until the car took off.

Annie could hardly contain herself. "What was that about?"

"Did you know she hung around Elkview for a couple of days, but didn't notify the station house that her son went missing in Alaska?" Chris asked Annie, very much the reporter.

Annie shook her head. "I guess I just assumed. We know how busy everyone is at headquarters, and this is just one guy from out of state, so I figured she — I mean Irene — wanted us — I mean me and Charlie; well, I asked Charlie — to help her, but I didn't know we'd be the only help." She blew out a breath. "Oh, dear. Can anyone think of one reason Irene wouldn't have gone to the police right away?"

Annie's question might have been rhetorical, but the Bear Claw turned into a grade school classroom. In the kitchen, three hands went up, fingers waving.

Why did I always forget there was no soundproofing in the diner? The through-window for passing food out to the waitstaff was large enough for the waitstaff themselves to pass through. They heard everything that went on at the counter, and when the Bear Claw was empty as it was now, they heard booth conversations.

The kitchen workers didn't wait to be called on.

"She's worried that he's off doing something illegal," Victor said.

"Like, selling something."

"Or buying."

"And that the police are already looking for him."

"And if he answered her calls and the phone was bugged, the cops could trace where he was."

"Or, if not the cops, then the competition."

"Yup, there's that." Back to Victor again.

"Well, that clears that up," Annie said.

But it didn't quite. Chris had more.

"It seems Mrs. Bloom was flagged as she came through the airport in Anchorage. One of Troop's more zealous volunteers routinely goes through the list of people entering the borough and checks for records."

"Irene has a record?"

I feared Annie was going to faint. She'd stood to say goodbye to Irene, and now she held on to the coatrack extension to steady herself.

"Misdemeanor in Wisconsin. She paid a fine of one thousand dollars," Troop said.

"So Mrs. Bloom wasn't about to walk into a police station and test things out if she didn't have to," I said. "So she chose Annie." *And Annie chose me,* I thought.

"Now what?" Annie asked, looking around, as if everyone in town knew more than she did.

She was probably right.

We regrouped later in the Bear Claw's back booth, a familiar quartet: Troop, Chris, Annie, and me. The kitchen group stayed put, adding the occasional whir of a blender or mixer to the background noise.

"Okay," Troop said. "We need to get busy." Troop seemed rushed, probably mindful of the approaching dinner hour, when our off-site meeting room would be busy and the civilians among us would have to return to our regular jobs. "I need to tell you my upcoming schedule. My availability for this case."

"Uh-oh," Chris said.

"Oh, no," Annie said.

"Great," I said, meaning just the opposite.

Troop continued, ignoring our groans. "I've been called to a training post down by Big Lake. There's a larger-than-usual class of VPSOs and I've been 'selected' " — Troop used his fingers to draw quotation marks in the air around the word — "to help out."

"Village Public Safety Officers," Victor told Rachel.

"Deputy Peters has a group of volunteers here to help him with locating the boy," Trooper said. "And in fact, it will probably be his volunteers who do most of that work, since the deputy has to be ready to go wherever else he's needed in Mat-Su."

"Noah Bloom," Annie said. "The boy's name is Noah Bloom. And why does everything take a back seat to finding him?" Observing her and the high pitch of her voice, I felt she was still reeling from the new information about Noah's mother.

"What I need is you two" — he waved his long fingers between Chris and me — "to keep on the Johnson case."

Chris and I looked at each other, trying hard not to jump for joy.

"Okay," we said, in a casual tone.

But Trooper knew better. "That does not mean that you spend your time tracking down a killer. Is that clear?"

Trooper stood as we nodded.

"One of your main tasks is to determine the motive here. Why was this young man, Ethan Johnson, targeted? And is the seeming disappearance of another young man, Noah Bloom, connected in any way? But that doesn't mean you put yourselves in harm's way, in any way, shape, or form. Is that clear?"

We nodded again.

"You have proven yourselves good investigators, and I just need you to gather some intel, anything to give us a lead on how Ethan Johnson's death came out of the blue." He paused. "I don't want the investigation to idle while I'm gone, which I hope will not be long." His hands had been on his hips, and now he relaxed them. "I guess I'm clear."

We smiled. "I have a question," I said, and I could have sworn Troop held his breath. "Is it common knowledge that Ethan died of mercury poisoning?"

"I wish I could say no, but it's Elkview, and you know how hard it is to keep something from making the rounds."

"Don't blame me," Chris said, though I hadn't noticed that Troop had singled him out. "As long as the old editor in chief is still kicking, I have no control. Just saying."

Though it wasn't always so, I believed him this time.

"Are you going to arrest Irene?" Annie asked Trooper.

"Not unless she commits another crime. She was already arrested and paid her debt for the one she committed in Wisconsin."

"Oh, right. Then what can I do to help?"

"Be on the lookout for Noah Bloom. He's going to want his mother to know he's safe but he'll be afraid to come out in the open."

"You want me to spy on Irene?" Annie asked, eyes wide, a pained expression on her round face.

"Do whatever you're comfortable with."

"You think Noah's running from the law up here?" Chris asked.

"I don't know what to think," Troop said. "And I wish I could stay to find out. I have a lot of wishes lately, but duty calls me elsewhere."

In the next few minutes, the team, as I thought of us, broke up.

Troop took his leave, but not without a snack pack from the kitchen.

"With double elk jerky, the way you like it," Victor told him.

Chris excused himself to finish up an article on school funding before he could join me for a strategy session. "I'm trying to position myself on a statewide platform," he explained, the Pulitzer-seeking part of him never sleeping.

Annie donned her jacket, her expression a combination of pouting and confusion.

Leaving me and my diner. I felt a soul-searching session coming on.

Everyone was going back to their main jobs, reminding me to take care of mine. I'd enrolled in a seminar before assuming ownership of the Bear Claw on the responsibilities of a restaurant manager or owner. Dad, who wrote the book on management, had insisted. Mom had agreed with me that having grown up in the Bear Claw, I didn't have much to learn. "But why not do it to please Dad?" we said, as a way of honoring his lifelong career.

Of course, it turned out that I had a great deal to learn, like choosing a style of leadership and being consistent. I tried to use the best of Dad's strict policies of staffing and inventory and his reliance on the latest technology along with Mom's way of winging it by paying attention moment by moment to who needed what, whether an employee, a customer, or a vendor. Or me.

One thing I had neglected lately was cooking — an odd choice for a member of the Cooke family. Keeping in touch with the core of the business was on everyone's TIPS list for good management.

I headed for the kitchen. "Move over, guys," I said, donning an apron. "Guess who's going to prepare the special for tonight?"

The round of applause was embarrassing. I took a minute to survey the menu Victor had written on a mid-century blackboard that had been one of Mom's first purchases. I chose Victor's salmon cakes recipe to start and ignored the cheering on the sidelines as I lined up the ingredients. Butter, eggs, mayo, bread crumbs, red bell pepper, parsley, Worcestershire sauce. Victor, a genius at using leftovers, had already flaked last night's cooked salmon, and I had a great time dicing the pepper, mixing everything together, and forming the patties.

I reconnected with how much pleasure I got from food prep, focusing on all the senses, from the delicious aroma as the batter came together to the mix of colors from the seasonings to the click of the spatula against the mixing bowl to the occasional taste as the ingredients were added, and to the feel of the whole as the mixture took shape.

Today, however, working with salmon reminded me of what could go wrong in what should have been an upbeat, thriving industry. Ethan Johnson had been part of that industry, and now he was dead. If his death was connected to that environment, I needed to find out how.

I lined up the patties on a tray and hung up my apron. I was ready to meet my other responsibility.

"I'll take care of the tartar sauce," Rachel said. "You have cop work to do."

I was impressed at how quickly she caught on.

Nina had prepared a small bowl of flaked salmon, a rare treat for Benny, and a bag of cookies for my meeting with Chris.

We were overdue in getting organized with our investigation.

Ten

I'd read that cats can get addicted to salmon and then they won't be willing to eat regular cat food. I took that chance and brought salmon home for Benny whenever we had it in stock. As long as I believed what Doc Sherman told me, that mercury levels in salmon are among the lowest found, I'd give my cat what he liked. If I ended up with the world's most finicky feline, so be it.

Benny was sleeping in his condo, on the top level of his tower. I stowed his salmon in my fridge and started a pot of coffee.

Troop had left us his notes from brief interviews with Garrett Marsh and Kevin Hunter, Ethan's roommates in the J and M dormitories. I noted that Garrett was a chemistry major in college. *Aha,* said the amateur side of my brain, jumping to a quick conclusion. A chem major would be able to separate out the healing parts of mercury-something, a compound, leaving only the bad mercury to poison a person.

Troop had three pages of notes, one sheet each for Ethan and his inner circle, J and M Fish Processing, and Noah's disappearance. I made copies and had finished printing out a few pages from the Internet that might be useful just as the doorbell rang.

I opened the door to Chris, who looked at the setup and smiled. "Coffee, cookies, copies. The Cookes do things right."

"Did you rehearse that on the way over?"

He nodded. "Except for the 'copies' part. A bonus. Thanks."

"Did you finish your Pulitzer Prize article?"

"A Pulitzer for Alaska school funding? I don't think so. But at least it has to do with the state budget, and that's sometimes used in TV news."

We settled at my dining room table with our three Cs. Chris had been leafing through the pages of notes. "A chem major. Whoa. How close can you get to the murder weapon?"

"That's what I thought, but before you throw up a flag on Garrett, maybe we should check alibis and so on. And don't ask me what the 'so on' might be."

"Still. We have to start somewhere, and Garrett would have access to all kinds of chemicals, and who knows what could be poisonous in large amounts, even if it's innocuous in small amounts. And didn't Trooper mention that the mercury compound that killed Ethan was used in medicine to treat bacterial infections and as a wash in surgical procedures?"

"Not in modern medicine," I said. "Though there are famous cases of mercury poisoning in the past. We read about them in chem class: A successful young actress in the nineteen twenties accidentally, maybe, drank from a bottle of mercury chloride. Her husband was using it externally to treat his syphilis sores. Then there was this wealthy heiress . . ."

I saw that Chris was no longer focusing on what I considered fascinating stories.

"You took chemistry in college?" he asked. He sounded as surprised as if I'd said my major was Slavic languages and I was fluent in Slovenian.

"Chemistry and cooking go hand in hand," I said. "And, truthfully, since this was a general class, not for chem majors, there was a lot of this kind of storytelling."

"Where the idea was to lead you to believe that's what chemistry was all about. Interesting stories."

"So we'd want to major in it," I said.

We both laughed at that.

Chris had picked up one of Nina's cookies and now put it back on the platter. "Never mind," he said. "This is just chemistry."

I smiled, snagged the cookie he had rejected, and took a big bite. "We should definitely look into the presence of mercury in today's labs," I said.

We settled down and spent the next hour going over Troop's notes, highlighting our copies, writing in the margins. We both had laptops open and created new files. I printed resource sheets, like the first pages of the J and M Fish Processing website and information on the summer program, led by Louis Preston.

More than a few possible avenues presented themselves as needing further investigation. We discussed them all. We started with Ethan's death and made a list-cum-plan of action for the investigation:

1. Garrett's chemistry-major background; does he use his major studies in his summer project for J and M?
2. Kevin's admission (to Troop) that he and Ethan had fought at a party over the weekend; what was the

fight about? Zoe, perhaps?

3. Zoe, her parka, and her attempt to leave town; why? Did she worry about being harmed herself?
4. Louis Preston, in charge of J and M summer programs and student dorms; how much interaction did he have with the students once they arrived at the plant for the summer?
5. Ryan's real reason for coming to Elkview. Was his client, J and M, worried that Ethan's family would sue them, hold them responsible for Ethan's death?
6. More from the medical examiner about the mercury in Ethan's system.

It was tempting to think our work was done once we'd finished making the list. Lately, I found myself falling into that trap: make a to-do list and immediately congratulate myself as if I'd already completed the tasks.

Chris and I agreed to quit, but just for the day, the one that had begun for me with a stakeout at Millie's Dry Cleaning and seeing Zoe taken unceremoniously to the police station.

"We can sleep on this, make some notes,

and go into action tomorrow."

"Nothing like starting the day at a fish plant," I said, holding my nose in anticipation.

"I'll pick you up around nine?" Chris asked. "I think I've had it for tonight."

"Me, too."

But I was lying, and I had a feeling Chris was, too.

There was no way I was going to call it quits at eight p.m. If I didn't have so much to do, I'd have followed Chris to see where he was going. Not to turn in for the night, I was sure of that.

I looked ahead a few hours. I felt the need to show up at the Bear Claw, send Victor and whoever else was there home, and wait for Tammy and Bert to check in for the graveyard shift. Traffic in the diner would be minimal, and I could answer emails and get paperwork done on-site. I might actually be able to open the fridge and freezer in the back room to check on inventory instead of relying on database charts.

I could call Ryan from there also. One more stalling tactic, I admitted, but if I called from the diner, I could always hang up quickly, claiming a customer had entered.

I knew I was the Queen of Stalling. I had to steel myself. But what could be more daunting than asking one's ex out for a drink? Since we were both teetotalers, "drink" in our case meant coffee and a slice of pie. *All for a good cause,* I told myself. How else was I going to determine what, if anything, J and M Fish Processing had to do with Ethan's death or Noah's disappearance?

One more stage, I told myself. Quality time with my cat first, then the call. I needed the grounding Benny could provide, along with a sense that, in the long run, everything would be right with the world.

Benny marched out of the guest room, which held his town house residence, and hopped onto my lap. Just where I wanted him, since I had a new book to show him. Annie, who was an inveterate shopper and gift giver, not just at holidays, had given me a coffee table book with art photographs of celebrities with their cats. This was the perfect time for Benny and me to look through it together. I didn't have a coffee table, but I had a lap made for large books, thanks to my long legs.

I had a delightful, relaxing time turning the silky pages, holding them at an angle to suit Benny's vision. I knew animal scientists claimed that cats' up-close vision was blurred, but not Benny's, I was sure. He was able to push around a little white twisty tie on a white floor and perform similar antics that required excellent near vision.

Among my favorites in the book on my lap now were a famous cook with her calico, a young actress's enormous white Persian, and a movie action hero with his tiny all-black rescue kitten. I listened to Benny's purrs at every turn of a page and could have sworn I heard a laugh at some of the photos in the chapter called "Carriers," where an older actor posed with a kitten on his head and a hulky football player held his cat on his lap in a mesh bag on an airplane. Another favorite was that of a well-known talk-show host showing off with the ever-popular cat-wrapped-around-the-neck pose.

Now and then, Benny would reach for a page and paw it, and I'd wait before turning to the next one.

Some of the pages were dotted with cat quotes. I liked the one from Leonardo da Vinci: "The smallest feline is a masterpiece." I made a note to check images of da Vinci's paintings to see if any of his own masterpieces had cats in their composition.

We stopped at the section that included painters and scientists of yore, leaving that for another session. I restocked Benny's feeder in the living room and lined his condo rooms with fresh terrycloth towels.

I sensed a nap coming on — for him, not for me. I opened the door to my coat closet a bit to give him a choice of sleeping venue. Curling up in a corner of one of my closets was not only a preferred hiding spot for him but also a frequent napping post.

Whereas his day was done, I still had miles to go.

Back at the dining room table, I remembered that I'd deleted Ryan Jamison's contact information a few months ago. I did recall the name of his law firm, however, and hoped their website would lead me to the individual lawyers.

I needn't have worried — Smithern and Dodd and Associates had names, phone numbers, and email addresses for all its lawyers. I was amazed at how the firm had grown, with fifteen members under the letter J alone. And there was Ryan, between Alan Jacobs and Bethany Johnson. I thought probably the phone number displayed was for a work cell phone, but what major-league lawyer didn't have all his phones on hand all the time?

"Why wait?" I said to an empty room.

"Why not call now and get it over with? Here I come, Lawyer Jamison."

I got as far as punching in the area code, then stopped. If I was going to do this, I needed another cookie. I took a ginger cookie from the plate of leftovers from my meeting with Chris and worried that I didn't have a reasonable script for the call. I now regretted being so cold to Ryan. How could I justify asking for a meet-up after I'd shunned him so completely? Maybe I could start with apologizing for being curt with him? I wasn't sure I could pull that off, since I wasn't really sorry.

I was starting to think that setting Ryan up wasn't such a good idea when my doorbell rang. My first instinct was to shut the cover of my laptop and sweep up the papers on my dining room table, a display that would be one of the first things the visitor would see. It was the fastest tidying up I could remember since I moved in. I pushed Troop's pages, which now had scribblings from my meeting with Chris, plus printouts I'd made, into a pile, and moved them facedown to a small table. A useless activity if it was only Chris returning for some reason, but I couldn't take that chance.

I was on my way to the window to see who the visitor was when my cell phone rang.

The number on the screen was the number I'd started to access, the number for Ryan Jamison.

Startled though I was, I managed to walk to my door and also say, "Hello?" in my most pleasant voice, pretending I didn't know who was calling.

"Charlie? This is Ryan." I could understand why Ryan would think I didn't have caller ID. In his mind, if I did, either I wouldn't pick up or I'd sound hostile. He recovered and went on. "I was wondering, on the off chance, if you'd be willing to have a chat."

"Okay, we can do that." A brilliant response.

"Is now okay?"

"Now?"

"I'm outside your door."

ELEVEN

I couldn't count the number of conflicting emotions that attacked my body as I sat across from my ex-fiancé for the second time that day. Sadness that I'd lost him. Resentment that he'd cast me aside. Annoyance that he had shown up in my town. Confusion over what he wanted from me. Dismay that I thought he looked good in a blue sweater that matched his eyes. A sweater that I'd given him. *Wasn't that cheating?*

Cream and sugar, I remembered, and set them out. I was grateful that I was able to pour our coffees without either spilling anything or giving in to the temptation to dump a cupful on his lovely sweater.

"I had an excellent salmon dinner at the Bear Claw this evening," Ryan said. "You have some fine staff there."

"Yes, I do."

We succeeded at about four more minutes

of small talk — how his parents were visiting Yosemite and mine were whale watching in San Diego, how we liked or didn't like the weather — when Ryan looked down at the floor. He'd felt something under his foot.

"Looks like you dropped something." He leaned down and picked up a sheet of paper, now decorated with his footprint. He glanced at it and showed it to me.

The home page from the website of the J and M Fish Processing Plant.

I'd captured an image of assembly-line workers filling cans of what looked like salmon. They all seemed to be women, but it was hard to tell, given the large plastic hairnets and shapeless aprons they wore over heavy jackets or vests. Many wore hooded rain slickers.

Ryan laughed, more acerbic than pleasant, more sarcastic than polite. He waved the page at me. "I might have known. You've been tracking me."

"No, apparently you've been tracking me. I'm home." I opened my arms to encompass my humble abode. "You're not."

I gave myself a point for that, and then hated that I was keeping score. I grabbed one of Nina's cookies. It felt good to chew on something. I hoped I had enough of them to get me through this meeting. If not, I could resort to the elk jerky that was in the snack pack I'd picked up earlier. I had a sudden urge to look up the word "jerky" to see if there was any connection between the cured meat and my unwelcome guest.

"What's your interest in my client?"

I leaned forward. "You first," I said. "What's your interest in my diner?"

"We're always attentive to a client's needs. I came to see how I could help."

"Know a lot about the fishing industry, do you?"

Ryan blew out a breath. Frustrated? I hoped so.

"Let's cut to the chase, Charlie. A worker in our client's plant died in your diner. Is that clear enough for you?"

"Not yet. You failed to mention that your worker, as you call him, hadn't eaten anything from my kitchen when he fell over. The medical examination showed that his poisoning started long before he entered my diner, from an unhealthy amount of a mercury compound, which is an ingredient in exactly none of my recipes. Is that clear enough for you?"

"You must not believe that. That you're disconnected that way. Why else are you skulking around with your reporter friend?"

My curiosity was aroused as to how Ryan knew so much about my activities, but I wouldn't give him the satisfaction of asking. I chalked it up to small-town culture and the adage that there's not much to see in a small town, but what you hear makes up for it.

"Not that it's any of your business, but . . ." I trailed off. Did I really want to tell Ryan that Chris and I were unofficial deputies, helping out an overworked Trooper? That, in fact, we had generated a plan to investigate his client, a likely place for Ethan to have been poisoned? I didn't think so.

I sighed and stood up. "I really do need to get to work, Ryan. If you have something else to say, please do it now."

Ryan followed suit, grabbing his very expensive winter coat from the back of the chair next to him. The garment was overkill for the weather. Apparently, the careful researcher had not done his meteorological homework. "Nothing further at this time," he said.

I managed to hold my laugh till he was out the door.

June was the month of the highest daily temperatures in our part of Alaska, mid- to high sixties on average. Perfect walking weather now, especially when sunset wasn't for another couple of hours, around eleven thirty p.m. I loved strolling by the variety of trees in my neighborhood. Spruce, cottonwood, birch. Tomorrow, I told myself, when I had more time, I'd take a more leisurely pace.

Tonight more than ever, I approached the Bear Claw with a sense of gratitude. That I had a place in the world, a business I could call my own. I could putter around and do the somewhat menial work of organizing shelves and collecting laundry. I could whip up a tray of bear claws or any casserole or cake my mood called for. I could sit in a booth, surrounded by sun-faded photos mounted by my parents, with a cup of coffee and look at the mountains in the distance, snowcapped even in June.

After my so-called visit with Ryan, the best therapy I could think of would be to take out any residual aggression on a bowl of batter and a heavy whisk. I said as much to my kitchen crew.

"That guy from Frisco found you, huh?" Victor asked.

I nodded and winced at the same time. Calling San Francisco "Frisco" was a dead giveaway that the person speaking wasn't a native and was hardly acquainted with one. It gave me guilty pleasure that the name of Ryan's town was under attack in Alaska.

"You can whip up the batter for French toast," Victor said. "We're going with the thicker German style these days."

"German French toast. I like it," I said, and took a clean apron from the pile on a shelf.

"We haven't finished the salad for tomorrow, either," Nina said. "How about getting started on a spinach-and-strawberry salad with poppy-seed dressing?"

"Will do," I said, scrubbing my hands as if for surgery.

The international toast batter was the workout I needed. I took pleasure in getting it thick and smooth, covering it, and storing it for the morning.

It was always a challenge to make a salad with fruit in Alaska, unless you could lay your hands on the one-pound apple or the five-foot goji berry that won prizes at the State Fair. But I took the dearth of fresh fruit as an opportunity for creativity. I prepared the greens and cut up strawberries and placed them separately in the big refrigerator for assembly in the morning with feta cheese and a poppy-seed dressing. I washed and prepared two kinds of cherries for a garnish for a last-minute fluff or cobbler.

Ethan Johnson and Noah Bloom weren't entirely missing from my mind while I played chef. The events of the past two days showed up like a steady video. I saw myself talking to Garrett and Kevin the first day, taking Zoe to my mom's, watching her get carted away in front of Millie's Dry Cleaning, visiting her at the station house.

The list Chris and I had made up ran through my head also. I needed to put together a set of questions for tomorrow's trip to J and M. The plant was about a half hour away, so we wouldn't have too much time to brainstorm on the way.

"Hey, boss, we were starting to tell Rachel the banana story," Victor said, cutting into my pondering. "Why don't you tell it?"

"Rachel doesn't believe us," Nina said. "I guess the story didn't make it as far south as Los Angeles."

How nice of Victor and Nina to make sure I had every kind of distraction from my interaction with Ryan, the guy from Frisco, though they couldn't have known the details of why I needed one.

"You mean how bananas were banned on boats as a result of a superstition that dates back to the seventeen hundreds?" I asked.

If this didn't sound like an old-time comedy routine, I didn't know what did. But I was up for resurrecting the old legend.

"Tell me, tell me," said Rachel, who was likely prompted.

"I feel like I should have stage lights and a stand-up mic," I said.

In fact, I'd told the story many times, as my veteran staff knew, when I worked as a docent at national park visitors' centers back in the day. Invariably, a tourist would ask me if there had been bananas on the *Titanic,* and I'd have to admit it was said that there had been one thousand of them.

"We can arrange a mic," said Victor, grabbing a mop and holding it out to me head side up.

"Never mind," I said. I made a note that we needed a new mop, plus a bucket of bleach for this one. Then I cleared my throat and launched into the story that would never leave my memory. I could tell it as if I were reading from index cards.

"The sailboats that transported bananas from the Caribbean had to move quickly to prevent the bananas from spoiling before they reached their destination. As a result, the fishermen on board struggled to catch enough fish to make the trip worthwhile. Their lack of haul was due to the speed of the boats, not the bananas on board, but a superstition was born. Also, many boats sank in those days because of faulty construction and inadequate equipment, and fishermen began to associate bananas being on board as the cause. Boatmen then chimed in and blamed the bananas for bad luck, and the tradition that 'bananas cause a boat to sink' received a lot of press, such as it was in those days."

I accepted a suitable amount of laughter and applause, and continued briefly.

"And if you want more bananas and fishing-boat stories, you can search Google," I added for this modern audience.

I took a bow and felt infinitely better. I'd been right to bracket my meeting with Ryan with story time with Benny on one end and fun with my staff on the other.

I sent my crew home and took a seat in a booth. I went back to my musings of earlier and tried to develop a reasonable agenda for Louis Preston of the J and M Fish Processing plant. I had the unhappy realization that it was possible, if not likely, that Ryan would be there. I pushed that thought away and moved on.

I wondered how much a manager like Preston would know about the technical workings of the plant. It didn't take much knowledge to list the duties of a worker in an employment ad and for interview candidates, whether it was for a diner or a processing plant. I hoped he was also savvy about mercury, how the presence of it in the fish they processed was monitored, whether there were regulations in place, and, most important, whether there was ever a need to have a compound of mercury available in the research lab attached to the plant?

A call from Annie came in to my cell phone. I'd meant to fill her in on Ryan's appearance at my doorstep, but cooking and playing games with my staff had taken over.

"Charlie, how did it go? I know Ryan was at your house." She took a breath as if she and/or I had been under attack and she was just catching up.

"I know you're well connected, Annie, and that you have spies everywhere, but how did you know Ryan was at my house?"

"Oh, my cousin Vinny, the one that sounds like the movie, he lives across the street from the guy who used to live next to you with his sister and now he dates his sister. Not the guy, but my cousin."

As usual, I was sorry I asked. I gave Annie a briefing, in the true sense, since that was all I had, and asked for my own update.

"Any news about Noah? And his mother? Last I knew, she was being taken away by Troop."

"Well, that turned out okay. She doesn't have any outstanding warrants or anything like that, and she wasn't carrying stuff across state lines. I think Troop wanted to show off or something, tell her who's boss in this state."

I had the same thought but decided not to share it. "And Noah? I presume there's nothing or you would have told me."

"None. And Irene is beside herself, as you can imagine. She wants to go back to the plant and the foreman or whoever was so nasty to her but I convinced her to wait until you had a chance to scope it out. You're going there, aren't you?"

"Tomorrow." I looked at the clock on the wall, noting that it was past midnight, and amended to, "Later today. And thanks for getting Irene to hold off. Tell her I promise to call as soon as we're finished there."

The bells over the door tinkled, and Tammy and Bert walked in together, discussing what might have been a serious topic. This companionship, even showing up together, was a new development of the past month or so. With Victor and Rachel a couple, and now possibly my overnight staff, the Bear Claw could soon become the setting for a rom-com. It almost made me want to partner up. Almost.

"Charlie, we have a proposal," Bert said, sliding into my booth.

"Yeah," Tammy said, sliding in beside him. "This is cool."

"Is this an ambush?" I asked.

They laughed.

"Yeah, we want a twenty percent raise."

I gave them a sideways glance. "Is this the trick where you get me all anxious about something really big and then hit me with what looks doable by comparison and is what you actually wanted to begin with?"

They nodded and looked surprised that an old person like me might have heard that one. I shuddered to think how I'd look in only a few years when — scary thought — I'd be old enough to have a kid in college.

"What do you think of reindeer dogs?" Bert asked. "I had one the other day, grilled, with onions, and on a steamed bun. I loved it."

"I skipped the onions, had just a little mustard, and it was delicious," Tammy added. "Also, you have to split it down the middle before you grill it."

"It's much more dense than the usual hot dog."

"Yeah, what's in the usual hot dog, anyway?" Tammy wanted to know.

Laughs and shrugs all around.

This enthusiasm for our menu was also new for Tammy and Bert. Typically, they spent their nights at the Bear Claw doing homework or whatever else on their laptops, serving the few customers from our regular menu. Coffee, grilled cheese, pie, snack packs for the road. Often the customers were what we called the Bathroom Brigade, since what they really stopped for was a restroom, but they felt guilty enough to buy at least coffee and a bear claw to go.

"Who are the overnight customers lately?" I asked. "How many are regulars?"

"A few regulars, like truckers or people coming off late shifts," Tammy said. "I'd say about half of them are still going to want their bacon and eggs, but the other half are interested in something new."

Maybe there was something to this majoring in business, I thought.

"We get a lot of tourists on their way somewhere who didn't prepare enough food, or they did, but their food spoiled," Bert said.

"Also, a lot of the tourists want to try

something 'Alaskan,' as they call it."

Bert nodded in agreement. "They even ask us that," Bert said. "'Do you have anything Alaskan?' " Here Bert gave his impression of a tourist, if a not-too-intelligent one.

I was aware of a new class of visitor to Alaska, who, unlike former travelers who wanted to reproduce the comfort food of their hometown or even of classic diner food, were eager for something more adventurous. If they couldn't scale Denali, maybe they could take back a new recipe or claim to have eaten something unavailable in the lower forty-eight, even if they ended up spitting it out.

"How about this?" I suggested. "You do the research. Find the best place to buy caribou meat. Figure out if we have the equipment to make up a good dog, how we'd price it, and so on, and we'll talk."

They high-fived each other. Another successful staff meeting.

The first hours of darkness had set in, and I was glad I'd driven to the Bear Claw and not walked. My feeling had nothing to do with the cold that attacked my cheeks, but with the apparent emptiness of the parking lot and some noises that weren't immediately identifiable.

I hurried to my car and drove away, unable to shake the feeling that someone was watching me.

Only when I had closed my door and locked it behind me and Benny had trotted out to greet me could I take a good breath.

That was what a few minutes with Ryan Jamison could do to me.

TWELVE

From the beginning, Benny, my attentive tabby, had a sense of what time I wanted to start my day. Maybe he could tell by where I'd positioned my laptop. When it was on my night table, it meant I wanted to boot it up and get to work early, and today was like that. Benny woke me by using my back as a highway, walking up and down, from my head to my toes and back, planting his soft, fuzzy paws on my upturned cheek at each turn.

Eventually, I sat up and pulled my computer onto my lap. Benny had brought me a treat, which he sometimes did. *Thanks, Benny.* A cuddly cotton mouse or a bird stuffed with feathers, just right for tossing. This Friday morning, Benny dropped a pink and gray rat from a set of ten chew toys on me. I would have preferred a chocolate-filled bear claw, but there was only so much I could expect of a cat when I wouldn't let him out of the house and discouraged him from interacting with the stove. I was aware that he spent the better part of the day on the top level of his tree house, looking out the window at whoever or whatever walked or flew by.

What a life.

I read an article about an extreme cat lover who laid out one whole wall of a room with short staggered shelves for her cats. I didn't have immediate plans to do that for Benny, but still, *what a life.*

Now I moved him gently from a position on my right ear to my lap, in front of my keyboard, my hands and lap forming a nest for him. With his paw on my wrist, I was set to type, and so was he. I gave him a final massage on the lovely strip of white fur under his chin.

My goal was to get a head start on the day by checking out summer employment in the fishing industry in our great state. I accessed a jobs site and clicked around, as if I were considering a stint in the industry. I never thought of myself as squeamish, but one informative website told me and showed me more than I needed to know about opportunities working the "slime line" in a processing plant or cannery.

Lucky me, I could be doing a variety of

jobs, like belly slitting, gut pulling, or decapitating. I gulped, especially at the last suggestion. I'd done my share of fish prep in restaurants, but I'd never had to kill one. My cat, however, felt no such repulsion at the images, but, in fact, pressed his nose to the screen as if he'd seen his ideal career portrayed. I resolved to fetch another helping of salmon for him this evening, but from a sterile kitchen, the more intimate work having already been done.

I realized I hadn't appreciated enough the summer jobs I'd had, rotating through the visitors' centers of the national parks, dressed in a dull brown uniform, long hair pulled back and stuffed under a cap, entertaining tourists with fun facts and stories. The facts I learned those summers played like familiar songs in my head, the kind of songs you know the words to, though you might not have heard them since high school. *The largest national park in the country is Wrangell–St. Elias National Park, in Copper Center, Alaska, covering more than thirteen million acres. The smallest national park is Hot Springs National Park in Arkansas, covering fewer than six thousand acres.* And so on.

As for the less appealing fish processing plants, I saw that most were located in major seaports like Seward or Ketchikan, but a few smaller facilities were sprinkled around other bodies of water.

It was toward one of the smaller facilities that Chris and I were headed by about nine fifteen a.m. on Friday. He wanted to drive my car this mild June morning "in case it turns cold," as he put it. How could I deny him the chance to take advantage of my heated steering wheel?

I'd promised Chris that I'd report on any meeting with Ryan, and I kept my word as we made our way toward the plant. The bottom line, of course, was that there was no report except that, as we guessed, he'd been sent by J and M to determine whether they had any liability for Ethan's death.

"Do you think they also care about the loss of a person in their employ, if only a part-time worker?" Chris asked.

"That sentiment wasn't obvious from Ryan, but I'm not the best judge of that."

"You'd think they'd want to make sure it couldn't happen again, whether or not they bear any responsibility this time."

"You'd think. To be fair, there's not a lot we know yet. Let's see what we can find out today. I'd like to know more about mercury," I said. "Is it locked up in a lab and used for some legitimate purpose? Is it sitting around in jars so everyone has access to it?"

"Or none of the above. My only experience with mercury was when I was a kid and I broke an old thermometer."

"And the mercury ran out in little balls. I remember," I said.

"I chased the beads around the floor, and my mom freaked out that I was going to be poisoned. I don't remember how we found out it wasn't going to kill me unless I ate a lot of it or breathed in the vapors. Or something like that. This was pre-Google."

"Now you have a digital readout for your temperature, or the nurse just swipes a sensor across your forehead," I said.

"You know, for today, when we meet Preston — if we meet Preston — I can say I'm doing a feature article for the *Bugle* on the presence of mercury in processing plants."

"Would he be that oblivious?" I asked.

"Probably not."

I shuffled through the web pages I'd printed out. "What if we pretend to be tourists?" I asked. "Their next tour is at noon. At least that would get us in past the office."

"That could work. I don't think anyone would recognize me," Chris said. "You have a higher profile because of the diner."

"Not as much as my staff does. I think we'd be safe. Unless Ryan is there. Then we'll just play it straight."

"Where shall we say we're from?" Chris asked.

"Frisco," I said.

Chris laughed. "Like that wouldn't be a giveaway."

I smiled, then felt it turn into a frown, my nose twisting briefly. "This is lame. I wish we had badges."

In other words, we pulled into the wide, nicely maintained J and M parking lot with no strategy.

Without preamble, we entered a large, well-appointed lobby. No tinkling bells, like the ones on the Bear Claw's door, announced us. No greeter, as in a big-box store. No one behind the high counter with a sign-in sheet on a clipboard. There was, however, an oversize sign behind the counter, with large letters the color of the ocean: J AND M FISH PROCESSING.

We were free to sit, or to scan the walls of dramatic photos, which were in stark contrast to the nicely upholstered, comfortable chairs. I hadn't realized how much of a landlubber I was, in spite of learning to swim at an early age at Miss Patti's Kids'

Klasses. One photo in the J and M lobby showed a woman in an olive green chest wader, knee-deep in salmon. Another pictured two workers in yellow slickers lying on a deep pile of large unnamed fish. At the company picnic? Not very appealing. Except to Benny, I remembered. I smiled, wondering if there were huge NO CATS ALLOWED signs in the interior of the plant. They'd lose half their profits otherwise. On the other hand, thinking of Benny, I thought it would be fun and pleasing if J and M gave away salmon samples to visitors.

I continued meandering, as did Chris, who had a similar reaction to the fish photos, sending me a thumbs-down signal. Like me, he probably preferred the scenic views of the sea, of the oceangoing vessels, and of Denali and the surrounding mountains.

It was almost ten a.m. and there was still no one monitoring the area. Not that there was anything to destroy or steal in the minimally furnished lobby. There were, however, several doors, one on each side of the counter that I guessed led to offices, and two other doors closer to the middle of the room. Chris and I took turns surreptitiously trying to twist the knobs on all the doors, to no avail.

On one side of the lobby was a small alcove with a television monitor set up on a high table. One had only to press a button to watch a video that showcased J and M Fish Processing.

"Do you think this is it?" I asked, waving my hand at the monitor. "This is what they mean by 'a tour of the facility'?"

"I don't know, but we might as well take a look."

Chris hit the button, and after a few moments of colorful but dizzying attempts, an image stabilized and the video came to life. A narrator ran through the various people and steps involved in bringing a piece of salmon or halibut to your favorite seafood restaurant or your dining room table. We heard from everyone from administrative staff to deckhands and beyond.

We were about to virtually board a catching and processing ship where fish were caught, cleaned, and frozen immediately on board the vessel when a young woman appeared, apparently having entered through one of the middle doors.

The woman greeted us with a wide smile. She verified that her name was as printed on her badge, barely squeezed into the allotted space: SAVANNAH.

We introduced ourselves, first names only,

but I was surprised to hear Chris ID himself as a reporter. I thought we'd scrapped that idea. My guess was that he figured someone as young as Savannah would buy the story that he was writing a feature on processing plants and perhaps be impressed that she herself might be quoted in the newspaper. The *Elkview Bugle,* covering events in and around Elkview, with a circulation of two thousand, carried some weight, it seemed, even in the age of digital news feeds.

"I see you've been watching footage of our newest venture," Savannah said. "These vessels are known as at-sea catcher/processors, where we sort the salmon by species. Chum, sockeye, king, silver, pink." She tapped the varieties off on her fingers, which had newly manicured nails.

As she spoke, I remembered the mnemonic I had learned as a kid in science class, or maybe at a science fair, to name the species. Using our fingers, we recited, in order, chum that rhymes with thumb, and then on to sockeye for poking an eye with an index finger, king for the longest finger, silver for where you wear a ring, and on to the pinkie at the end. It had been a while, maybe twenty years, so I found it amazing that I remembered.

Savannah continued, reiterating what I'd

read on the J and M site and elsewhere. "They take the heads off and the guts out and freeze the fish to about minus twenty degrees." She used her boundless energy to hug herself and give a fake below-zero shiver.

I had yet another flashback to my national park days. It seemed I was doomed to relive my youth, my docent years, but I doubted I'd ever put as much energy into my little speeches as Savannah was doing now. I wondered whether I had sounded so falsely excited. I hoped not.

I hadn't noticed that Chris had taken from his pocket a stubby spiral notebook in an old-fashioned stenographer's style with the spiral at the top and had begun writing. I assumed he felt this gave him a reporter's legitimacy more than using a cell phone app would have, though I felt the distinction was lost on Savannah.

"How long do these trips last, with the fish needing to stay frozen?" Chris asked, and dutifully wrote the answer — approximately five to seven days — in his notebook.

Chris asked several more questions, including "Approximately how many people come to Alaska to work in the fishing industry for the summer months?" (thirty-one thousand) and "What are you doing in terms of conservation of the species?" (the fish are closely regulated by dates, region, and the method we use to land them).

I was very impressed with Chris's performance, to the point that I thought maybe he really was writing a feature article.

Then he moved toward the question we'd come here to ask.

"How do you handle the problem of the mercury content? Aren't fish the bearers of toxic mercury in our diet?"

Savannah was ready for this question. She walked to a corner table that held stacks of slick handouts, one of which was a chart showing how mercury gets into the food chain. She pointed to flowcharts showing effluent from factories, plants, volcanoes, and bacteria in the water, enumerating levels for various species.

There was nothing new here, nothing I couldn't find by myself online. I was getting itchy to go through at least one of the four doors that must protect the plant itself from people like me and vice versa. I hoped J and M's idea of a tour was not a pitch session in their lobby. I needed to up the ante.

I gestured toward the unseen area beyond the doors. "I wonder, Savannah, does the plant have any mercury onsite? I mean, not in the fish, but in bottles, in a lab, say? I remember we had some jars in our chemistry lab in high school."

The last was a total fabrication. I had only the most distant of memories of my high school chem class, which I had passed in large part due to help from the smart kid in the seat next to mine, whose name escaped me. The only exposure to anything remotely similar was through my culinary classes and a "Cooking is Chemistry" lecture by a famous TV chef.

I thought Savannah was going to fall over backward as she stepped away from me. Fortunately, she was in front of a row of chairs, so if she had lost her balance, she would have landed safely.

She started with a visible swallow, then, "Well, we do have a laboratory, of course, and I know a little bit about our research grants, but —"

Bam. A middle door opened and slammed against the wall.

A tall man, oozing a great deal of hair and importance, strode into the lobby.

"Mr. Preston," Savannah said. She couldn't have sounded more relieved.

"I can take it from here, Savannah," he said. He placed his hand on her back and led her toward the door that was still on its way to closing.

"Yes, sir," she said, all but saluting, and disappeared through the doorway.

If I'd bothered to glance around earlier, I would have noticed the cameras in the ceiling.

THIRTEEN

The three of us — Chris Doucette, reporter from the Elkview *Bugle;* me, owner of the Bear Claw Diner; and Louis Preston, human resources manager of the J and M Fish Processing plant — shared an awkward moment in the lobby of J and M's building.

"You found us," I said, pointing to the cameras.

Preston's smile sat at an impossibly wide angle between his nose and his chin. Not at all a happy face. *Smarmy sixty-year-old,* I thought in my inimitable prejudging way. *Making up for being short,* I also thought, but not without an apologetic nod to my five-foot-two mom.

"You know how it is these days," he said. "You can't be too careful."

"I assume you've come to answer the question about the presence of mercury onsite," I said, chiming in. I had to admit I had sort of blindsided Chris with my question, but only after he had blindsided me by up-fronting that he was a reporter.

Had Preston been listening in to our conversation with Savannah? Or was some security guy watching monitors behind closed doors, ready to alert his boss when questionable, or questioning, visitors dropped by? Were there some key words that got his attention? Like "mercury," or who knew what else?

"If you don't mind," Preston said now, "I've asked my counsel to join us."

I minded, but in came Ryan anyway, and thus began the second awkward moment in as many minutes.

The good news was no one was in the mood for small talk.

"J and M has a research grant. The work is being done on-site and therefore we've curtailed all but virtual tours for the time being," Ryan said.

Had he been practicing that crooked Preston smile?

"I didn't see that mentioned on your website," I said. *And neither did you mention it when you dropped by my house last night.*

"We're in the process of updating that."

"So sorry you've been inconvenienced," Preston said.

"Can you tell us a little about the research?" Chris asked, his pen poised over his notebook. "You can consider it a piece of free advertising." As if fish processing plants advertised.

"That's not possible at this time," Ryan said. "You understand that the grant lays out strict guidelines for an ongoing project."

"But there is mercury on-site?" I asked.

Both men remained close-lipped, and they were herding us, as if we were an unruly flock of sheep, or a class of preschoolers, toward the exit. I so wished I had a badge, or even a letter from Trooper, but that might have been too much like a note from my mom. As it was, I had neither, and I was left scrambling to avoid being shoved out the door.

"I would have thought a larger plant than this would be more likely to have a research grant," I said, sidestepping Preston's shoulder, considerably lower than mine or Chris's.

Preston couldn't resist commenting, defending the size of his facility, though I was sure he just wanted us out of his building. "Quite the opposite. We don't have the input/output volume of a larger plant, so we can focus on the science."

Chris made a show of writing in his notebook. "I'm taking it as a 'yes,' then. That there is mercury on-site for research purposes."

A brave move on Chris's part. I could tell when Ryan was about to blow up. His face was red, his jaw throbbing. He screwed up his nose and all but spat out the words. "Be careful what you write, or you'll be —"

Preston's hand shot out, landing on Ryan's arm in a steadying gesture. "Contact Mr. Jamison's secretary here at the office with any further questions," he said. He opened the door and ushered us out with a not-so-grand wave.

I couldn't help wondering: if Smithern and Dodd had sent any other lawyer from its firm — a barrister I had not been engaged to, for example — whether they might have been the calm one in the lobby, instead of the one needing care.

Back in the car, with Chris at the wheel again, we headed for the exit to the street. Lucky for me, I was buckled in, because only a minute or so into the drive, Chris hit the brakes.

"What?" I asked, bouncing back in place. "Do you think the J and M cameras are following us?"

"No, but look. Your three o'clock."

"Aha," was my brilliant response. A crude

wooden arrow pointed to what looked like a set of old barracks, maybe left over from WWII. Or even WWI.

The printing, in dripping white paint, read, DORMITORIES.

"Our lucky day," Chris said, turning in the direction of the arrow.

"There's one thing I'd like to do first." I tapped my watch. "If I remember correctly from browsing the pamphlets or website, lunch will be served at noon in the dorm cafeteria."

"And institutional food is the same everywhere, in all time zones, past and present, civilian or military. Tolerable at best. Ask someone who knows."

"I'd never question a veteran's opinion."

Chris drove past the road to the dorms. "Let's bring them some real food."

I called ahead to Victor and ordered four specials of the day, to go. "No fish, however," I added.

I was impressed by the useful signage, making it easy to locate the dining hall, as it was called. We made it just in time to intercept Garrett and Kevin inside, where they were waiting in line with stained and battered trays that looked like they'd come with the building. Garrett was thrilled at the prospect of a Bear Claw lunch, but Kevin declined.

"You're nuts, buddy," Garrett told him. He handed his tray off to the next worker who needed one.

"A previous engagement," Kevin said, indicating a young woman sitting alone at a table.

Garrett shrugged and pointed to the Bear Claw bags. "More for me."

"What happened to your hand?" I asked, pointing to the bandage wrapped around his left hand, but with considerably less gauze than Nina had pointed out in the diner two days ago.

He smiled and lifted his arm. "Occupational hazard."

Here was the downside of being a deputy. A bandaged hand on a guy who worked with knives, cleavers, slicers, and metal hooks all day could still raise suspicion.

It wasn't too hard to find a table, but it was impossible to get away from the noise. The chatter, backpacks thunking on chairs, plates and glasses clanking on the tables.

"This is familiar," Chris said.

"You worked here?" Garrett asked.

Chris shook his head. "Army. I joined out of high school, eventually stationed up at Fort Wainwright in Fairbanks."

"Wow. My dad was stationed at Richardson."

"Anchorage," Chris said.

"Yup. That's what made me want to come up here in the first place. My dad loved Alaska. My brother and I were teenagers before we realized Dad hadn't actually ever climbed Denali; he just talked about it."

Chris assured Garrett that his dad was hardly the only father who wanted his kids to think he'd climbed North America's highest peak.

I pulled two cheesesteaks and two fried chicken sandwiches, and fries with each, from the tote Nina and Rachel had prepared. Chris and I decided to split a chicken sandwich; Garrett took a full cheesesteak.

"You should have seen this place yesterday," Garrett said. "Empty. After, you know, Ethan and all. Lots of people were afraid he got sick here."

"What made everyone trust it again?" Chris asked, indicating the crowds in line and at the tables.

"Mr. Preston. He's in charge of us in a way. One of his jobs is running the summer program. He called us all into the auditorium in the main building and explained that it wasn't food poisoning that got Ethan. It was some other kind of poisoning that takes a long time."

"Did he say what that was?" I asked.

Garrett shrugged. "Nah. He said it could have happened before Ethan even got here a month ago."

I paused to process Preston's theory, then offered Garrett the two sandwiches on the table to take to his room.

"We do have a little kitchen area with a fridge, but you have to label your food. Like with this" — he laughed — "I'll put a sign on it. 'Radioactive! Do not touch.' " Garrett stuck his head a good distance into the tote from the diner. "Pie, too. What do I have to do to earn this?"

It was time to own up to why we were spending lunch hour surrounded by young people who all smelled like fish — and not the well-seasoned, cooked kind.

"We know you don't have a lot of time, but we're working with Trooper Graham — I think you met him at the Bear Claw," I said.

Garrett's expression turned somber. "Yeah, the day Ethan was taken away." Garrett swallowed. "In the ambulance. The trooper asked us a few questions."

"Did Ethan live here?" Chris asked. "I assumed he lived in the subsidized housing?

Sorry if I'm repeating the trooper's questions."

"It's okay. And, yeah, almost everyone lives in the dorm. Unless you're rich, but then why would you be here at all? J and M provides four- and six-person bunkhouses, or just dormitory style, which is perfect as far as I'm concerned. You know there's a chance you'll find camaraderie with at least two or three of the guys, right? We've got laundry facilities and a rec center with all kinds of equipment in another building." He pointed to the young people around him. "And food is included. Though maybe not like this," he added, and followed the sentiment with another healthy bite from his Bear Claw cheesesteak.

"Quite a deal," Chris said.

"I think they figure, keep us close, make it easy for us to work long hours and not worry about food or laundry or transportation. That kind of thing." He laughed. "It's hard to be late for work when you live here."

"It makes sense." I had the feeling Chris was thinking of his own army days as much as the fish processing days Garrett was talking about.

"Did Ethan live in your building?" I asked.

Garrett frowned. "Hey, is this official, like? Should I have a lawyer or something?"

"No, no," Chris and I both said.

"We're just trying to help," I added. "Gather as much information as we can and pass it on informally to Trooper Graham."

"Well, I want to help, but I don't know how much I can." Garrett took a final bite of his cheesesteak and started on a chicken sandwich. It was possible there'd be nothing left for his fridge. "Ethan kept to himself, until he started hanging around with Zoe. Then he even joined our coffee run. Zoe was part of it, though girls are in another building."

"You all went out for coffee together?" I asked.

"No, no. Believe me, there's no such luxury as that. The coffee here is very bad, as you can imagine. Sitting in that metal vat all day. So we set it up to take turns getting out of bed early and going to that little shop down the road and bringing back a real coffee for everyone. Right now" — he paused — "well, there used to be me, Kev, Noah, Ethan, and Zoe. It was nice, having your caffeine brought right to your bedside four days out of five. After a while we didn't even need cheat sheets, like Kev wanted a latte with soy, Noah wanted extra whipped, et cetera."

I was only a little disappointed that the

Bear Claw wasn't chosen as the best place for coffee, but I got that the café was closer. I also wanted to hear more about everyone, but especially when I heard Noah's name.

"Do you mean Noah Bloom?" I asked.

"Right. Do you know him?"

"Yes, I was hoping to see him here, too."

Garrett looked around. "I don't know if he's here. I haven't seen him in a couple of days, maybe longer. But I don't think he left, like Damon. There were five of us on the same schedule to begin with. Me, Kev, Noah, Ethan, and Damon, a guy who didn't stay long."

"Is that usual? For someone to leave before the season is over?"

"It's hard work, and Damon couldn't take it." Garrett pushed up the sleeves of his sweatshirt, consciously or not, revealing his considerable muscle and an American flag tattoo. He cast an admiring look at Chris. "Damon never would have made it in the army."

That was my cue to let Chris take over.

"When did Damon leave?" Chris asked.

"Oh, long time ago. Back in May. He lasted maybe four or five days."

I mentally ruled Damon out. Whoever poisoned Ethan had to do it over a period of time, and up to the present.

We continued asking him questions.

Did anyone have a grudge against Ethan?

Not that I know of.

Did some other guy like Zoe and was therefore jealous of Ethan?

Nothing like that.

Was Ethan a favorite of the bosses for any reason?

At this, Garrett tilted his head, thinking. "Well, Ethan and Kevin got to spend a few hours a week in the office since they'd been here the longest. The bosses found out they had some experience with —"

Chris put his hand on Garrett's arm. "Say, Garrett, you're a chem major, right? What do you know about the mercury research? Do they keep some in the lab?"

Chris rushed through the sentence as if he had a plane to catch and needed the answer before he boarded. I was stunned. We'd had an agreement that we wouldn't hit Garrett with any reference to his knowledge of chemistry until later. Maybe even waiting for another meeting, when Kevin or other coworkers could be present and bolster our query.

Meanwhile, I heard a low-level murmur that swept through the hall. Normal conversation seemed to come to a halt.

Garrett missed the scene, since he started

in on an answer to Chris's question. "Yeah, I get to play with some of the supplies for the researchers once in a while. I'm very —"

The next hand to land on Garrett's arm was a familiar one.

Ryan Jamison's.

He and Louis Preston had entered the dining hall, thus the employees' reaction, and thus the end of our interview with a J and M employee, for the second time in less than two hours.

"We'd rather you didn't say anything further, Mr. Marsh," Ryan said.

"In fact, you're needed on the floor, so if you wouldn't mind coming with us?" This from Preston, and not a request.

"Okay." Garrett rose, understandably flustered, and started to gather his things.

"You can leave the food," Preston told him.

"Okay."

Preston turned to me and Chris and pointed to what was left of the Bear Claw's offerings. "You'd better take that away. We don't allow outside food or drink in the dining hall. Regulations. I'm sure you understand."

"We don't want the bother of taking it to a lab for testing," Ryan said.

Two smarmy smiles followed us out the door.

In an unusual show of displeasure, Chris banged his fist on the steering wheel. My steering wheel. And I was the one who was supposed to be short-tempered, according to Trooper, who'd known me since I was a child. Maybe it took what Chris saw as an attack on freedom of the press for him to react as he did. I didn't blame him, but neither did I want him driving in an agitated state.

We'd left the property and were heading toward the Bear Claw.

"We'll find a way to contact Garrett outside the J and M property," I said. "They can't follow us home."

"Ryan already did follow you home."

"Good point. But they can't keep doing that."

"Who says?" Chris asked.

"I say."

I was grateful that Chris didn't pursue the conversation.

FOURTEEN

It hadn't been a good day so far. Chris and I had been silenced at every turn. Or, rather, those who would speak to us and answer our questions had been silenced. Which amounted to the same result.

We decided to stop at Aly's coffee shop instead of forging ahead to the Bear Claw, to give me some time before I had a different set of problems to face. Besides the normal course of business, like our bills, vendors, maintenance, advertising, upgrading, and scheduling, I was aware that I'd agreed to help Annie with her own project, Irene Bloom, who was looking for her son. It wasn't that I didn't want to assist Irene in her need to find Noah; it was simply that I could do only so many things at once.

There was also Zoe, still in custody, as far as I knew. I still hadn't heard from Willow. That was not a good sign.

Chris and I needed to get our thoughts

together, figure out what we still had to learn about J and M, and make a plan to accomplish our goal concerning the availability and accessibility of mercury on the processing plant site. In other words, the likely murder weapon. Then there was the not-so-small matter of motive — who had a reason to want Ethan Johnson dead? And could his murder be connected to the disappearance of Noah Bloom? It wasn't a huge stretch to think of Noah as a suspect in Ethan's murder, though I'd been careful not to suggest that in the presence of Annie and Irene.

I liked that Chris appreciated my need to check in with Benny, and the relatively quiet hours between lunch and dinner at Aly's offered the perfect opportunity. By now Aly was used to having us stake out a table and was generous with coffee refills. Chris set out his laptop, checked his email, and made some notes for an article on increasing news coverage in the more rural regions of the state while I tapped in to my cat.

I saw that a package had been delivered to my house and was now sitting in front of the Bennycam, with Benny snoozing on top. I re-created the most likely scenario, starting with Linda, our mail carrier, who had placed the box inside my front foyer. Because there was no need to lock our doors in Elkview, we had the benefit of weather-proofed deliveries. The box was apparently light enough for Benny to push around and eventually position in the family room, in a spot optimized for viewing with the Benny-cam. Benny knew exactly what he was doing — ensuring that he and I could make contact, then asking me why I wasn't around to open a box he assumed had a new toy for his enjoyment.

I could read the logo on the side of the box — KTY TOYS, printed in bold letters between thick, cartoonish cat's ears and curved so it looked like a cat with a smile on its face. Benny was right. I had indeed ordered a new toy. Every time I thought there wasn't a single bauble or novelty or game left that I hadn't already bought for Benny, an ad would appear in my email or on my social media feeds. The newest one would be more colorful, more interactive, more interesting in some way, and I wouldn't be able to resist.

My mom accused me of making up for the lack of physical time I spent with Benny by showering him with goodies in the form of food treats and playthings. She had a point. But when I took over the Bear Claw, I didn't expect to also have what amounted to a part-time job with the Alaska State Troopers in my neighborhood. *Not complaining, just explaining,* I told myself.

I was fairly sure that what had arrived today was a crinkly tunnel with a cube at each end. The tunnel length was adjustable, and the cubes were detachable for nesting anywhere in the house. Of course, it wasn't unusual for him to prefer the plain brown box to the more colorful toy even after the box had been opened.

As much as I wanted to wake him and drag out the old laser dot interactive game, I resisted and let him sleep. Depending on how the rest of the day went, I might have a greater need for his company and expertise later.

Chris made a coffee and muffin run to the counter for us, a signal that he was ready to resume our duties as Trooper's deputies. Since Benny was unavailable for games, I was ready, too.

"We sure came close to finding out more about mercury today, and I don't mean the planet," Chris said, moving his chair around to face the door. He accompanied the move with an explanation: "In case our stalkers come back."

For me, I couldn't guarantee I'd be able

to maintain any level of decorum if Ryan Jamison showed his face again today, unless he was accompanied by a cop and either a warrant for my arrest or a big sign that said, I APOLOGIZE FOR HINDERING YOUR INVESTIGATION INTO THE MURDER OF ONE OF OUR EMPLOYEES.

Chris and I started this session by parsing the questions Chris had asked Garrett and Garrett's partial answers. Chris thought his memory of the rushed Q and A session was pretty accurate.

"I know I wanted to verify that Garrett was a chem major and I asked what he knew about the mercury research. I know I also asked about mercury stored in the lab, and now I wish I'd asked only that. I should have tried to get it in before the bullies came."

I nodded. "Because we don't know exactly what Garrett was responding to when he said, 'Yeah.' He might have been agreeing only that he's a chem major."

"We have to find another way to answer the question for sure, but it seems highly unlikely that we're going to learn anything about that research grant. Maybe I can go back in" — here Chris sounded like this was a Special Forces op — "under the auspices of the newspaper. I can call it a feature on security that we're doing. I'll look into going around Preston. There must be a PR person, or a communications liaison, that kind of person, who can tell us how much mercury is on-site. And tell us, is it under lock and key? Is there a sign-out sheet?"

"If we had to sign out an ounce of silver nitrate in my high school chem lab, I'd expect mercury would be equally controlled on this site."

"Except that's probably because teachers wanted nothing unaccounted for in the hands of teenage boys."

"And the occasional gutsy girl. I have another lead for someone to speak to." I told Chris about Irene and how she'd found her son's boss at J and M. I paused, trying to recall another moment that offered a clue. "Way back in the Bear Claw, when Ethan was being escorted to the hospital, Garrett and Kevin thought they heard last words from him. One was 'archer.' It should be possible to find out if the rec center activities that Garrett mentioned include archery. Another was 'harbor,' which of course could just mean that they did some fishing."

"But why would Ethan mention fishing at the end? He probably knew these were his last words, and saying 'harbor' would have been meaningless."

"So would 'archery,' I guess, unless it was an obsession of his," I said. "And Kevin thought he heard 'arc,' like an electric arc." I shook my head. "I'm getting nothing."

"Okay, what about rhyming words? Harbor, arbor, barber, starter."

"This is impossible," I said. "But, oh, starboard. A boat term."

"It's not clear he was on a boat this summer. I guess it's worth checking out. As for archer, that goes nowhere."

"Departure, Macarthur," I said, and with that we called it quits on the rhymes.

Chris dropped himself off at his office, leaving me alone with my car. "I have to show up for a staff meeting now and then," he said.

On my part, I finally had a text from Willow (good news) and was eager to see her and Zoe. I headed for the station house, where Zoe was still holed up (bad news, which I understood Willow would share in person).

The plan was that later, Chris would find his way to his pickup in my driveway, and maybe we'd "catch some dinner," he said. Dating terminology? Or just fishing talk?

I couldn't imagine why they'd still have

Zoe at the station house. Were they keeping her for questioning? And who were "they" anyway, since Trooper and Deputy Josh were supposed to be busy, the former in Big Lake, the latter tracking down Noah Bloom? So busy that Chris and I had been enlisted to help.

The parking lot in front of police headquarters was sparsely populated, not because there was no crime or crime fighting going on, but because the lot was about four times as big as it needed to be. I often invented in my mind a fantasy world where all the extra space in Alaska's parking lots would be transported by boat to the docks in San Francisco, where it would then be distributed across a city that really needed it.

I pulled into a spot in front of the flagpole and entered the main door of the station house. The inside wasn't as deserted as I had expected, however, and I wondered about the clientele, several of whom seemed to call the PD home, since they had been here yesterday. Then again, so had I.

A few people were slouched on the chairs or were sleeping on the benches in the lobby. I hoped they hadn't been here all night, waiting to be served. I wasn't surprised that Ms. Assistant had been replaced by a much tougher-looking middle-aged woman, one who could have been a bouncer on the mean streets of Elkview. I didn't even try to sound confident when I asked if by any chance I could please talk to Ms. Zoe Michaels.

Before the serious woman could bounce me out of the station house, Willow came bounding out of an interview room, the same one Chris and I had been in briefly yesterday.

I managed to ask Willow how things were going down there in Anchorage and to utter a word of thanks before entering the room to see Zoe. She looked considerably better than she had yesterday, mostly because of the fresh clothes Willow must have brought her. Clean jeans and a fresh T-shirt with a California logo partly hidden by a down vest. Why hadn't I thought of that? I hadn't even remembered to bring Zoe's own pink parka.

She stood and hugged me. I took it as a sign that she was feeling isolated and desperate for support. I hated the idea that she was being questioned while in such a vulnerable state.

"Will you tell Charlie, please?" Zoe said over her shoulder to Willow.

My mouth went dry. "Tell me what? What

is she still doing here, Willow?"

"She'll be released in the morning," Willow said, ushering me out into the lobby. "They think another twelve hours will get more out of her. I want her to be co-operative, given what we now know."

I swallowed hard. "What do we now know?"

She gestured toward a seat and took one herself, but I didn't want to stay in the building an extra minute if we couldn't have time with Zoe again.

"This will be faster," Willow said, crossing her willowy legs. Too many people throughout her life had asked how her parents could have known how perfect their name for her would turn out. "And I need to get back to Anchorage for an early appearance in the morning."

I took a seat and a deep breath. "Okay, tell me."

"They dumped Zoe's phone. She's either an innocent or not smart enough to have dumped it herself, though these days that probably wouldn't have mattered. I'm sure they have their ways of digging even into deleted messages."

"And?"

"She and Ethan had been dating."

"I guessed as much. She took it very hard.

But what's wrong with that? Is there some law against intracompany dating? At J and M, perhaps?"

"Nothing like that. They have separate dormitories, but no one polices them, according to Zoe. The problem is that they were about to break up, and Zoe was not happy about it. There are a lot of texts between them, some over-the-top."

I blew out a breath. "But that's no reason to get excited — unless she threatened him?"

"Not in so many words." Willow continued to pack her briefcase with paperwork. "But it is enough to search her dorm room and a few other places before they let her go, along with a warning not to leave town, I'm sure."

"What about the idea that Ethan was poisoned over a period of time? Do we know when Zoe and Ethan started their text wars?" I asked, determined to clear Zoe. But my immediate goal was to get her home, or at least to her dorm, as soon as possible.

"I don't know offhand when the relationship went south," Willow said. "But as you know, poisoning is rarely an exact science — or, I should say, rarely an exact weapon, so the dates don't really matter that much."

"Right."

"I'll be back after my morning meeting. Don't worry, Charlie. All you have to do is find out who really fed Ethan that poison, and Zoe can get on with her life."

We both smiled.

"I'm on it."

FIFTEEN

Usually, I loved to hear from my parents when they were on vacation. Last spring I went on a vicarious cruise on the Danube through their postcards and phone calls, for example. Although it was hard to beat Alaska for stunning, majestic scenery, I was glad my mom especially could experience life and vistas in another part of the world.

But now there were a few reasons why I wanted to avoid talking to my parents, especially to my mom, who had some of Benny's superpowers and was able to discern my mood and what was going on with me even from a distance.

Back at the Bear Claw in time to help out with the hopefully large Friday evening dinner crowd, I took a chance and answered my phone, even though the screen showed Mom's number.

"I haven't heard from you," she said. "Everything okay there?"

"Yep." Using a word I never used was a sure giveaway that everything was not okay. I swallowed before diving further into a white lie. "I didn't want to interrupt those relaxing, sunny days at the beach."

"Well, it is pretty sunny. The Russells love it here, did I tell you that? They say they don't know why they waited so long to move away from the cold."

"They don't miss Palmer and the rollicking nightlife of Anchorage?"

She laughed. "They don't miss the ice, that's for sure. 'Not good for old bones,' they've been telling us."

"It's a good thing you're not old," I said.

"And it's a good thing everything's fine there, Charlie. If I believed you, that is."

Uh-oh. How much does she know? "What do you mean?" A placeholder.

"We're still in the US, you know. Alaska news reaches the contiguous forty-eight."

"We're handling it."

"Out with it. Whatever 'it' is."

Of course, I ended up spilling the whole story, with the entire cast of characters from J and M Processing and beyond. The young victim, his girlfriend, his roommates, and his parents, who were probably on their way from Boston to claim his body. The fish processing plant, Annie's guest, and her missing son. I was tempted to hold back on the reappearance of Ryan, but why bother? She probably knew already anyway.

"You poor thing," she said. It wasn't clear which item in my litany put her over the top. "I certainly didn't know all that."

"Do not worry, Mom," I told her. "Chris and I are working together; and Willow Yazzie, you remember her, is helping out; and Victor and the staff are really stepping up. By the time you're back, it — that is, all the 'its' — will all be settled. When are you coming back, by the way?" I tried not to sound as though I needed her desperately, though it was close.

"Probably right after the weekend. Monday or Tuesday. I'd like to attend Stella's book club down here on Monday evening since I read the book and I've met some of the women in the group. Your dad might stay a little longer. He loves the golf club that Barney belongs to. It could be because Barney lets him win a lot of the time."

We signed off with "I love you more" on both sides, and I smiled as I reached for an apron. Talking to Mom did that for me. I'd have to arrange a slide show for her San Diego photos when they were back.

I wasn't surprised that my parents were aware of what was going on in Elkview.

Stella and Barney Russell were very connected, whereas both of my parents avoided all social media — my mom because she was concerned about being spied on, and my dad because his job as a management consultant involved enough people interaction, he claimed, and he didn't want to keep it up during his personal time.

Then it hit me.

I should have heard the signs as Mom had been talking about their visit all along. Sun and sand. Golfing. Pleasant weather year-round. Old friends already there. New friends in a book club.

Mom and Dad were moving to San Diego.

I plopped onto a chair, my apron falling to the floor, my heart joining it.

I shifted my thoughts as quickly as I could to the customers entering the diner, but the idea of my parents living almost four thousand miles away crowded out other, more practical thoughts. I listened as well as I could as Nina briefed me on the menu and on the small tour group that would be here for the next two days. Tomorrow was the birthday of one of the members, and the tour guide had requested a birthday cake for her. I agreed that we should honor that request.

I went through the motions of preparing

batters for the morning's omelets, muffins, and special pancakes. I ran a load of dishes and prepared the laundry for pickup. I geared up for the usual run of mooseloaf and mashed potatoes for tonight's dinners. I checked the booths for condiments and napkin holders that needed refilling.

What I didn't do was answer my phone calls and texts. I was on hiatus as far as communicating. My staff seemed to be aware that I was in attack mode on our ingredients and limited their interaction with me to necessary reporting or querying.

Nina approached me tentatively. "Anything we can help with?"

"Not just yet, thanks," seemed to satisfy her.

The busyness of the Bear Claw helped somewhat to distract me from the idea of losing my parents to Southern California. Of course, I myself had moved away for a few years — but I felt that was different. I was young, and my leaving was never meant to be permanent. I was all too aware, however, that when older people moved away, older people like my parents, they never came back. The move wasn't to earn a degree, to explore the world, or to beef up their résumés. It was to relocate.

Permanently.

I had to remind myself that I didn't need my parents as I had as a kid. I'd proven I could manage the Bear Claw as well as my own life. (More or less, on that latter one.) Mom and Dad deserved to live where they chose, and without responsibilities. They'd paid their dues, working hard, living in a harsh climate, giving me all the love and support a person could want.

I came to my senses more starkly when I realized the awful permanence of Ethan Johnson's parents losing him forever. I could fly to San Diego for a weekend whenever I chose. My parents could visit me. We could be together for the holidays or any other time. My family would be separated, but not destroyed, as Ethan's was.

The realization made me more determined than ever to seek and find justice for Ethan. But first, I needed expert counsel. As soon as the rush was over, I grabbed a salmon snack for Benny and headed for home.

I sat on my rocker and watched as Benny enjoyed his salmon. "Tomorrow," I told him, "you're getting only regular cat food." He gave me a "We'll see" look. "And you're going to eat it in the kitchen, where cats are supposed to eat," I added. He didn't dignify that with a response. I rubbed his back but not so much as to disturb his eating.

I wished I knew more about cats' memories. Benny certainly recognized people he liked and people he didn't like. When my mom was on her Danube cruise with Dad in the spring, she'd been gone almost two weeks before laying eyes on Benny again. He seemed to have no problem remembering her, sticking with her for the time she'd stayed with me when she got back. Was it her scent he remembered? Her looks? Her voice? The toy she brought him? Maybe all of the above. Whatever reinforced Benny's memories, I hoped I was providing pleasant ones and not always coming to him with problems to solve.

A framed photo stood on the end table next to my recliner — a snapshot from last summer's staff picnic in a small Elkview park. I picked it up, remembering. I'd been back from San Francisco for only a few months. It was hard to tell from the picture that the baskets were filled with anything but standard picnic food — watermelon and kiwi crisps, smoked salmon wrapped in lettuce, Greek salad, olive bread, and coffee dream bars for dessert. Some of the temporary staff were students who'd gone back to school, but the main crew was there. Victor, with his dark hair peeking out from a mock chef's hat, since he wasn't titled at the time; Nina, dressed only one level below the haute couture she usually changed into at the end of her shift; Tammy and Bert at opposite ends of the group (probably not the spots they'd be standing in today). Mom was seated front and center, all smiles. I'd kept to the back of the group, against all efforts to move me next to Mom.

Another *aha* moment, this one more positive than the relocation one that had sent my head spinning. We needed another picnic. Once Ethan's killer was caught and Noah was reunited with his mother, we'd celebrate. I planned the menu for the celebration, to include deviled eggs with my mom's secret ingredient. No one ever guessed it was as simple as celery seed.

In my mind, she and my dad flew up for thc occasion. It occurrcd to me that I had no idea when they'd be moving. "If" seemed uncontested, though we hadn't spoken about it. It was like my mom to drop hints and let me figure it out. She might even be waiting for me to broach the subject with something like, *Hey, Mom, have you and Dad ever considered retiring somewhere warm and sunny?*

Benny finished his salmon and hopped up on my lap. I thought I heard, "Time for another book," in purr-talk.

But not right away, since my phone rang with a call from Annie.

"Checking in," she said. "Remember it was my job to track Irene's son, Noah."

"Was? You found him?"

"No, but Irene did."

"Wow. That's great. Where was he? Or should I say where is he?"

"She hired a private detective. I guess she didn't have confidence in me. Not that I blame her. I wasn't getting anywhere."

I was used to having to repeat questions to get Annie back on track. "Where was he?" I prompted.

"In a cabin up north. Irene didn't say where exactly."

"Who was the detective who found him?"

"She won't say. I think she's embarrassed that she went over me, or around me or whatever, although I don't mind at all as long as he's okay."

"Why did he stop writing or calling his mom?"

The better question would have been, why didn't I stop pursuing this case? I should have called it a win and crossed it off my list.

"Irene says he just needed a break and lost track of time. I guess the dorms get a little crowded or something."

"Did Irene go up there to see him?"

Back off, Charlie. I would have been better off if Annie weren't so obliging.

"No, he called her and sent some selfies so she could see where he was staying. I guess he's going to head back here to Elkview soon, but she's not sure when."

It seemed strange to me that Irene would travel more than three thousand miles to look for her son and not travel another couple of hundred to see him. But who was I to judge what was strange behavior?

"When did you say she was leaving?" It was no use pretending I could drop it.

"Tomorrow, mid-morning. She ordered a car to take her to Anchorage for her flight."

"Maybe we could get together for breakfast? I'd like to say goodbye."

And a whole lot more.

"That's a great idea. I'll let her know." Did I feel sheepish messing with Annie this way? Of course. I'd make it up to her with an overdue movie night. "Shall we meet you at the Bear Claw?"

"Or I can bring the Bear Claw to you if she doesn't have a lot of time." So considerate as I plan my third degree on her.

"Even better. Thanks, Charlie. I know you've had a long day, so I'll let you go, and

I'll see you at eight-ish? And we can talk about the tour that's coming in."

I'd had a long day indeed, starting with a back-and-forth to J and M and including a back-and-forth to the Bear Claw, a trip to the station house, and a life-changing phone call from San Diego.

I headed for my bedroom, Benny close behind me.

I barely made it through one chapter of a favorite cat book when I fell asleep. I can't say whether Benny left his pillow during the night, but he was there in the morning, his paw holding the place for chapter two.

Sixteen

Like me, Annie had inherited her parents' property and business. Jensen's Elkview Inn had quickly become known as Annie's Inn, in a way that the Bear Claw would never be called Charlie's Diner. Annie had put her mark on the business by effective advertising and smart marketing. For all her ineptitude at verbal sparring, she was a tireless promoter and had grown the business by leaps and bounds.

Annie found a way to woo customers with very different needs. Her property housed a midsize Victorian with a row of small cottages on either side. On the west side were cabins with minimal creature comforts, aimed at the mountain, rock, and ice climbers and at the professionals and semiprofessionals who came to reach the top of Denali and break records for hiking and kayaking. For them she offered a night or two in a bed with a real pillow instead of the back of an SUV with a duffel bag for a cushion, but in those cabins there were no luxuries to be embarrassed about when they shared adventure stories later. The hot showers were a well-kept secret.

On the east side were cabins outfitted with enough amenities to match the finest hotels, with heated towels, coffee at the ready, and mints on the pillows. Annie promised comfort to tourists who wanted to see Alaska, but with the buffer of a tour guide to take them fishing, birding, canoeing, dogsledding, and general sightseeing. They were guaranteed exposure to the charm of Alaska, spectacular views, and wild animal sightings, plus a swag bag of souvenirs, from postcards to mosquito repellent in the summer and face shields in the winter. I contributed to the swag with an elk jerky recipe and the Bear Claw's renowned snack pack — made famous by Annie's Inn, I might add.

Fortunately for me, Annie decided not to expand into a bed-and-breakfast lodge.

"For one thing, I don't like to cook. That's number one, and that's also the other things," she'd told me, "so they're all yours."

I'd assumed she meant her guests and was offering me the chance to feed them. We agreed on a plan to share the cost of shuttle service between Annie's Inn and the Bear Claw, which were only a short, view-filled ride apart.

This morning, I carried my signature breakfast bag with our Alaskan bear logo up the steps to the main house and entered the inn's lobby. Annie had chosen a soft blue decor for the sofas and chairs, with a wood-burning fireplace and inviting conversation corners. A small reception desk was off to the side, staffed at the moment by Annie herself.

Annie's cat, Yulie, a beautiful flame-point Siamese with piercing blue eyes, greeted me. I was ready for him, having dropped a felt mouse into my tote. While Annie finished with her newest guest, Yulie and I had some fun with the new mouse. The only problem was that, unlike my quiet Benny, Yulie was a yowler, emitting loud sounds whether he was unhappy or very happy, as now. Annie had gotten him from a rescue center when he was seven months old, and as she liked to say, he'd never stopped yowling. She motioned for me to quiet him down while she talked to her guest, but it was no use unless I found a way to get him to nap.

"Oh, Charlie, I tried to text you," she said, when she'd sent her visitor off with an inn worker. "But I don't think it went through." Annie held up her phone and made slapping motions. "I think it's the battery."

"What's up? Is Irene ready?" I pointed to my deep brown carrier, which I knew Annie would recognize as full of flour, sugar, nuts, and cinnamon in one breakfast form or another.

Annie threw up her hands. "Irene left."

I frowned, confused, and pointed to the clock over the check-in desk. Seven forty-seven. "I'm early," I said, as if Annie couldn't see for herself.

Annie closed the large registry book and stopped straightening items on the desk. "I know," she said, massaging her fingers. "She said she was sorry, but in case the traffic is too much, she wanted to get ahead of it."

Did she now? I was peeved, but not at Annie, and not because I'd gotten up early, driven to the Bear Claw, and baked for this occasion. I was peeved because I knew Irene had not been truthful with us from the beginning. Was Noah Bloom even her son? Was she really from Wisconsin? I had the thought of asking Trooper to dig deeper, in case Irene and her alleged son were a piece of the puzzle that was Ethan's murder. Maybe she'd come to murder another summer worker. There was no end to my speculations.

"I'm really sorry," Annie continued, probably waiting for me to respond instead of standing there motionless, entertaining conspiracy theories. "I know you baked and all."

I gave brief consideration to jumping into my car, racing to the Anchorage airport, running along the shiny, vast hallways past shops and life-size stuffed animals, searching for Irene. I came to my senses, deciding that the odds of finding her before she boarded a plane were slim without exact information as to her airline, flight number, and time. And there was no way she'd be forthcoming with the truth on those details without a warrant.

Not worth the effort.

"Never mind, Annie," I said. "Let's you and I have some breakfast."

Annie made us excellent mugs of coffee from a self-service setup in a corner of the lobby. She was on duty, so we used a small seating arrangement near the check-in desk as our breakfast bar. The inn's special roast and the Bear Claw pastries improved my mood considerably. We spent some time recounting stories about Benny from me and about Yulie from Annie. Yulie had the run of Annie's Inn. He could be anywhere at the moment. Roaming the hallways, hiding in an interesting broom closet, curled up in one of the sitting rooms off the lobby. The thought that I was depriving Benny of such wide-open spaces prompted me to ask Annie if she had a couple of ounces of catnip to spare, since I'd run out. Benny loved to sniff the catnip-filled pillows Mom would sew for him, often in the shape of a mouse. I'd often thought it was too bad cats didn't do playdates, the way dogs did. I smiled as I thought how there would never be such a thing as a cat park, like the dog parks in town. Benny and Yulie were simply not destined to meet and play together. Neither would come out unscathed.

When a sudden rush of business interrupted us, I offered to take care of welcoming a couple who'd arrived from Portland, Oregon, while Annie ushered a family with two small children to a cottage on the east side of the property. I knew that at least one of those cabins was outfitted with games and puzzles, in case Alaska's high summer humidity was too much for them.

I was glad to help out with the next guests, to reciprocate for the many times Annie had donned an apron at the Bear Claw when I needed an extra hand. I took care of a credit card transaction for the new couple and answered the usual questions from first-timers.

"Yes, it's true that there are thirty-five species of mosquitoes in the state at this time of year," I told the chatty young woman. "But they're not as bad as the myths surrounding them."

Her male companion read out loud from one of Annie's many pamphlets, displayed on a multilevel oaken rack.

"As long as we stay away from 'stagnant ponds and moist tundra,' " he read, and laughed.

"What's a tundra?" she asked.

"I assume these spots are well labeled?" He sounded hopeful.

I assured him that they'd be safe following the other tips and recommendations, such as wearing long-sleeved shirts and avoiding scented soaps, lotions, and shampoos.

"And you'll find repellent in your cottage," I added.

I handed the pen to the young woman to sign in and watched as she half printed, half wrote: "Sally Pierce." She then twisted the pen to read the writing along its barrel.

"This is weird," Sally said.

Her companion looked over her shoulder

and addressed me. "Sally collects pens from all the places where we stay on the road." His tone was teasing. I pegged them as newlyweds, thought of Ryan, and felt my jaw clench. "She even has one from a hotel in Dubai. She must have a hundred of them."

"Not that many," she said, nudging him. "This one says 'Marcus King Detective Agency.' " She smiled and looked around the lobby. "Is there something we should know about this place? Like, does a PI have an office here?"

I let out a small gasp and forced a laugh. "So sorry," I said, taking the pen from her as gently as I could and stashing it in the pocket of my jacket. "Someone must have left this behind in this morning's crowd." I reached under the desk to a box of Annie's logo pens and other souvenirs and fished around. I handed Sally a bright blue and silver pen from the multicolored assortment. "Here's an Annie's Inn pen for your collection."

"Oh, nice colors, thanks."

I dug another pen from the box. "In fact, take two," I said.

As soon as I was alone, I retrieved the click pen from my pocket. I turned the barrel and read the imprint, white on a burgundy background: MARCUS KING DETECTIVE AGENCY, with an address in Elkview and an eight-hundred number. I recognized the street as one on the outskirts of town. A private eye in my own hometown. I never would have guessed, but then, I'd never needed one.

Until now.

While I waited for Annie to return to determine if there was any possibility that the pen was left behind by someone other than Irene Bloom, I constructed a plan. First, visit Marcus King. I didn't expect him to disclose private information, of course, but I thought there might be something I could pick up about a client named Irene Bloom. The second part of my so-called strategy would be to share this information with Trooper on the off chance that he could look into whatever publicly available particulars Mr. King had discovered. The zeroth position in the strategy, I realized, belonged to Chris, whom I needed to loop in.

I explained all of this to Annie, who was positive Irene had left the pen, because it was the only time this morning that a guest had to use her own pen to sign out.

"And that was Irene," she said, with

multiple head nods. "I hadn't opened the new boxes of my own pens yet," she explained.

The timing was good in that Annie expected a busload of tourists before the day was over. We never had been able to track the pen's route to the inn once they arrived.

"Shall we go into Irene's cabin?" she asked me, in a near whisper. "I don't think Juan has cleaned it out yet."

"I wouldn't mind." The understatement of the year.

Off we went to the east side of the inn's property. Annie had outdone herself in trying to make these cabins pleasing, inside and out. Attached to the exterior of each were a jacuzzi and a porch from which to view the lake and the mountains in the distance. On the interior, Annie had matched quilts to draperies, hung photos with interesting shots of the gardens and of the willow ptarmigan, the official bird of the state.

The room that had been assigned to Irene was a two-person cottage with two twin beds, a sitting room, and a kitchenette. The door was unlocked, and upon opening it we caught a whiff of a familiar, refreshing scent. It was pleasant, but one that was sure to attract mosquitoes. Apparently, Irene had not read the tips and recommendations on every Alaska pamphlet and website. NO SCENTED SOAPS, LOTIONS, ETC.!

I saw that Juan would not have a lot to do. The room looked as neat and clean as if Irene had never slept here. Maybe she hadn't, I thought, picking up on the covert life I'd constructed for her.

Annie checked the closet and all the drawers, even fishing around in back in case something had gotten stuck. I looked in the bathroom and saw that the shower had been used, with wet towels piled up, probably from this morning, and scratched the theory that she had been operating from another post.

I'd watched a few TV shows featuring amateur and professional sleuths with my mom. Now I wished I'd paid more attention. I tried to remember how the detectives went about searching for clues in cases like this. The wastebasket, I thought. There was always a clue in the wastebasket. I found two metal trash containers, one by the desk, the other under the bathroom sink. Tipping over both yielded nothing. No shop receipt or letter or sticky note with a phone number. The same for feeling around under the mattresses and the pillows on the bed and on the easy chair.

Not a single clue as to Irene's activities surfaced. I recognized that twenty-first century living didn't lend itself well to the tricks of the past. We used our own cell phones, not a human-operated phone that would have traceable calls. We made notes on a phone app, not hotel pads. It seemed that crime-fiction shows were just that. Fiction. I planned to point that out to my mom. If we ever watched TV together again.

At that point, I almost let Annie in on my theory that my parents would never live in Elkview again. But we had bigger fish to — I smiled before finishing the metaphor.

Annie and I each sat on the edge of a bed. She showed me her palms, as empty as mine were.

Which made me think of fingerprints. If Juan was as good as Annie claimed, the only fingerprints in the room would be Irene's. Plus Annie's and mine, of course, because, unlike TV detectives, we had touched everything with our bare hands, leaving prints everywhere. Still, Trooper or his crew might be able to sort through them.

"What's next?" Annie asked.

I pulled the ballpoint pen from my pocket and indicated Marcus King's name and address. "We follow the only lead we have."

"What if Irene really is just a kind lady

who came looking for her son, found him, and is now on her way back home?" Annie asked.

Maybe Annie was right, but Irene's behavior wasn't normal by my rules.

"If you're right, we'll find out," I told Annie. "I'm going to pay a call to this private eye."

Back in the lobby, our attention turned to a group of three men and one woman who entered the lobby. They were dressed in heavy clothing in spite of the mild temperatures and were easily identifiable as climbers who knew what they wanted.

"We're hoping you have a west-side cabin or two," one of the burly men said.

"Absolutely," Annie said. And then to me, "You'll have to meet the private eye on your own, and I'll come later when Henry arrives to work the desk. Unless you want to wait for backup."

"That won't be necessary. But text me first, in case dropping in and asking about a lost and found gets me nowhere fast."

"No way. You're a natural crime solver, whether it's a missing person or a murder."

The confidence my friend had in me was at once undeserved and inspiring. On the other hand, her newest guests looked confused and concerned. I hoped they wouldn't get the wrong idea and take off.

SEVENTEEN

As good as Annie's coffee was, I needed a cappuccino from Aly's. In truth, I also needed a break from the busy Annie's Inn and time to absorb the additional branch of an already full, treelike case — the absconding Irene Bloom and the newly awakened Marcus King, private detective.

I thought I'd start with a simple search for King, his promotional pen being the only potential clue as to what had kept Irene busy during her time in Elkview. A little recon never hurt. I opened my laptop and found King's website without a problem.

The "About" section told me that King had set himself up in Elkview this year after serving as an MP in the army, a Los Angeles cop, and a former member of a SWAT team, all of which gave him impressive street credentials. The bio also explained why I'd never heard of him. In a way, he was as new to town as I was. He was a professed expert at Alaskan terrain and remote investigations. He could serve papers via cars, boats, planes, hiking, and other modes of transportation, which I pictured as riding a moose or an elk when necessary. He claimed to have an abundance of resources at his fingertips.

And he was ready to serve us.

I read down the list of services King offered and guessed Irene would not have needed assistance with background checks, tenant/landlord negotiations, covert surveillance, or suspicions of infidelity. Probably the closest would be skip tracing, defined on King's site as "locating a person's whereabouts."

There was no photo on the website, and I knew cops could retire young, so I had to be prepared for any look. I was ready. I packed up my laptop and stray papers and started toward the dirty dishes tub with my mug when I saw that I'd waited a few minutes too long.

"Hey, you weren't going somewhere without me, were you?"

"Of course not."

Chris Doucette had found me, no doubt through well-meaning Annie. As I thought about it, I was grateful for the help. Some interviews required a good cop/bad cop approach.

I briefed Chris on my morning so far and meant it when I said, "I'm glad you caught me."

"I guess I'm hard to reach, huh?"

I supposed that was my cue to apologize for not keeping him in the loop, but it was hard for me to admit that most of the time, I preferred to work alone. But not this time.

"Things happened fast," I said, as I added my coffee mug to the large gray tub. Chris was kind enough not to note that I hadn't been rushed enough to order my drink to go.

In Alaska, the terrain can change abruptly. One minute, you're driving on what the lower forty-eight think of as a normal road with houses and trees, and the next minute you're on gravel, with what looks like a dry cabin every half mile or so. Some of these plumbing-less, running-water-less abodes were isolated; others were clumped together into what might be called a development, though in some sense they were undeveloped.

As we turned onto Marcus King's property, we saw only a small cabin, separated from any other homes, with a wooded area behind it, enormous solar panels on the roof, and a large gravelly lot in front of it and to the sides.

With Chris at the wheel as usual, we approached King's tiny home and saw a sign next to the steps that read, RESERVED PARKING. I wondered if this was a reflection of King's sense of humor, since there wasn't a car or a person within earshot for at least a mile as we'd driven in from the road. Three semis could have pulled up together and parked without a problem.

The house looked brand-new, its metal exterior freshly painted brown from the peak in the roof to the middle vertically and white from the middle to the ground. From the window arrangement and the slant of the roof, it appeared to have a second-story loft. A similarly designed and painted outhouse was at the end of a pathway that stretched out from the side.

We obeyed the sign and left the reserved space free, climbed four steps, and knocked on a white door. A man's voice called out for us to enter.

I was surprised to see a youngish man, by which I meant only a few years older than I was, behind a desk with a laptop open and not much else either on the desk or in the room. Two folding chairs were set out on a highly polished laminate floor.

Where was the PI of old movies? The one in a rumpled suit, sitting at an old desk with papers and books stacked floor to ceiling, a cigarette burning in an ashtray, and a bottle of something strong in the bottom drawer? This desk didn't even have drawers, just a flat surface with a shelving system attached to the wall above it.

"Just moved in, as you can tell," the man said. He pointed toward the back of the property. "Tore the old eyesore down and set this up. It'll be a while before I bring my stuff in from storage, though."

Maybe there would be a six-foot pile of papers and a bottle of spirits, after all.

"Very nice looking," Chris said. I figured he meant it, since he had spent some time in foxholes.

The man closed his laptop, stood, and reached out to shake our hands. "Marcus King. How can I help you today?"

King was a match in height for Chris and me, and from his outfit, jeans and a long-sleeved bright orange T-shirt, you could surmise he'd just come in from a logging gig.

Chris and I had agreed on a strategy that might give us a clue as to what had transpired between Irene Bloom and PI Marcus King.

King had moved his shiny mesh-backed chair around to face the other two seats, and soon we were in an uncomfortable circle. I tried to imagine the more proper Irene in this setting, pantyhose, pearls, and all.

"Can I offer you a drink?" King asked.

He'd removed the cover from a red cooler and showed us the contents. What we saw were bottles of water and cans of soft drinks. We declined. I didn't know Chris's reason, but I wasn't taking any chances on having to use the outdoor facilities.

"We're friends of Irene Bloom," I said.

"We know she hired you to find her son, Noah," Chris said. "And that you found him for her."

"But now Irene has gone missing," I said. "So we're very concerned."

"We know you can't tell us anything confidential, but —" Chris began.

"I'll bet you're Trooper Graham's unofficial deputies," King said, with a wide, pleasant grin.

That stopped our prepared dialogue cold.

"Yes, we are," from me, surprised, but pleased to have been acknowledged as acceptable visitors.

"Uh-huh," from Chris, who'd been cut off mid-sentence.

King laughed. "Trooper does this a lot. Sends me his crew."

I tried to hide my shock. Trooper had other unofficial deputies? My friends and I were not special in that regard? I felt betrayed in a way, like a wife who learns she's not the only one, that her husband has another, in fact many other families. I had a vision of Trooper sitting at his desk at the station house all day with his feet up, dispatching dozens of pseudo deputies to do his work.

Chris recovered more quickly and took advantage of the situation.

"Then you know how important this is, connected to a murder case back in town."

"Uh-huh," King said. "Can't tell you anything about this Mrs. Whoever, of course."

"Of course not," Chris said.

"But I can help you and Trooper Graham out with some useful information, stuff that you would have come upon on your own eventually."

"That would be great," Chris said, filling in for the still-stunned me.

"What you do is, when you leave here, the best way back to town is if you take a left and follow the signs."

"But wouldn't that be —"

Chris managed to bump my ankle, a sign to quit while we were ahead, and possibly with an eye toward getting even with me for the light kick I'd given him a few days ago.

"Thanks, Mr. King," I said, and headed out the door with Chris.

"A left, then follow the signs. But which signs?" I asked Chris as we headed off King's property in my car.

"I think we'll know them when we see them."

"Can you believe that Trooper has a whole crew of 'deputies'?" I made a show of putting the word in airborne quotes.

"It makes sense when you think about it. Underfunding is not news."

"I suppose."

I decided I'd hold off on any more pouting and do the job I was asked to do.

We continued on without another sign or driveway to turn into, either to the left or to the right. We followed groves of fir and cottonwood, the whole scene reminding me of a Christmas tree lot. I tried to relax and enjoy the beautiful road. When we cracked the windows an inch or so, the crisp air poured in.

"There," Chris said, too loudly. He slammed on the brakes. "There's a general store. Maybe this is our goal, or someone in there can tell us where we're supposed to get our information."

"This is way too much like a scavenger hunt," I said. "And I'm really not in the mood for one. I'm not sure why we care about Noah anymore if his mother doesn't care enough to share."

"Good thing you didn't try for a job in journalism."

"Or the law," I pointed out. "In any case, I'm all for going into" — I squinted and read the sign, surprised we were still in Elkview: ELKVIEW BROTHERS GENERAL STORE — "that store. It has something I need if we're going to keep driving deeper into dry country."

"Restrooms," Chris said, guessing correctly.

I gave him a thumbs-up and tried to bear in mind the reason this trip might be useful — as a clue into the murder of Ethan Johnson, who'd died in my diner soon after he'd walked into it.

The sprawling general store was set back on a huge lot. Not for the first time, I compared the parking situation anywhere in Alaska to that in the San Francisco Bay

Area, where residents had to apply for permits to park near their own homes.

Inside the store, the Elkview brothers offered a little of everything in the massive, ultra-high-ceilinged space, from produce and groceries on one end of the store to postal service on the other.

The endcaps of each aisle had advertisements, postings of special deals, and the like, causing me to wonder if I should have more signage in the Bear Claw. One notice was a helpful plan for preparedness in the event of a power outage. I read down the list and thought I could reproduce it from memory with no trouble.

- Stock up on bottled water (WATER, Aisle 3)
- Have paper plates on hand (PAPER GOODS, Aisle 7)
- Have a large stockpot on the stove for soups (HOUSEHOLD, Aisles 9 and 10)
- Have some easy freeze-dried meals on hand (FROZEN FOODS, Aisle 15)

There were many other tips, most tied to the store's inventory. Maybe this kind of public service posting, minus the aisle designations, could find a place at the Bear Claw.

Chris and I found our respective restrooms in a back corner and met up afterward in the food service area. The gray metal tables and attached benches were crowded with singles, groups, and families with young children. Things hadn't changed much since I was in high school. Stores like this were where it was happening at lunchtime on a Saturday in Elkview, as the closest destinations we had to a big-box store.

"Checking out the competition?" he asked.

"Always. Their selection of jerky is impressive." I swept my arm along the shelf. "Beef, buffalo, elk, moose. Also, teriyaki, sweet and spicy, garlic, black pepper, and more." I was aware that I sounded like a commercial.

Off to the side along one wall was the sign we wanted: CUSTOMER SERVICE.

"How are we playing this?" I was getting into the game.

"We'll ask the clerk if there's a community of dry cabins nearby. Sometimes they take in guests who are trying to lay low for one reason or another. The owners usually deal in cash. Some don't even have a utility bill."

"Shall I ask how you know this? The laying-low thing, I mean. Are you sure you weren't in WITSEC?"

"If I were, I couldn't tell you."

"Funny."

"Seriously, I did a feature on dry cabins. You didn't see it?"

"I must have missed that issue."

"It wasn't in the *Bugle.* A magazine bought the story. There were some interesting takes on tiny houses. One woman lived in a converted school bus. She was teaching an ecology course and wanted to practice what she was teaching."

"I thought living simple was cleaning out your closet once a year."

"Nope. Four hundred square feet is what we're talking about most of the time."

"We have to get inside," I said. "How about this? We're looking for a friend who's here for a little R and R, and we don't have the exact address."

"We can say, 'He just told us it was beyond the Elkview Brothers place.' "

"Check."

On duty today was someone's Grandpa. Old, dumpy, with overalls and a pleasant smile.

Until we made our pitch.

"Don't rightly know of any such place," he said. He turned to a woman at the other end of the counter. "Clara, you know anything about some dry cabins nearby?"

"Can't say I do," Clara yelled back, continuing to collect bills from the register and stack them neatly. Their chief financial officer, I guessed.

A youngish tuxedo cat, who'd been hidden till now, jumped onto the counter and walked toward us. He was the essence of tuxedo, with shiny black fur everywhere except for the white strip that started between his eyes, twisted around his nose, mouth, and chin, and ran straight down his tummy. His body ended in four white paws at the end of black legs. He could have played the groom in a wedding movie.

I waited until I was sure he was comfortably squatted near me, then greeted him warmly with a "Hi, there" and a smile. He didn't turn and flee — a good sign. Once again, I felt a twinge of regret that Benny did not have the run of a huge space like the Elkview Brothers store. I pictured him stretched out along Aisle 6, the pet food aisle, waiting for some tuna.

"He's beautiful," I said of the tuxedo cat. "What's his name?" I asked Clerk Grandpa.

"He's Cutaway."

"Perfect." I took a chance and offered him my hand. He sniffed it and accepted me, allowing me to run my finger down his back.

"This is strange. He usually runs and hides when there's anyone here," Grandpa remarked.

"Maybe he smells Benny, my orange tabby, and he's curious."

I proceeded to talk about Benny and how his real name is Eggs Benedict because I manage a diner.

Grandpa thought that was pretty funny and laughed as only Santa and certain grandpas could.

I revealed how I'd just found the most fun toy that Grandpa might want to look into. And the special tree house was also a winner.

"I'm sure you have that condo look-alike for Cutaway," I said.

Chris had wisely stayed off to the side during this exchange, fingering a rack of watch bands in various designs, though as far as I recalled, he hadn't worn a watch in the several months that we'd worked together.

"I wish I had a treat for you," I said to Cutaway. He stood, lifted his tail, stretched, and yawned. "Maybe I'll come back with one, okay?" I added. Even though he was no Benny, I was sure Cutaway understood me.

"You know," Clerk Grandpa said, "I might

have an idea where you can find those cabins."

EIGHTEEN

We drove out of the Elkview Brothers General Store parking lot, our purchases in the back seat. We'd felt it only fair that we show our gratitude for their excellent customer service by carrying away a bag or two of their goods. Chris had walked to TOOLS on Aisle 11 and found an extra set of hand tools to carry in the bed of his pickup. I bought a package of three rolls of paper towels and two pot holders for my home kitchen. We might have looked like an old married couple.

"Well played," Chris said, tapping his fingers on the steering wheel.

"But I wasn't playing. Cutaway walked over in his built-in tuxedo and I just responded to the moment."

"Okay, then good responding."

Chris tipped his cap in my direction, exposing part of his shaved head. Today's logo cap was from the Alaska Aces — maybe a collector's item, since the hockey team hadn't played here for a few years.

"I'll bet those two aren't at all as dumb as they were pretending to be. I'll bet they're back there now at their daily game of chess," I said.

"And without the bluegrass accents," he added. "They probably shed their overalls, too, as soon as they're out of the public eye."

I pulled out the map Grandma-slash-CFO Clara happened to find for us under the counter. Without saying a word, she'd circled a small area down the road a piece and given us a friendly wave goodbye.

Another fifteen minutes with fir trees on both sides of a narrow two-lane road, and Chris hit the brakes again.

"Sorry, these so-called roads sneak up on me," he said.

I saw it, too: a crude sign that read FOUNDER'S VILLAGE. Chris had to back up to be able to turn into a development, if it could be called that, of tiny houses — a technical term according to some Realtors, and in some boroughs — all about the size of Marcus King's, some with an added porch, and most with zero bathrooms, as evidenced by the outhouses in the rear. The path from the road opened into a ragged semicircular arrangement of cabins with varying distances between them. Mountains rose up behind the area.

"I don't quite get this," I said. "I thought the idea was to have a couple of acres of your own. To be cut off from the world."

"Not necessarily. Some people want the best of both worlds, meaning a small space with minimal living but a sense of community also. They'll join a gym where they can hang out, and by the way, take a shower. Or they'll go to a laundromat for conversation as well as for washing clothes."

"You sound pretty familiar with this lifestyle."

"I knew a guy once" — we both laughed at that old catchall — "when I was stationed up near Fairbanks, where there are a lot of these communities. He was a musician. His whole cabin was filled with guitars, some very expensive. But he had no running water."

I shuddered at the thought. "I saw those water stations back there outside the store. A woman was filling a five-gallon container with water from a hose, like through a gas nozzle. That wouldn't last me a day."

I looked ahead at the cabins. Some were very rustic; others had elaborate scrollwork on the doors and trims. One cabin had hubcaps of different sizes and designs nailed to the outside wall. But each had a loft that I imagined was a lookout post.

"Shall we just knock on a door and ask if anyone knows a Noah Bloom?" Chris asked.

A nervous shiver ran through me. "What if this is a compound? The kind where they're all armed and ready to shoot anyone who encroaches on their property?"

Chris laughed. "Wow, is that the kind of thing your mom reads in her crime books? Is that where you're getting this?"

"Don't bring up my mom, please." I was having trouble compartmentalizing today and thinking of her and my dad a lot, picturing them packing up and selling the house I grew up in. "But no, that's not the kind of book she reads. They're more the whodunit genre."

"What's wrong with bringing up your mom?"

"She may be moving to San Diego." Once the statement was out of my mouth, I couldn't believe I'd said it, and not to my best friend, Annie, or Trooper, or even to my Bear Claw staff. But to this only slightly more-than-casual friend, and a reporter, at that. "It's not definite, so don't say anything, please."

"I won't. I'm sorry to hear it, though. I know you guys are close."

"Do you think Noah's holed up in one of these tiny houses?" I asked.

Back to work.

"Possibly. But why? I wonder. To meditate? Maybe just to get away from the dorm, especially if it's all crowded."

"The bigger issue is, why didn't Irene come up here to see him?" A question that had been bugging me since I heard Annie's story about Irene's quick exit.

"Let's try one of these places," Chris said, pulling off to the side of the wide path that was called a road. "Lenny's Road," in fact.

Chris opened his door and stepped out.

I clicked the buckle on my seat belt open.

Chris stopped, turned, and hopped back into the Outback in one swift movement.

"What's wrong?" I asked.

Then I saw it. A sleek brown Doberman pinscher came roaring toward us, barking loudly, its long muzzle ready for action.

My heart went into overdrive. I sat still in my seat, noting Chris's heavy breathing. The only relief came when we both let out a laugh as Chris pushed the door lock on the car.

"He can't get in now," I said, through my laughter.

We were still for a minute or two as the Doberman continued to bark loudly, his paws scratching at the driver's-side window, his watery breath steaming it up. It seemed forever, but he, or she, finally let up and trotted away.

"What do you bet that's Noah?" I asked as I saw a man race out of one of the cabins and hop onto a motorized bike.

Chris maneuvered the car away from a most likely perplexed Doberman, and a car chase ensued.

"Who do they think we are?" he asked. "Siccing their guard dog on us."

"Tax collectors? Narcs?" I suggested.

"Hard to tell. At least we didn't see any artillery." Chris pulled onto the lot and turned back to the road. "I'm going to see if I can overtake that bike."

We passed a sign indicating ANCHORAGE one way and FAIRBANKS the other, with no indication of how far either was. We kept going straight, almost closing in on the biker. But he made an abrupt course correction, crossing over to join the small amount of traffic traveling in the opposite direction. I turned in my seat and kept track as he rode for a few yards. Chris couldn't make the same maneuver, of course, with my large Outback. I watched as the biker turned into the woods.

I shook my head. "He's gone."

Chris hit the steering wheel. "That's that."

We eventually turned around ourselves, heading back, sailing past enough firs to cover Christmas for the rest of the century. I hit HOME on the GPS. "Lunch at the Bear Claw," I said, a command decision, wanting Chris to come down from the thrill of the chase. "I hope Trooper is there."

"So we can brief him on all this," Chris said.

"So I can ask him to call a meeting of his full complement of deputies."

When we reached the Bear Claw, I used my laptop to check my emails, and a live phone call came in while I was scrolling, from Willow. She called to say that Zoe was almost certainly about to be released. I was overjoyed.

"It's not definite, but I thought I'd give you a heads-up. Any chance you can pick her up?" Willow asked. "I absolutely have to get back to Anchorage for a deposition."

"No problem. The least I can do."

"I'm so sorry I don't even have a minute for a coffee with you. One of these days."

"Yes, and I promise I'll drive to you the next time. And buy you coffee."

I was happy to be able to salvage the day by doing something useful toward solving

Ethan's murder. Sometimes it was hard to remember what our gallivanting was all about, Chris and mine, when we came back with next to nothing.

"I'll text you when I know for sure," Willow said. "And by the way, a volunteer is going to drive your mom's car to her address. Maybe you could see to putting it back in the garage, or wherever she keeps it."

"Of course." My mom's car! I'd forgotten all about it. Zoe had driven it to Millie's to pick up her parka and then got taken to the station house in a patrol car. One of Trooper's volunteers, not to be confused with his civilian deputies, had driven Mom's car from Millie's to the station house and now would return it to Mom's, where it would be safe, no thanks to me.

"And I'm assuming we're sticking to the story that she had permission to borrow it, so no charges, et cetera," Willow continued.

"That's right."

"You forgot, didn't you?" Willow laughed. And when I did also, she knew she was right. We hung up on that note.

I debated whether to call Mom and Dad — not to talk about the borrowed car, however. I realized I'd built up a new lifestyle for them out of whole cloth. Why had

I been hesitating to call and ask them directly what I suspected? I needed another session with Benny, but for now I had to be satisfied with a quick visit via the phone app. As usual, he was in front of the camera. I told him I missed him and had a treat for him, though I shelved the word "catnip" for a time when I'd be with him.

Victor came by our table.

"Any problems?" I asked.

"The usual delivery hassles. The new guy left the milk at the door without ringing the bell, but I handled it."

"That's what I like to hear."

"I want to show you this," he said, and opened the *Elkview Bugle* to an ad. The special slow cooker he'd been wanting was on sale from a store in Fairbanks. He launched into a campaign about its amazing features, ticking them off on his fingers. "It has eleven functions and comes with a stir tower," he said, "so you don't have to keep —"

"Buy it," I said, just as he got started.

"Okay, then, boss." He cut off his speech, gave me a salute, and wandered off. Smart guy.

Every day I had greater and greater insight into how managers make decisions at times. All the planning in the world, all the seminars on supervisory skills and smart fiscal management, fall apart when your patience runs out and you have things other than your budget on your mind. Or when your staff can tell when you're most likely to acquiesce.

"Can I get a grilled cheese deluxe, or whatever the latest name is?" I called into the kitchen — something I would do only if the Bear Claw had no one other than regular customers, as today. I pointed to Chris, who nodded. "Two, please," I said, and Nina gave me a thumbs-up, either for the order or for the new appliance.

I gave Benny a final five minutes with a remote-controlled mouse I'd found online, then bit into my own treat, a grilled cheese supreme, which was as good a name as any.

When the text came from Willow with the go-ahead to pick up Zoe, I wrapped half of my sandwich to take to Zoe, figuring even a cold grilled cheese was better than a hot meal at the station house.

Chris opted out of the trip to the station house to pick up Zoe. "I'm bummed to miss her, but I had a message from Wally, and he wants to see me. I think he's just pulling rank, making sure I show up at the office once in a while."

I stopped off at my house to load my car with a couple of the snack packs I kept in my home fridge and a clean, lightweight San Francisco sweatshirt of mine that Zoe could change into, though it would probably hang to her knees. I was comfortable with my unlined windbreaker, and at the last minute I threw an extra one in the car in case Zoe would prefer it to a sweatshirt.

A surprise awaited me when I went to collect Zoe's pink parka, in its Millie's dry cleaning bag, from my coat closet. Apparently Benny had already had a party in there. The bag had dragged on my closet floor just to the point where it got in the way of my cat and his toys. He seemed to have treated it as if it were a piñata. In Benny's defense, the plastic bag was extra long, thus covering some of his toys, the ones I routinely tossed in there for when he had a yearning for a hidden-away spot in the house.

Thus, the closet floor was littered with items formerly wrapped in Millie's plastic, all in a jumble with a fleece mouse, an old wand, and several brightly colored balls of various textures.

I spotted a few coins and pieces of paper. I was eager to pick up Zoe and didn't want to take the time to gather the miscellany and dust it off. I grabbed the parka and left the floor as it was, to be culled another time. I reasoned that Zoe wouldn't be desperate for something she'd already left behind at the cleaners.

My mind continued to play tricks on me, making up worst-case scenarios. What if Zoe had left, was no longer at the station house? Willow had had to leave once the process of signing Zoe out was complete, at which time Zoe was free to call a taxi or a ride service to take her to the airport and to anywhere from there. I blamed Ryan and his reappearance in my life for these irrational fears washing over me, that everyone was leaving. Mom, Dad, Irene. Why not Zoe?

But Zoe hadn't left; she was pacing the lobby of the station house when I arrived, no doubt concerned that the powers that be would change their minds and usher her back into holding.

"Charlie!" Zoe put all one hundred pounds or less of herself into her hug. "Let's get out of here," she whispered, although there was no one around.

I went to hand her the sweatshirt, thinking she could use the women's room to change into it, but she simply grabbed the garment and almost ran for the door. The brief glimpse I had of her showed how much she seemed to have aged since I met her at the Bear Claw only three days ago. Her face was pale, her long hair darkened and lifeless. But she had enough energy to nearly skip to my car.

With no clerk visible, I determined that I didn't need to worry about any formality in leaving. I assumed Willow had taken care of whatever checkout was needed. We'd already settled the issue of my mom's car, so I followed Zoe out to the Outback.

Once in the vehicle, Zoe fell on the floor of the passenger seat. She was small enough to fit in the space between the seat and the dash and come up clad in my sweatshirt, the image of the Golden Gate Bridge wrapped around her torso.

I pointed out the food that was available in the cooler in the back, though I didn't figure Zoe as an elk jerky fan. I thought the cheese sandwich or cheese sticks might be appealing, but she rejected all options.

"I really want a shower first," she said.

"I understand. How about at my house?" I asked.

To my disappointment, she shook her head. "I really need to get where my things are."

"I get it."

"Don't get me wrong. It's not that I

wouldn't prefer your house, sight unseen, to the dorm. But I have to see what's happening with my job and stuff. I wonder if there's some kind of service planned for Ethan, you know." Zoe choked up, but recovered quickly with a loud throat-clearing. "Also, I want to be there when his parents come for him." She frowned. "I might have missed them. Do you know?"

"I don't think Mr. and Mrs. Johnson have gotten here yet. I'll find out for sure and let you know."

Zoe put her hand on my arm, tense on the steering wheel. "Don't worry, Charlie. I promise I'm not going to try to run away again. I learned my lesson."

I smiled. "You're reading my mind now?"

I felt cruel doing it, but I wanted to get as much out of Zoe as possible before letting her off at the dorm. And in spite of her promise, I couldn't trust her completely. She'd tried to escape from me once. I preferred that it not happen again. There was no telling how long Zoe would be available for questioning.

"Do you know Noah Bloom?" I asked, deciding that her grace period was over.

"Yeah, he worked with Ethan a lot because he was a veteran."

"A vet?"

"I mean at J and M. The year that Ethan took off to work here? Noah was here that year, too. That's why we called them the veterans. Kevin, too. There were only the three of them — at least in our crew — and they got special assignments."

"Have you seen Noah lately?" I tried to sound cool, especially since I was driving, but actually my mind was working like a calculator, the old-fashioned kind that was now an app on my phone. Could this be some kind of clue? Ethan, who was dead, and Noah, who was missing, had something in common: They were both special employees, veterans, at J and M. Kevin, however, was okay, at least as of yesterday in the dorm cafeteria.

"No, I haven't seen Noah, but he was here early, like back in May, so he may be taking a little break."

"What kind of special treatment do the vets get?"

"I wouldn't say special treatment, but they got the clean jobs mostly, like working on the loading dock or even in the office sometimes."

"So they probably got to be good friends."

"Oh, yeah. Ethan had this heavy Boston accent, leaving off the last R in a word, like he'd say 'sistah' instead of 'sister' or 'hoss' instead of 'horse,' and we'd all laugh. He'd mess up Noah's name, too."

"I've known Bostonians, so I know what you mean. But how did he mess up 'Noah'?"

"By adding an 'R' where it didn't belong. So he'd say, 'Noahr and I' did this or that, and we'd laugh again."

"That's funny. Do you know if Noah, or Noahr" I paused for effect, to show I was enjoying this conversation — "was around that day, when Ethan got sick? Before he, uh, passed away? Otherwise, he might not even know that Ethan is gone."

"I'm not sure. Now that you ask, I don't think I've seen him around for a few days, maybe." Zoe shifted in her seat. She'd been scratching her arms and legs off and on all through the ride, probably itchy from her life in jail without a shower. She turned in her seat and looked out the window. "I'm not familiar with the route you're taking."

"Not much farther," I said, without admitting I'd taken the long way around. "Have a snack pack."

I wondered if I could claim the engine of the car was acting funny, to extend our time together. There were enough lights and icons on my dashboard that I might be able to pull it off, but a better opportunity presented itself.

"I just remembered that I left Garrett's parka at my mom's," I said, hoping she'd remember the part where she'd used it to trick us into thinking she was still in bed and feel a pang of guilt or that she owed me a favor. "Would you mind if I stopped to get it, so I won't have to make this trip twice?" In other words, *It's your fault that I'm making it at all, and you're the one who left it behind in the first place.*

"Uh." Zoe was thinking, maybe reading my mind again, realizing she should make something up to me. "Okay, I guess so. A few more minutes won't hurt."

"Great. Thanks." I made a few turns on roads I knew to take us to my mom's.

Not wanting to push my luck, I wasted no time retrieving Garrett's parka from Mom's guest bedroom. I made a note to return and make up the bed before she came home. If she even came home. Maybe they were planning to just stay there in San Diego in their new home and send movers for their belongings. Never mind that they hadn't told me they'd bought a house. I gave myself a mental slap and blew out a long breath, an action that was happening a lot this week.

We were fast approaching the barracks-like

structures called "the dorm" in J and M brochures.

"Would you have any idea where I could find Garrett?" I asked Zoe.

"Schedules are all different. I think Garrett is on the three-to-eleven this week. But I can leave his parka on his bed." She pointed in the direction of the last barrack to our right.

"That's okay. I've held you up long enough. You're probably ready for a shower and a nap."

"Most definitely. And you probably want to interview him, too, right?"

Kids these days, I thought. *So smart.*

"Busted," I said.

And I hadn't even gotten to the part where I was going to ask Zoe about the alleged breakup with Ethan, as evidenced by the texts on her phone, according to Trooper. As lively as she was today, she still looked vulnerable to me, and I didn't have the heart to ask her about a breakup with a deceased boyfriend and make her feel even worse. I hadn't wanted to hit her with that immediately, and now it was too late. I'd ask Trooper for details the next time I saw him.

I could hear Trooper now: *Some deputy, not wanting to hurt the feelings of a potential suspect, or witness at the very least.*

Zoe laughed at my "busted" confession as she released her seat belt and turned to exit the car. She opened the back door and pulled her parka off the seat. She leaned in to say goodbye and stopped, pointing to a man walking along a pathway that ran through the buildings.

"Oh, look. There's Mr. Jamison, coming out of Garrett's building. Cool guy."

"Who? Coming out of where?"

And, finally, to myself, *Cool?*

Nineteen

I couldn't have been more startled. Zoe had recognized Ryan Jamison walking on J and M property, near the dorms. But how? Zoe bounded away before I could ask. I'd had the impression that Ryan had just arrived from San Francisco when he wandered into the Bear Claw on Thursday looking for me. There had been no reason to think he'd been hanging around Elkview before then.

But Zoe had been in custody one way or another since Wednesday afternoon. First with me at the hospital, then at my mom's, then scooped up by Trooper in front of Millie's Dry Cleaning, and at the station house until I picked her up an hour or so ago. Ryan had either caught up with her while she was on the run in Mom's car, or he'd visited her in the holding area.

Zoe was out of my car, dragging the plastic bag with her clean parka enclosed. I worried that she'd have a problem with the tattered plastic at the bottom, evidence that Benny had torn it up on one of his exploratory trips to my closet, but I couldn't imagine that she'd care. The plastic was destined for the recycle bin anyway.

She'd waved goodbye to me immediately after spotting Ryan, so I couldn't very well run after her and ask her how she knew this cool Mr. Jamison.

The only thing I could do right now was try to find Garrett Marsh, return his dull green jacket, and interview him as Zoe had known I'd want to do. I also needed to follow up with Kevin Hunter, who'd made a point of avoiding Chris and me in the J and M cafeteria, and who was known to have argued with Ethan the morning before Ethan died. I'd wanted to go over Trooper's notes on those two men first, but I was onsite now, and I was determined to get the most out of the trip. Even if it meant running into Ryan again.

I needed Garrett's parka from the back seat, as well as the Bear Claw tote that held the snack packs. It wasn't easy. Zoe had managed to wrap the sleeves of the extra windbreaker I'd brought for her around the handles of the tote. Garrett's parka was inexplicably tangled with everything. I had the feeling Zoe was the kind of person I had known in my own college dorm living — perfectly put together on her person, but leaving a trail of chaos wherever she'd been.

I pulled Garrett's parka out of the mess, planning to straighten things out later. Before I closed the door, I noticed a few stray items on the seat and floor that might have fallen out of Zoe's package from Millie's. One task at a time, I reminded myself. No one was going to look in my car window and mark me down for sloppiness.

I thought I remembered correctly which of the many barracks Zoe had pointed out as the one Garrett lived in, the one cool-guy Ryan had come out of. The building, a two-story wooden structure, must have dated back half a century and seemed to be the oldest on the property. But the paint job looked new, a light brown with a darker brown trim on the windows. Two sets of steps were in front, one at each end of the building, one for each story, I presumed. I'd been in such barracks before, where there was an entrance and a flight of stairs that led directly to the second floor.

As with the main J and M building, this one was not locked, nor was there any kind of foyer once I'd climbed the steps and pushed open the door. I found myself with beds, mostly unmade, on either side of me, and there were several young men, some napping, some accessing a small countertop with drinks and a vending machine, and others in conversation in an open area at the other end of the floor.

Much of the conversation stopped at the sight of me. I turned to leave before my glance landed on someone in a truly compromising state of dress.

My hand was on the doorknob, Garrett's parka still stuffed under my arm and slipping around like an energetic toddler, when I thought I heard my name.

"Hey, Charlie. You lost?"

I took a breath. I risked raising my eyes. I was relieved to see Garrett all but galloping down the narrow pathway between the beds, his long blond hair falling here and there on the way. Perhaps his enthusiasm was related to the sight of his parka finally being returned. I held it out for him.

"Oh, yeah. Thanks," he said, taking the parka from me. "I almost forgot about this. I have a bunch of them."

"A bunch of parkas?"

"All different weights. Just because it's summer here doesn't mean it's hot, but it never gets so that you have to use the heaviest jacket, except if you're working in a freezer."

I didn't bother pointing out that I'd been born and raised here and had been through a few more summers than he had.

"Two other things," I said, holding out a Bear Claw tote with the snack packs. "First, these are for you."

"Oh, hey, much appreciated. He sniffed the bag. "Any chance there's some of that elk jerky in here?"

"You bet. And I also wanted to finish up our conversation from yesterday," I said.

Garrett led me back toward the area that passed for a combination foyer, kitchenette, and den.

"When Preston cut us off in the cafeteria? What was that about?"

"I thought you might know," I said.

"Nuh-uh. Except he gets weird sometimes."

"Weird how?"

Garrett shuffled his feet, as if he was sorry he'd spoken ill of his boss.

"Never mind," I said. "Can you tell me how well you know Noah Bloom?" This brought my agenda to three things instead of the promised two.

"Not like Ethan does." He stopped. "Did. Noah and Ethan were the chosen, you know, since they came back here a lot. They had, you know, clean work that some of us wouldn't have minded now and then."

"I take it clean work means clean parkas."

"You got it. I couldn't have done what Ethan could do, though. He was good at numbers, and they let him help out in the office. Most of the summer workers are business majors, looking to learn about the business, beefing up their résumés. I might be the only science major."

"Do they let you in on the research?"

"Starting to." He looked up at the enormous clock over a row of beds. I wouldn't have been surprised if it was connected to a fire drill alarm. No excuses for being late in this house. "I better get going."

"Oh, I meant to ask. Have you seen Noah this past week?" A casual question, in a casual tone. "His mom left something behind at the inn and I wanted to find him."

Way to get creative, Charlie.

"I can't remember when I saw him last. He might be taking a break. But you mean his mom was up here? Irene?"

Uh-oh. I knew I shouldn't have lied. *Garrett knows Noah's mom. From another visit? What if he's even dating her, in a cougar scenario?*

"I might have that wrong. The innkeeper is a friend of mine and I may have misunderstood when we were chatting." I felt

Garrett was looking through me, seeing my untrustworthiness. "One more thing," I said, now up to five or six. "Do you know where I can find Kevin Hunter?"

I followed Garrett's gaze, looking around the building. Every bed seemed to be visible, separated only by a small table between each one. I could see why a worker would need to escape for a time.

"I guess he left already. And I better be going, too. We start at three o'clock sharp, or else." When he drew his hand across his throat, I noticed only a small bandage on his hand this time. I started to ask him about it, but he'd continued on right away. "Of course, we don't end at eleven sharp. That's the great thing about this job, is that you can have all the overtime you want." He handed me the tote, minus the snack packs, which he waved near his mouth. "Thanks for these, Charlie. I'll see you around."

Garrett took off, and I headed back to my vehicle with nothing but a few crumbs of information that I didn't have yesterday. I walked briskly, with the hood of my windbreaker up and my head down, to lessen the chances that I'd see Ryan or he'd see me. It was a toss-up whether I'd rather be confronted by Ryan or by the Doberman pinscher that roamed the tiny-house property. I got to the car safely, without facing either my ex or a guard dog. It was depressing to realize I never got to talk to Zoe about her breakup with Ethan and I never got to quiz Garrett on his knowledge of chemistry and any chemicals on-site, or the last words that Ethan spoke in the Bear Claw, words that Garrett and Kevin claimed to have heard. And I never got to talk to Noah or his mother at all.

I made a note to ask Trooper how his other deputies were doing.

What I needed was a long session with Benny.

After an uneventful drive along Elkview's main roads, with only one phone call from Annie, who wanted to know if I'd found Noah, I arrived home.

I found a piece of cherry cheesecake mousse in my freezer from who knew how long ago and took the dessert and a mug of coffee to the edge of the family room so I could watch Benny play with a soft, old mouse.

Some people take notes when trying to analyze a problem, and I did that occasionally also, but the best insights came to me when I talked things out with Benny. This time I felt I had only losses to share, from striking out on progress in the investigation I'd hoped to facilitate to dealing with an ex who could still rattle me to possibly losing my parents to Southern California. I hoped that by the time Mom and Dad returned from their trip, I'd be big enough to be happy for them and not break down and bestow an inadvertent guilt trip as they packed for their future.

I was annoyed at the residual resentment I felt at seeing Ryan "cool guy" Jamison again and being on the opposing side once again. Ryan was representing a client who was not cooperating with an investigation into the murder of one of its employees, albeit a part-timer. Surely there was some kind of ethics violation in there, or a simple obstruction of justice. I wondered if the Johnsons were planning to bring a suit against J and M. It was possible that was the main reason for bringing Ryan here from San Francisco.

I tried to focus on the positives this afternoon, like the excellent staff at the Bear Claw — where I should be headed soon to do my part for the Saturday dinner rush with Annie's new tour group in attendance. Most of my staff had been hired by my mom, however, so all I could take credit for was not messing it up.

While Benny was pushing and pulling on his mouse, encouraged by scattered applause from me, I went through my mail. There was a reason I sat near a wastebasket while doing this daily task. Catalogues with a holiday theme — already? Christmas, a month before the Fourth of July? — went into the trash. An ad for gardening services, trash. A free sample of shampoo, trash. An invitation to my high school reunion, maybe. An order form for food from a San Francisco deli, mistargeted. Didn't they know I had my own deli food? A postcard from San Diego from Mom and Dad, *uh-oh.*

I looked for a clue. The San Diego postcard was the standard four-by-six with large block letters, each of which was filled in with a photo of a different highlight of the city. I identified a beach, a park, and a ship that was probably the USS *Midway.* I looked for something that spoke of senior apartments, but couldn't find it. The message on the back was a simple having-a-good-time type, with no further hints about their future.

Benny was on my lap now. Tired of his mouse? No problem. I was considering a new item for him, an ad for which had come in yesterday's mail. I picked up the flyer from the table, close to making a decision to buy my cat a combination warmer and scratcher. The description pitched it to older, possibly arthritic pets. Benny was neither old nor suffering from arthritis, but I was running out of new toys and comforts for him. And how could I resist this? It was a sort of pouch, lined with soft microfleece, that he could crawl into and enjoy a heater that "produced mild warmth plus a scratching pad," said the ad.

When I started studying details like its nonslip fabric and machine-wash feature, I knew I needed withdrawal therapy. Mom had told me more than once that no number of material things would be as good as physical interaction and conversation with Benny, and it was time I took her seriously. I tossed the flyer in the trash and promised Benny more time as soon as Ethan's killer had been found and brought to justice.

Once I stood and lowered Benny to the floor, I noticed he'd been sitting on another piece of mail from today's delivery: a plain white envelope addressed to me, but with no return address and no stamp. I knew that, technically, a mailbox, once installed, was federal property, and anyone who deposited mailable matter into a box without postage was subject to a fine. I did occasionally get an invitation, minus stamp and label, to a neighbor's barbecue or to a PTA meeting, even though I was neither a P nor a T. Elkview was not known for its adherence to the laws that we felt were written for big-city dwellers. So what if seven-year-old Lily from down the street dropped an invitation to her birthday party directly in my mailbox? But if this envelope contained a solicitation of any kind, I told myself, I was going to report it, notwithstanding the fact that I couldn't identify the sender. Not that I was cranky today after all that had gone wrong, all the way back to being stood up by Irene Bloom.

I pulled out the sheet of paper and unfolded it.

I opened my eyes wide and studied the large block print letters.

LAY OFF.

It was a good thing Benny was paying attention. He hopped back on my lap, climbed to my shoulder, and sat with me, cheek to cheek.

Otherwise, I might have been afraid.

Twenty

My first inclination was to drop the threatening note, if that's what it was, into the trash. Not that I was nervous — but I picked it out and threw it back three times. It could have meant anything, or nothing, I reasoned. Maybe it was a message to union workers. LAY OFF DUE SOON. BE READY. Or some sport was in the middle of a PLAY OFF, and this, minus its "P," was to gather support for the home team. All of the above misdirected, the result of a glitch in some mailing list.

As far as I knew, I wasn't a threat to anyone, such that I had to lay off anything. If the message was related to the investigation of Ethan's murder, whoever the killer was had nothing to worry about from me. And if they had been following me around today, they'd know that for sure.

In the end, I decided to keep the note and its envelope and determine later whether I wanted to show it to Trooper. He already had enough on his plate in Elkview, combined with his commitment to his training gig down in Big Lake. I dropped the note into my bag, which I'd be taking to the Bear Claw later. Chris, Trooper, and I had talked about meeting this evening at the diner, but we hadn't gotten around to setting a specific time. I thought I could call them during a lull.

I thanked Benny for his comfort and set him in front of a catnip-filled fish that he could chase around, courtesy of Annie's larder, while I got ready to greet Annie's new group of tourists for dinner at the Bear Claw.

I changed into something more befitting a diner manager who was to receive a new tour guide and her charges, which meant clean pants and a newish sweater. I hoped a load of clean aprons had arrived from our laundry service. But it wouldn't be so bad if the load had been shredded in the machinery, giving me an excuse to order new ones without the cartoon bear design.

When I left my house, I did something unusual — I locked both my front and back doors.

I was always cheered by the sight of the Bear

Claw humming along with regulars on stools in front of the cake stands and the tiered pie display cases. This evening several booths were occupied by families who seemed to be tourists. I smiled at all of them as I passed, and I greeted Elkview residents that I'd known for years.

Victor reported that Annie had called to say the tour bus she expected was delayed. She couldn't tell us when it would arrive, maybe not even tonight, so she said we shouldn't plan on dinner for a crowd. In other words, I didn't have a lot of control over the evening, whether it concerned Chris, Trooper, or a busload of tourists. Or the meaning of an unsigned note. Or, ultimately, where my parents would choose to live.

I was getting better at handling unpredictability and spontaneity, though I far preferred a more orderly schedule with known entities. All the more reason to admire my mom's ability to look organized and unflappable all those years when I was twirling myself on a stool until I was dizzy or helping out in the kitchen. I didn't remember my mom ever coming unglued when a delivery went wrong or an appliance broke or the behavior of a two-year-old or a boisterous adult sent all the other patrons packing. I wondered if I had ever thanked her for not sharing any anxiety she might have felt. I doubted I had.

"We're leaving the elkloaf frozen," Nina told me. "Until we hear for sure. If we're gone by the time they arrive — if they arrive — you'll just have to pop the loaves in the oven. There's the usual selection of singles and doubles and family size."

I assured her I'd be able to handle it. I knew that if the bus did show up late, Annie would step in and help. This was the newly flexible Charlie talking.

Perched on the last stool this evening, I noted, was my new mail carrier. I caught her mid-mouthful of Dutch apple pie with a question I didn't think I'd get to ask so soon.

"Sorry to interrupt your dinner," I said. I checked her nametag. "Chloe, nice to meet you up close. I wonder if I can ask you a quick question."

"Sure. Something wrong with the box I shoved in your foyer?"

I was surprised at this reply. Our new mail person knew who I was, my address, and that I had a delivery yesterday. Impressive.

"No, not at all. Thanks for doing that. How did you know who I was?"

"They make us learn the route pretty well.

Try to avoid screwups."

Not today, I thought, but it wasn't Chloe's fault that my box had been intruded on.

"By any chance, would you remember if there was already a letter in my mailbox when you put in the stack from today's delivery?"

"Uh-oh. Did I mess up some outgoing mail you had in there?"

Poor Chloe, showing all the signs of insecurity. I needed to help her build confidence in her ability to carry out the duties of her new job.

"Not that, either. You're doing great. I've been meaning to tell you. Can you say about what time you got to my house?"

"The usual, around one o'clock. I stayed in my vehicle and ate my sandwich. Did I leave scraps around? Or drop the wrapper from my sandwich?"

"Nothing like that. It's just that there was an unstamped business-size envelope addressed to me in my mailbox, and I wondered if you'd noticed it. If it was already there by one o'clock."

"No, but don't worry about it. If that ever happens, there's no way I'd charge you for the postage."

Time to call it quits. "That's a relief. Thanks," I said, understanding that there would be no more information from Chloe. I believed her observation that she'd put today's pile of mail into an empty box.

She flicked her fork toward the remains of her pie. "This pie is outstanding, by the way. You make it?"

"I'm glad you like it." I motioned to Nina, who came to join us. "Here's the lady who made it. Nina, make sure Chloe's pie is on the house."

Nina accepted the decision without question, though she had to be wondering what was up. I wished I knew.

By ten o'clock, I was alone in the Bear Claw, going about the usual nighttime chores. I had a service for the heavy cleaning, of course, but I enjoyed keeping things tidy, filling containers, now and then whipping up a batch of cookies to test a new recipe. Chris had called to say he was trying to reach Trooper and that they'd come by together whenever they could find a time that was good for both of them. He knew I'd be here until Tammy and Bert arrived at one a.m. Annie had called around eight with an update. Her tour guide had notified her that there had been a breakdown, and the bus was not going to arrive until much later.

"Sorry, Charlie," she said. "I don't know

why tonight is so busy at the mechanic's. We were supposed to get preferential treatment, the bus, but I don't know. Did I miss the rest of June? Is it Fourth of July or something?"

So it was just me, contemplating my own dinner while I dusted off the shelving and canned goods in the back room.

I had my back to the door when I heard the tinkle of bells, signaling that someone was entering the diner. I turned to see a taller-than-me young man in a short-sleeved T-shirt, muscles well defined, sauntering down the aisle.

Kevin Hunter. Another one of Ethan's dorm mates.

I almost didn't recognize him. He looked older, and more serious.

"Hi, Charlie. Nice to see you again."

Why did I not believe him? Somcthing in his manner? Or in mine?

"Kevin," I said, with more spring in my voice than I felt. "Welcome to the Bear Claw."

He took a seat on a stool. "I hear you've been looking for me."

"Yes, I wanted to ask you some questions if you don't mind." I sat three stools away, so that our respective long legs, if stretched, wouldn't touch.

It was still light out and would be until about eleven thirty. But the parking lot was deserted, and I found myself ill at ease.

"Shoot," Kevin said. Not the best choice of words.

Did I really want to face down this budding NFL specimen about his argument with a friend who'd been murdered? I told myself I was being silly, that the stupid LAY OFF note was making me unnecessarily uneasy about even a college kid who stopped by, in Elkview, in Alaska's version of broad daylight.

"Can I get you a cup of coffee or a soda? A snack?"

"I just got off work. Skipped my breaks and took off early. I was hoping you'd have a spare bear claw."

"I can certainly do better than that. How about some fish soup and my special sourdough bread?"

"You're joking, right?"

"Because?" I thought a second. "Oh, fish!" I laughed, which relaxed my shoulders for a moment. "As if you didn't have enough of it all day."

"And all night."

"Elkloaf and mashed potatoes, then?" I moved off my stool.

"Now we're talking." Kevin had turned

and put both elbows on the counter between two dessert displays. The pies had almost been depleted, with only one slice left, but there were several slabs of cake at the ready.

"I'll get that heated up."

It felt good to situate myself on the other side of the through-window, putting two counters between Kevin and me.

I found Nina's stash of individual elkloaf servings and worked on Kevin's dinner.

"So what did you want to ask me about?"

Now I really wished I'd looked over Trooper's notes. What if he'd already asked Kevin about the fight he and Ethan had? In any case, did I really want to ask Kevin that question now?

I started in neutral. "As you probably know, I'm trying to help Trooper Graham clear up some loose ends. He'll be here in a little while with Chris Doucette, the journalist for the *Bugle*." I stopped short of giving Chris's height and weight. "To put all our information together."

"I thought it might be because you heard me and Ethan had a fight."

An on-the-nose comment that might have thrown me for a loop if I hadn't been distracted by his grammatical error. What did they teach in high school these days?

"Oh, yes, that, too," I said. Spoken casually. I wondered how much a fully grown Doberman pinscher would cost.

"It was your typical triangle. Ethan and Zoe had a thing. Then he breaks up with her, and not very nicely. Zoe and I are friends, and I was upset because she was upset."

"So it was about how badly he'd treated Zoe?"

"Uh-huh. You can check that box."

"Done." We laughed as the *ding* of the oven confirmed it, and I brought Kevin's meal to him, still leaving one counter between us.

"How about Noah Bloom? Do you know him well?"

"Oh, yeah. Nice guy," Kevin said. "From the Midwest. You know they're all nice guys down there."

"I guess he's taking a break?"

"Maybe. We all have different schedules, and then there's all kinds of overtime if you want it, so we don't keep track of each other that way."

Kevin fiddled with the potatoes and gravy until every potato morsel was covered. Only then did he move food to his mouth. He looked like a hungry teenager now, so I ventured another question.

"I remember you said you heard Ethan's

last words, before he was moved to the ambulance." *Before he died.* "Were you ever able to make sense of them?"

"Yeah, you know, I've been thinking of that. 'Barker' is the closest I could come to figuring out a word. But there's no Barker in the dorm. Maybe it could be a J and M employee, I guess. A regular one. We don't run into too many of them except for supervisors."

"It's beginning to look like some stranger, someone passing through, found a way to do some damage. Who knows why?" I shrugged, as if I were happy with that solution, not pointing out that this itinerant stranger would've had to come back over and over to give Ethan the doses needed to eventually kill him.

"Guess so." Kevin was more than halfway through his elkloaf dinner and was eyeing the cake slices in the stand.

"Oh, this is interesting," I began. A last-minute thought, Columbo style, as my mom had taught me. "I ran into an old friend of mine from San Francisco today. What are the chances, huh? Turns out he's a lawyer for your company."

Kevin laughed. "My company. I wish."

"Maybe you've seen him around. His name's Ryan Jamison. Youngish guy. Well, not as young as you."

While I looked for a tell, Kevin shook his head. "I try not to hang around lawyers," he said. And the former wariness came back, accompanied by a no-more-fishing look, to be taken many ways.

"If you don't mind, Kevin, I need to make some calls and possibly get ready for a busload of tourists and a committee meeting of sorts. Help yourself to some dessert. All on the house for hardworking college students." I smiled, easier to do now that I felt the threat had passed.

I wished I could have found a way to get a sample of Kevin's handwriting. I imagined saying, *Hey, Kevin, would you mind printing out the alphabet for me?*

If the fight had been about not upsetting Zoe, then my name was Julia Child.

Twenty-One

All my backup groups had fallen through. It was a good thing I hadn't really been counting on them to save me from Kevin Hunter, who left the Bear Claw shortly after his second dessert, which was after his second helping of elkloaf. Eventually, I got comfortable while he was in the diner. What attacker, I asked myself, eats so much food right before lunging?

Annie's people were now scheduled for tomorrow morning. Trooper was tied up way down in Kenai Fjords National Park, where a kayaking expedition had gone wrong in the frigid waters. Chris gave me no details for himself other than "It's not going to work tonight."

Tammy and Bert burst in about one fifteen in the morning, apologizing for the fifteen-minute infraction. I told them they could make it up by prepping for a busload of at least two dozen for breakfast in the morning.

"No prob. We're on it," was the response.

"You can leave us alone now," Bert added. At least I wasn't too old to get the subtext of that.

I left the Bear Claw in the middle of the four-hour period of darkness. The sun had set about eleven thirty p.m. and wouldn't rise until four a.m. No different from most nights, so why was I tense as I drove along Main Street with its closed-up shops? I saw shadows everywhere, figures that turned out to be trees, and crawling shapes that were simply old Lucas's outdoor collection of broken wheelbarrows. The appearances of LAY OFF and Kevin Hunter in one day took their turns in nearly doing me in. I kept hitting the door- and window-lock buttons on my car.

When I arrived at my house, I zipped up the steps, key at the ready, and slammed the door behind me. Benny's loud *meow* didn't help, but it was my fault for pounding on the steps and banging the door shut. A cat had the right to peace and quiet in the middle of the night in his own home.

And it wasn't over yet, as my landline rang, louder than ever, it seemed.

Poor Benny. He marched to the back room, tail flicking, a mild hissing sound audible, without so much as a twirl around my ankles to welcome me home.

Chris was calling. He knew I'd just be getting home. "Sorry about tonight," he said. "My sister came down from Fairbanks for a surprise visit, and I haven't seen her in a while."

"No prob," I said. "Trooper wasn't available anyway."

"Do you believe the protecting-Zoe story?" Chris asked, after I filled him in on my conversation with Kevin.

"Nope."

"The 'random stranger' theory?"

"Nope."

"How about the I-don't-know-Ryan story?"

Chris had covered a lot, always with the same answer from me.

"Nope. I'm sure Ryan has gotten around to everyone in the summer program by now." I let out a tired sigh.

"Are you okay, seeing your ex around?"

"Definitely." *Was that a crack in my voice?*

"Hmm. If you ever want to talk about it . . ."

"Are we ever going to get anywhere on this case? That's what I want to talk about."

"Sorry. I'm not trying to pry. You've had a long day. At least I got to laugh with my baby sister this evening. She's here for the wedding of one of her high school buddies, and we all went out to dinner. Sorry to flake out on you."

"It's okay. I'm glad someone was having a good time."

"The groom is from Boston, and we teased him about his accent all night."

"Like Ethan," I said.

"What's that?"

I didn't realize I'd spoken the line aloud. "Ethan was from Boston, and a couple of times lately I've heard about how he got the same kind of teasing. Leaving out the R where it should be and adding it where it doesn't belong."

"This guy, Jerry, wanted to buy a parka while he was here, thinking they'd be so much cheaper here, like they were falling off the trees. He kept saying 'parkar,' of course, but not always, so maybe we were getting to him."

I'd once heard an explanation for when Bostonians added an R and when they omitted one, but I wasn't up to continuing the conversation with Chris. Besides, something he'd said jogged my mind about Ethan's case, but then I lost it.

"A lot of people think Alaska is strange, like with cheap parkas on street corners, or twenty feet of snow everywhere year-round," I said.

"Well, Alaska is a little strange," Chris said.

"How so?" I found myself wanting to defend Alaska, especially against the state I perceived as taking my parents from me.

"Let's start with its having the lowest population density of all the states."

"You have a point."

"Okay, when you give in that easily, I know you're tired. I hope you can get a good night's sleep tonight. What if we have our meeting, briefing, whatever we're calling it, in the morning? Trooper said he'd be free around ten."

"I have a busload coming in for breakfast, but the Bear Claw should be clear by ten. Usually tour groups want to get an early start out of town."

"Ah, but they haven't had Bear Claw bear claws."

On that note, we clicked off.

I didn't tell Chris the real reason I gave in about the strangeness about Alaska, which harkened back again to my docent days. At the time, I knew by heart details of the annual outhouse race, along with some of the more bizarre legislation concerning moose, such as never give one a beer and never push one out of a plane.

I was just as glad to give in before revealing that strangeness.

On Sunday morning, after a more or less sleepless night, I made it down my steps to my driveway, ready to climb into my car, when I saw my next-door neighbors. Dan and Beth Tucker, both of whom worked from home, were already deep into gardening in their front yard. With my ragged hours, I hardly ever ran into them. I took it as a sign from the universe that it was okay to query them about yesterday's mail.

We exchanged a few words about the weather and how beautiful their fireweed and asters were coming up. They were kind enough not to mention that nothing but weeds was coming up in my yard.

"I have a question for you," I said. "About the mail delivery yesterday."

"The new person, Chloe, is very good," Beth said. "She doesn't just shove the magazines in, the way old Gus used to."

"You should tell her that. She's a little nervous about her performance right now. I wanted to ask you about yesterday." I swallowed, ready to sound unconcerned. "I got an envelope without a stamp, as if someone hand delivered it to my box, without going through any post office."

"That's funny," Dan said. "A personal letter or a solicitation of some kind?"

How to respond?

"Somewhere in between. Someone wanting to surprise me, I think. I wondered if you saw anyone. Maybe a car you didn't recognize making a quick stop? It would have been after Chloe delivered the regular mail around one o'clock."

They both shook their heads.

"We were working around the back yesterday afternoon, so we wouldn't have seen anyone necessarily," Beth said.

My glance landed on their matching green gardening aprons, which I hadn't noticed before. *Somewhere between cute and weird,* I thought.

"It's really not a big deal," I said. "I just thought I'd check. I'm sure someone will tell me soon."

"We'll let you know if we see someone," Beth said.

"I think that's illegal," Dan said. "Putting something in a mailbox if you're not a postal employee. It's federal property. You're even required to have a return address or they're not supposed to take it."

"Oh, that's just so no one will put a bomb or something like that in the box," Beth said. "I'm sure it's okay if it's just handy, or for fun. Didn't Alice let Tommy do that for his birthday party?"

"Tommy's six," Dan said.

"Makes sense," I said, not knowing what I meant.

"We should get together for lunch or something sometime," Beth said.

I confirmed what a great idea that was and said I'd let them know my schedule for the next week or so.

It seemed to me we'd had that conversation about lunch, or dinner, or drinks before dinner, several other times, without ever following through. It could have been because we didn't have much to talk about besides their lovely flowers and my crazy hours.

It seemed like forever since I'd seen Trooper, but it had been only a couple of days. Maybe it was his big blue hat that I missed. He tipped it at me now.

"Charlie," he said. A little somber, I thought.

I gasped. What if he knew my parents' plans? What if they had told him, to test the waters, or so they wouldn't have to break the news to me? But that wasn't like my mother, especially, not to come right out with it, whatever "it" was.

"You okay?" Trooper asked.

I guessed I was the person you'd want to play poker with. "I'm fine. Just a little frustrated."

The breakfast crowd from the tour group had come and gone, leaving Rachel free to whip up omelets for the three of us. Annie joined us, but not to eat. She patted her stomach and claimed to be full from eating two breakfasts, one with each seating of the tourists.

"I'm turning in my badge anyway," she said, sliding into the booth, next to Chris. "I've been so busy keeping everyone in mosquito repellent, I haven't had a minute, but also I don't have any ideas and, plus, I feel really guilty letting Irene go without getting her to tell us where her private investigator found her son, or what he had to say, or absolutely anything."

Now I felt guilty, making Annie feel guilty by my stomping around in a bad mood when I missed catching Irene, and then behaving even worse when we lost Noah. "You couldn't very well have tied her to a chair," I said. "It's not your fault."

"Who does know anything?" Trooper asked.

I let Chris describe our visit to PI Marcus King in his tiny house and later seeing Noah ride off while we were entertained by a Doberman.

I offered my meager morsel. "I talked to Kevin, who said the fight he had with Ethan was about Zoe. He was worried she'd be hurt when Ethan broke up with her."

"That's funny," Trooper said. "He told me it was about hours, that Ethan had been taking a lot of time off, leaving the others to pick up the slack."

"I thought they liked the overtime," Chris said.

"Which was why I didn't like that particular alibi," Trooper said.

"So you think it might not have been about Zoe at all, too?" I said.

"Who knows? It was Zoe who ran, remember," Chris said. "Shouldn't she be prime suspect number one?"

"No, it couldn't have been Zoe who killed Ethan," I said, offering no reason in support of the claim. It wasn't as though I had proof, and Chris was right. If it weren't for the coup at Millie's dry cleaning establishment, Zoe would be as out of sight as Noah was right now.

"It could be nothing," Annie said, by way of something only she could fathom.

"It could be something," Trooper said. "Remember, everyone's a suspect —"

"Until they're not," we said in unison, confusing Rachel, in the act of delivering our omelets. She looked a bit forlorn, like she hadn't been invited to the sing-along. I noticed Victor and Nina in a huddle with her when she got back to the kitchen, likely catching her up on local customs.

Trooper ticked the suspects off on his hand. "We have the official J and M people, Louis Preston and Ryan Jamison. And the summer people closest to Ethan — Garrett, Kevin, Noah, and Zoe."

"Plus the random stranger," Chris said.

This was my chance to show Trooper the LAY OFF note I'd been carrying in my tote since I found it in my mailbox. What if the author was another possibility on the list of potential murderers? If I was ever going to share the threatening note, it would be now, with my whole team here for support.

"I found a —"

Chris interrupted with what he'd found by digging into Kevin's past using his *Bugle* databases. "A couple of fights in his dorm down in Oregon — frat party stuff — plus one DUI, but we know that sometimes little infractions can grow into big ones."

"You'd think they'd do a better job at vetting these kids," I said.

"Depends on how desperate the plants are

for help."

Trooper let us know that Ethan's parents were due in this afternoon and he needed someone to meet them. Chris and I raised our hands.

"They'll be staying with me," Annie said. "I have the best cabin ready for them, and I've contacted Doc Sherman's office to tell him and the staff, so they won't cheer or anything, that they'll be coming by to, you know, see their son."

We had a self-imposed moment of silence as everyone cleared his or her throat. We'd already heard that the Johnsons didn't want any kind of memorial service in Elkview; they wanted to escort their son back to Boston as quickly and quietly as possible. Completely understandable.

"They'll be arriving at the Anchorage airport around four this afternoon."

"Text us the details," Chris said to Trooper, who still relied on his pager.

"Will do," Trooper said, a grin spreading on his face. He took great delight in surprising us, holding up his new cell phone.

We all clapped as Rachel came by with coffee refills and a tear in her eye.

For a while this morning, I forgot to worry about reappearing exes, threatening notes, or abandonment by my parents. No wonder

I loved being part of this team.

Chris stayed behind so we could make plans for the drive to Anchorage to pick up Mr. and Mrs. Johnson. We went back and forth about what to say, whether to bring them flowers or leave a bouquet in their room at Annie's Inn, whether to talk to them at all about the investigation. We agreed we shouldn't share the progress we were not making but would instead promise to keep them informed. I made a note to put waters and snacks in a cooler in the car, since we didn't know how long they'd have been traveling to get here from Boston. Annie had said she'd take care of snacks for their room and give serious consideration to how cheerful the room should look.

"I've never had people here for death before," she'd said. As usual, we all knew what she meant.

Finally, Chris and I knew we had to follow the Johnsons' lead while they were in the car with us, answer any questions as best we could, and otherwise play it by ear.

"You know they're going to blame Alaska," Chris had said.

"And the Bear Claw," Trooper had added.

I'd simply nodded. But I secretly hoped

that J and M would be also be listed as sharing the guilt.

Twenty-Two

When Trooper and Annie left the Bear Claw after breakfast and our so-called deputies' so-called meeting, Chris ordered a second bear claw.

He took out his laptop. "I need to finish this article on the oldest guy to scale Denali. He's from California. I interviewed him online. I forget how old he was when he climbed it, but he's over ninety now."

"Better hurry, then," Nina said, then covered her mouth as if to undo the insensitive advice. "So sorry," she added. Chris never looked up or stopped typing.

I took a turn in the kitchen, loading the dishwasher, noting that it was time to order more logo mugs, and verifying that we had enough staples for our lunch menu, which today included freshly battered fish and chips. I had successfully pulled off a phone call and settled a pricing disagreement with our soft drink vendor when Chris called me over to his booth to show me a text he'd received from Trooper.

> The Johnsons will be arriving at Ted Stevens Anchorage International Airport at 3:50 this afternoon, on flight 5812.

We laughed at the texting newbie's grammatically correct sentence, wondering how long it would take for Trooper to learn the shortcuts, bringing the message down to:

> Johnson ETA 3:50p FLT 5812

We spent a minute or two tossing texting lingo back and forth, much the same way Victor and his kitchen staff sent diner lingo over the through-window now and then, especially when they had an audience.

LMK and ROFL were obvious, but Chris stumped me with @TEOTD.

"At the end of the day," he said.

I pointed out that the acronym my dad always used with his business associates, pre–cell phone days, for the same message, was shorter: COB, for "close of business."

For some reason, these abbreviations, not unlike special languages, brought me back to the Boston accent anecdotes I'd heard recently, but I still couldn't put my finger on why.

"I have to make a stop at the office," Chris said. "I'll come by your house at about one." He looked up at the large diner clock over the jukebox. A little after noon. "Which is pretty soon."

"I can pick you up," I said to Chris. "Office or home?"

"Are you ashamed to have that junk heap" — he pointed to his truck outside the window — "parked in your driveway at home?"

I laughed. Then a thought crossed my mind. It was possible that if the LAY OFF person came cruising by my house again, he might be put off by such a tough, masculine-looking pickup, complete with dents and rust spots, obviously not owned by a wimp. He might turn around and forget the whole project, whatever it was.

"I'd be honored to have your pickup in my driveway," I said, stopping before owning up to why it might serve my interests. "See you there at one."

With the others gone, I was tempted to tell Chris about my unwanted mail. If he hadn't been in such a hurry, I might have.

With Chris's self-described junk heap parked in my driveway, I fully expected next-door neighbors Dan and Beth would alert me to an intruder.

We climbed into my car and headed for the Anchorage airport, still laughing at how Trooper had spelled out its whole, long name. Maybe he was just a fan of Ted Stevens, long-serving, now-deceased US senator from Alaska.

Traffic was light enough on the AK-3 on a Sunday. It might have been the lull in the conversation once we'd covered every possible topic concerning the investigation into Ethan's murder, but whatever the reason, I found myself telling Chris about the note.

"Charlie!" he said, half-worried, half-accusing. He pulled off the road as soon as he could do so safely and repeated, "Charlie," this time with more concern in his voice.

"Nothing bad happened." I took the note from my tote, envelope and all, and showed it to him. "It wasn't exactly a threat."

Chris extracted the note and unfolded it. Unlike me, he handled it by the corners.

Again, too late, I thought.

"Not a threat? What's that mean? That it didn't say 'or else' or come with anthrax sprinkled in the envelope?"

"Right." I took a breath. "Look, I'm already a little freaked, so I need you to be calm."

"Okay, okay. You're right. I'm just concerned about you is all. You live by yourself."

"I'm aware of that." I didn't think it was the time to mention Benny, though he'd come to my aid more than once.

"We have to tell Trooper, and we have to get this checked for fingerprints, though I don't suppose you took any precautions."

I pointed to the clock on the car's dashboard. "What we have to do now is get to the airport."

"I'm going to let Trooper know he needs to put a car in front of your house tonight."

"No, Chris, I need to tell him myself."

"When?"

"When we get back this evening."

"Not good enough."

Chris opened the note again and took out his cell phone, ready to snap a photo of it.

I quickly slipped it off his lap. No more pleading.

He threw his hands up. "Okay."

I was part glad and part angry that he was so solicitous. My mind was busy acknowledging how strange it was that I told him, and not Trooper, first. I distinctly remembered the time a few months ago when I would have told Trooper first and not told Chris at all. If only there were a book on such changes of heart.

We spoke little the rest of the way to Anchorage, but I could almost hear the gears turning in Chris's brain as he tried to figure out who might have sent the note.

In another strange twist, I now felt much more relaxed, having shifted my burden onto Chris and eventually Trooper. So relaxed that I dozed off, sleeping deeply for the first time since I'd retrieved yesterday's mail.

If one of us had been smart, Chris or I would have tried to determine what the Johnsons looked like. We might at least have checked out Ethan's social media pages, a likely place to see family photos. Or we might have asked Zoe or one of his friends if they'd ever met them, though it was unlikely since they lived in Boston. But according to Zoe, Ethan had spent almost a year with J and M recently, and it was possible that his parents had come to visit. No matter, we'd neglected to do anything about it.

We stood with a group of chauffeurs at the foot of an escalator waiting for deplaning passengers to show. Within a couple of minutes, a middle-aged man in a business suit showed up and approached a uniformed older man holding a sign that read, FAR-

LEY. The presumed driver took the man's luggage, and the two turned to leave the area.

"Excuse me," Chris said, trotting after them, and I knew immediately what he had in mind. "Are you by any chance done with that sign?"

Two minutes later, he'd scrawled JOHNSONS on the blank side of the cardboard, and a few minutes after that, the saddest-looking couple in the airport came up to us. The man caught my eye and lifted his hand to waist level, as if that motion itself was exhausting.

They were both wearing dark clothing. No breezy summer pastel for her; no lightweight pants for him. Their clothes hung on them, as if they'd each lost fifty pounds in less than a week. They might as well have been expecting a funeral service in the airport. I was glad Chris and I had decided against picking up flowers for Mrs. Johnson. It would have made it all the more obvious to everyone in the airport that this was a couple in mourning.

They were each rolling a small carry-on, probably not planning to stay longer than absolutely necessary.

We introduced ourselves as the people sent by the innkeeper to take them to town, stepping around words like "state trooper," "police," "medical examiner," and "coroner." We each expressed our condolences, in those words that everyone says even though nothing said will help. But we tried our best, and were met with faraway looks and silence.

While Chris retrieved the car, I was left walking with them toward the revolving doors leading to the sidewalk.

Did they want to get a cup of coffee before we left?

No, thank you.

Was this their first time in Alaska?

No.

Were they exhausted from the flight?

No.

Chris couldn't return with the car fast enough. Then it was more of the same, with the Johnsons in the back seat of the car, after, "Would you like to sit up front?"

No, thank you.

Were they hungry?

No, thank you.

And finally, did they want to go straight to their cabin at the inn?

Yes, please.

Chris and I waited in Annie's lobby while she personally led them to their cabin. She came back shaking her head. They'd been no more forthcoming with her than they'd been with us, she reported.

"I did keep reminding them that I'm prepared to get them anything they need. Those poor people. They just wanted to go to bed, though they did say they had a lot of questions and hoped they'd be able to get some answers in the morning."

"Uh-oh," Chris said.

I let out a loud sigh.

Back at my house, Chris offered to return and stay the night in my guest room. After witnessing the Johnsons' grief, I'd almost forgotten my own problems. I couldn't imagine losing a child, plus having the death occur thousands of miles away. How hard it must have been to board a plane for twelve hours or so, not for a vacation, or to celebrate with relatives, but to ride back with your only child in a casket.

"No thanks," I told him. "And please don't push Trooper on the idea of having a car sit in front of my house. He has enough to do. And so do all his volunteers."

"So you've said."

I motioned him into his truck and went inside to change out of my city clothes. I hated that I could think of nothing to do to help Trooper with the Johnson murder, but at least I could give my staff some time off while I ran my own diner.

At six o'clock on a Sunday evening, the diner was not highly populated. Annie's bus group had already taken off for points north. I'd heard that they were going to stop to tour a gold mine before moving on to Fairbanks, and I had a strong desire to join them. You could never see the northern lights too many times.

The next couple of hours were relaxing for me as I made a batch of cookies, with an eye toward giving Annie a couple of dozen — some for the Johnsons, if they were so inclined, and some for any new sign-ins. Annie had come up with the idea, or rather stolen it, when she heard that a big chain hotel offered a freshly baked cookie to all newly arriving guests. Thanks to me, right down the street, we were able to work out a new deal, with cookies practically on demand.

Just before nine, I took a call from Annie. "Oh, Charlie, I know you're not going to like this."

I closed my eyes and mentally lifted myself out of my happy, sweet-smelling kitchen.

"The Johnsons want to talk to me," I said.

I heard Annie gasp. "How did you know?"

"It was inevitable," I said.

"Oh, Charlie. I didn't mean to, but —"

"They wanted to know where their son was when he died, and you told them."

"It just came out. The Bear Claw Diner. I was so surprised. They called me to their room and said could I bring extra towels, so I naturally ran right over." She took a breath that sounded as if she were still running. "I guess they'd taken a nap and a shower and suddenly they were all energized, and they asked me and it was the first thing that came out of my mouth."

"Because it was the truth. You can't be ashamed of that."

"Still, Charlie. I'm sorry."

"It had to happen sooner or later, Annie. Don't worry about it. When do they want to talk to me?"

"Ralphie was just getting off duty, so he's driving them to the diner now."

"Great." But not really.

"I whispered to him to drive slow, Charlie."

Annie had bought me about five minutes. She'd done her best.

Hadn't I wished for something to do? Now I had it.

Great.

TWENTY-THREE

To prepare for meeting the Johnsons, who were only minutes away, I first turned the sign on the door of the diner to CLOSED. On the way, I grabbed my phone, ready to text Chris and Trooper. I thumbed the text on the way to the restroom, where I hoped to make myself more presentable than I'd been in my kitchen.

Johnsons on way to diner from annies. need suport. Please!

Sure, it looked like a ten-year-old wrote it, but I was in a big rush. I hoped I was clear. Both men knew that Annie's was right down the road and they needed to hurry. There was no telling where either of them might be between nine and ten on a Sunday night while it was still daylight.

I made a to-do list in my head as I dashed to the back of the diner: undo ponytail, brush hair out to look more adult, remove splattered apron, remove chocolate droppings from sweater, lick finger and blot out particles of cookie dough on pants. And the toughest item on the list: *Breathe, Charlie, breathe.*

My anonymity as the Johnsons' driver on the trip from the Anchorage airport was over. How would they react when they learned that the person who had escorted them to the inn was the owner of the diner that was scene of their son's death? That they'd had two-plus hours during which to quiz me, that I'd been captive to them at that time?

A bigger question was, why hadn't I prepared for this moment? As I told Annie, I had known it was inevitable, so why no plan? It struck me that I had no idea to what extent the Johnsons had communicated with anyone in Elkview. Had they talked to Ethan's supervisor at J and M, Louis Preston, or his new pal the attorney from San Francisco? To Ethan's friends in the dorm, Garrett, Kevin, or the missing Noah? To Zoe, only recently estranged from him in girlfriend/boyfriend terms? How about Doc Sherman? Wouldn't the Johnsons have had to deal with him to make arrangements for the transport of Ethan's body?

I had learned enough about funeral practices over the years, but not one that was interstate. Assuming everyone knew that Alaska was actually part of the United States, the process of transporting the deceased should be simple, not requiring passports or embassy involvement. The Johnsons had probably taken the route of contacting their local mortuary in Boston and letting them handle everything. All Ethan's parents would have to do would be travel on the same flight, with their son in a container in the cargo hold.

I couldn't suppress a big gulp and a shudder at that thought.

At a little after nine thirty, a car pulled into the Bear Claw's lot. Not Chris's old truck. Not an Alaska State Trooper patrol car. Maybe a late-night diner? It was called denial, and I felt I needed a bit of it.

I watched Ethan's parents exit the vehicle, a sleek black car owned by Annie's Inn and providing limited service to and from the inn. For special occasions, such as proms and — another shudder — when parents came to pick up the corpse of their son.

"I'm saving up for a real long one," Annie said often, meaning the company car. "I can't decide on white or black. I guess I have to figure if I'm going to have more of weddings and proms or funerals."

If the Johnsons had changed their clothes, it wasn't obvious. They wore the same somber colors, to match their expressions. Their gait was purposeful, however, as they strode toward my front door.

I held the door for them and thought they seemed shorter than earlier this evening, considerably shorter than me. I greeted them and led them to a table toward the back, where there was less access to a view out the window. I wasn't sure they'd want to be reminded that they weren't in Boston.

I started in the usual way. "Can I get you something to drink? Coffee or a soft drink? Or maybe you're ready for some dinner? I can show you a menu or make some suggestions." I knew I was rambling.

"We're not here to eat," said Mrs. Johnson. "Charlie, is it?"

I didn't think so. I understood, even though I heard "heah" for "here" and "Chah-lie" for "Charlie."

I nodded. "How can I help you?"

I sat facing the door, with a better view of the Alaska parking lot than they had, wishing as hard as I knew how that Chris or Trooper, preferably the latter, would drive up and even the playing field.

"This is where he died? In this diner?"

Mr. Johnson asked. His tone was despairing, as if the Bear Claw was the last place in the world he'd want his son to live his last moments.

Dinah. I wondered why the accent mattered to me, why it seemed like a connection was there, but not fully. Maybe I was worried that my parents were considering moving to Boston, not San Diego, and that I would no longer be able to understand them. That's what one freshman course in psychology could do to a person.

I shook my head at Mr. Johnson's question. "No, he died in the hospital a few miles from here."

I based my comment on the fact that Ethan's friends heard him speak, possibly in the last minutes of his life, and I'd never heard an exact time of death. Once again, I was dismayed at my lack of detailed knowledge of a case I was supposedly working on, and it was through no one's fault but my own.

Mrs. Johnson let out an annoyed groan, as if she didn't believe me, or she'd been expecting me to point out the exact spot where Ethan took his last breath. "We meant where he ate his last meal, Chahlie," she said.

Now she was annoying me, grieving

mother or not. "That would have been at his dorm, I presume, in the morning. He ordered lunch here, as his friends did, but none of them were even served their food before nine-one-one had to be called and Ethan left in the ambulance."

"I see," she said, stumped for a minute or two anyway.

I struggled to walk that line between compassion and self-defense.

"Can I ask you, have you spoken to your son's employers, J and M Fishing? I believe his supervisor is Louis Preston?"

"We have a meeting scheduled with him in the morning," Mr. Johnson said. "We spoke on the phone, and he promised to tell us everything he knew when we got here."

Lots of luck, I thought.

"I hope we'll get some answers then. All your doctor told us, Chahlie, was that Ethan died from poisoning."

"Dr. Sherman, I presume?"

They nodded.

Not that there was another doctor nearby. Doc Sherman was not only everyone's physician; he was also the medical examiner for the area, and if there was an emergency when our town veterinarian was off, he took on that role, too. Still, it wouldn't be his place to say any more about Ethan's death than what would be public record and was reported in the *Elkview Bugle.* Only Trooper would be given the full report directly.

With little warning, Mrs. Johnson's tears flowed. My heart went out to her, and I was sorry I'd thought ill of her. Of course she'd be looking for someone to blame.

I left the booth and came back quickly with bottles of water, two for each of them, plus a box of tissues I had snatched from the paper-supply section of the closet. While I was searching for the tissues, I noticed our first aid kit and wondered if I should pull that out, too, in case they needed an aspirin or two. In the end, I decided the sight of it might make matters worse and simply nudged the container with the bright red cross on its top to the edge for easy access.

While I was gone, Mr. Johnson had moved closer to his wife, draping his arm around her shoulder, consoling her. I felt completely helpless, then immensely relieved when I saw a patrol car enter the Bear Claw parking lot. I'd locked the door when the Johnsons came in, but Trooper had a key and used it now. He walked down the aisle, exuding confidence that only I could see.

Trooper approached the booth, his uniform hat in his hand, and nodded to Ethan's parents.

"Mr. and Mrs. Johnson."

A slight bow, and as serious a look as I'd ever seen on him. It occurred to me that this wouldn't be the first time he'd had to address relatives of a deceased person. But I hoped not often the parents of a young man still in his undergraduate years of college, parents who'd had to cross the country to take their son home.

I yielded my side of the booth to Trooper and made my way to the kitchen to give them some privacy. And myself some emotional relief, I admitted. I started a pot of coffee that I knew Trooper would appreciate. I tried not to eavesdrop, but I heard their voices and might have inadvertently listened in on bits and pieces of Trooper's remarks. At times, he was loud enough that I thought he might be tuning me in purposely.

Sick for a few weeks.

Nothing to do with this diner.

Making an exception for you to take him home so soon.

We don't have all the lab results yet.

Another week before we can close [inaudible] and then let you know.

Only the last comment had me reeling. Did he expect we'd close the case in a week? What did Trooper know that I didn't? A lot,

I hoped.

I carried a tray with three mugs, a small cheese plate, and a plate of cookies in one hand and a pot of coffee in the other.

"I'll be at my desk in the back, if you need me."

I wandered off again and picked up a new cookbook one of my staff must have brought in. "Be the best griller you can be" was the inspiration and promise on the cover. It occurred to me that I should be reading one of Mom's mystery books instead. Maybe I'd learn some sleuthing tips from a fictional detective.

Trooper found me pacing some time later.

"We'll be off, Charlie. I'm going to drive the Johnsons back to the inn."

I looked out the through-window. The Johnsons had already exited. I could hear them now:

Let's get out of heah.

I guess they didn't feel the need to say goodbye. I wondered if I should find out where the Boston service would be and send flowers. They might never want to hear of, or from, me, Elkview, or Alaska, ever again, however.

I couldn't say I'd blame them.

I called Tammy and Bert, who happened to

be together and were happy to come in early. Tammy once confided that taking the late shift was a twofer: getting paid to work, and doing homework. Now that they were a couple, I saw that it was actually a threefer, adding being on a date.

Their early arrival gave me time to pull myself together, to stop dwelling on LAY OFF and San Diego and being hated by the Johnsons, and put serious thought into how Ethan was murdered and by whom. Otherwise Trooper was going to relieve me of my deputy duties and focus on his dozens of other recruits.

I drove home, relieved that I at least seemed to be technically clear of any blame from the Johnsons even though they'd treated me as if it were my fault that Ethan chose to be at the Bear Claw when the poison finally hit its mark. I told Trooper I'd be glad to drive them to J and M, Doc Sherman's, or wherever they needed to go, but he said they'd arranged for a ride service. Message received.

I'd just released my seat belt when my gardening neighbors Dan and Beth came up to the car, obviously waiting for me.

"Someone was here today," Dan said.

I thanked them for their vigilance and told them the truck in driveway was my friend

Chris's pickup.

"We know Chris's truck," Beth said.

"This guy was on a bicycle," Dan said. "We just happened to be having lunch at the window and saw him. He dropped his bike on the lawn, then walked around your property for a few minutes."

I swallowed hard. "Could he have been a utility person or anyone like that?" *Not on a bike,* I told myself, but I was grasping at straws.

"Nuh-uh," Beth said. "He was on a bike." She said this louder, as if I might not have heard her the first time.

"Can you describe him?"

I knew this was a long shot. The Tuckers' house was separated from mine by two expansive front yards, theirs and mine, and theirs had lovely flowers that partially blocked the line of sight. One vote for not taking care of your property.

"Not really," Beth said. "He had on a helmet. Otherwise, he was just average. Average height, average weight."

"Are you sure it was a he?" I asked, trying not to sound as freaked out as I was.

"Yes, from the legs," Dan said.

"Oh?" I said.

"He was wearing shorts."

"Anyway, we thought you should know."

I waved my arm, dismissive. "Thanks for letting me know. I'm sure there's nothing to worry about. Probably someone noticing my lawn needs attention."

"I'll bet you're right, and I'll bet there's a flyer in your mailbox or under your door," Beth said. "We get them all the time, and our lawn . . ." She stopped before identifying her lawn as not needing attention as mine did.

We parted, and I walked back toward my house, passing by my mailbox, assuming it was a usual Sunday, with no delivery of the official kind, and therefore there was no need for me to check inside. And even if it had been Saturday, I admitted to myself, I didn't feel up to opening my mailbox.

I entered my foyer and breathed a little more easily when I saw the alarm still armed and Benny trotting out, his tail in the happy position. I imagined the person with manly legs walking around my property. What if he was just a freelance gardener checking out my needs? It was no exaggeration to say mine was the least attractive front yard on the street.

I smiled. What if the Tuckers had made up the story so I'd do something about my land, what with property values depending a lot on the appearance of the neighborhood?

Nice try. When did I get so creative with my what-if reasoning?

Ultimately, I couldn't talk myself out of the notion that LAY OFF man was the same guy as Walk-Around Man.

I scooped Benny up right after I texted the number for Trooper's volunteer patrol drivers.

Please send someone to sit outside my house. Thanks.

As long as I didn't flag my message as an emergency, Trooper would never know.

Now all I had to do was stroke Benny's back while I looked out the window at the weeds coming up between the stones in my small-rocks landscaping and wait for Trooper's volunteer in a car with the special decal in the corner of the windshield.

Annie called me for a briefing after she had tucked in the Johnsons, as she put it.

"I didn't want to ask Mr. and Mrs. Johnson," she said. "But do you think there could be a body down with the luggage on a flight an ordinary person is on? I mean like us?"

"You mean like when you went to your

cousin's wedding in Kansas last year?"

"Yeah, like that."

"I do think that's a possibility."

"Don't you think that's a little weird?" Annie asked. I had an image of Annie screwing up her nose, as if the odors of an embalming room had reached her nostrils in the here and now.

"Not any more weird than being in a funeral procession on the ground, with the casket in the hearse in front of us."

"I guess you're right."

It was the kind of night that brought on shudders, and it was Annie's turn for one.

TWENTY-FOUR

At nearly eleven p.m. and almost dusk, I was in the middle of clearing up the assortment of items from Benny's piñata episode. When my doorbell rang, I was afraid Ryan was making another unannounced visit. I steeled myself to ignore the bell. Instead, a peek out the window revealed that Chris had come calling. I let him into my foyer, now littered with what I thought of as pink-parka remains, though much of it was from a buildup of my own hodgepodge of things I'd dropped and left on the closet floor until I felt like crawling in and cleaning up.

Chris pointed to the official car outside my house.

"Another scare?"

"What makes you say that?"

"Because I know it would take more than one for you to respond seriously and report it."

"Coffee and Dutch apple pie?" I asked.

Was I being passive aggressive, or was there another, more appropriate word? "Stubborn" came to mind.

"Only if you'll tell me what else happened." Chris seemed to just become aware of the debris on the floor, some of which he was close to either stepping on or tripping over. "Is this part of it? Did someone break in?"

I blew out a breath. "Not unless you consider Benny a burglar."

I explained the situation with Benny and Millie's dry cleaning bag. "Let me help," Chris offered, removing his jacket and rubbing his arms as if he were rolling up his sleeves. "Then I'll have earned my pie."

"Deal."

"And while we're working, you can tell me what happened to put you over the edge and call for a car."

"Sneaky. But I will tell you."

And I did, while we picked up and threw away mints that Benny had managed to claw out of their wrapping and dusted off one of my jackets that had come off its hanger in the melee. If I didn't know better, I'd have thought Benny had invited company over to play with him while I was out.

"Where is Benny, anyway?" Chris asked.

I pointed to the guest bedroom, where I'd

witnessed my cat's disdained posture. He'd curled up on the lowest level of his condo, his back to the bedroom door as if to say, *I don't want to talk about this. Call me when you're over it.*

I did my best to minimize to Chris the fact that a man had scoped out my yard for who knew what reason. "It could have been a harmless intrusion onto my property by someone who heard I was selling, for example. What if my parents told people they were selling and an interested party thought it was me instead?"

Chris frowned and shook his head and his finger this time. "No, no, no. And combined with that note you showed me, no way. I'm assuming you've finally told Trooper."

I shook my head. "Maybe the note was a prank and the guy on the bike was really looking for gardening work? And what hit man rides a bike to do the job?"

"I don't know," Chris said, his tone sarcastic. "The kind who's too young to afford a car? The kind still in college?"

I saw his point. Except for rude HR director Louis Preston, the murder suspects were all college kids. But even minors, I reminded myself, might be capable of murder.

"Tomorrow. I'll tell Trooper tomorrow," I told Chris. "I didn't see him alone at all this evening. He came, talked to the Johnsons for a few minutes."

"Okay, tomorrow. Which, by the way, starts in less than an hour. Don't let the daylight fool you." He grinned, taking the edge off.

We stopped arguing for a few minutes while I pulled a wastebasket closer so we could discard bits of tissue and lint that were likely from my unvacuumed closet floor, not from Zoe's parka.

I left floor duty to put together our late-night coffee and Nina's apple pie. That was the great thing with Alaska's seasons. At this time of year, with sunset just happening around eleven thirty, it was like having dessert right after dinner, say, seven o'clock. Much less restricting than in the lower forty-eight.

I was setting our snack on thc table when Chris came into the room. At the same time, the clink of plates and the smell of pie brought Benny from his cushy post. He walked toward the foyer, which was still not completely cleared up, sniffed a few items, turned around, and returned to the back bedroom.

We laughed at that, a nice transition to a break in the heaviness of the night so far.

■ ■ ■ ■

It didn't take long for Chris and me to return to the case at hand. We brainstormed a way to get to the J and M research wing, if that's what it was, and had some luck with the Finding Noah issue. We constructed a plan to return to the development we'd been led to by Grandpa Clerk in the Elkview Brothers store and agreed on convening a meeting in the morning.

"One more thing I need to show you. It might be nothing." Chris reached into his pocket and pulled out papers that looked cleaner than others that had fallen from Zoe's pockets or mine onto my closet floor. These were carefully folded, down to less than two inches on a side. "That's what made me take a look at them," Chris said. "They were taken care of, important in some way, and maybe recently."

He opened the sheets and smoothed them on my table. "They could be pages from a lab book," I said. "The kind we used in chem class for our pretend experiments. Except these look like third- or fourth-generation versions from a copier, so why take care of them so well?"

"What if they are from a lab notebook?"

Chris said. "What if we have our motive here?"

I looked at the blurry sheets, copied off-center to boot. Numbers, definitely, and a hint of rows and columns, but otherwise meaningless. "They're certainly not mine," I said. "But what would Zoe be doing with them?"

Chris stayed on his own train of thought. "By 'motive,' I mean what if Ethan was onto some kind of fraud at the lab, like they were sending false results to the money people, the people giving them research money?"

"Or embezzling, where there's a double set of books." I was into it now, ignoring the leaps and bounds we were undertaking over a couple of out-of-focus pages of numbers.

"Garrett and Zoe both talked about how the veterans at J and M, kids who'd been there more than one summer, got to do clean work, and that sometimes meant working in the office."

"Why would Zoe have these pages, though? Wouldn't she have mentioned it? And wouldn't she have turned them in to Trooper? Or else skipped town for real, afraid of being involved, not waiting around for a parka she could replace in a minute?"

I had no answer.

Alaskan daylight or not, we were both

showing signs of fatigue and realized our guesses and speculations were bringing diminishing returns. The effects of the coffee were wearing off. We gave up and agreed that without further information, the pages could be relegated to the trash, declared nothing more than someone's arithmetic homework.

They could be, but we didn't. Declare homework or trash them.

I heard myself thinking in Annie's syntax and knew it was time for bed.

It was hard to let go after my highly energetic session with Chris. I found myself wishing I'd taken him up on his offer to stay in the guest room, doubling up on my security. I stood at the window and watched him stop to talk to the man on duty before climbing into his pickup. I hoped he hadn't had to wake up my bodyguard first.

It helped to have Benny close. I'd followed the advice of vets and trained Benny to sleep near me, but not with me. I lured him out of his condo, reassuring him I wasn't upset at his closet antics. Once I got around to vacuuming the area, I planned to populate it with some of his toys. I told him as much and carried him to my bedroom, depositing him in his own plush round bed on the floor at the foot of my bed. My version of a guard dog.

Last night and tonight were the only times I could remember needing one.

On Monday morning, I headed for the Bear Claw early. What a concept, actually showing up to work. It helped that the diner was a place where I hadn't had any failures. Not lately, anyway. Our recipes, old and new, all worked out. Appliances were in good working order. Deliveries came on time. I had no personnel problems. Though not overflowing, my bank balance was healthy enough for me to consider my business a success.

A far cry from my side job involving a murder, impossible deputy duties, missing or silenced witnesses, bully management, threats from an unknown source, and ineffective communications.

At times like this, I was so grateful to my parents for trusting me with the Bear Claw and, most important, honoring me with Eggs Benedict, aka Benny, without whom things would have been oh, so much worse.

Rachel had asked me for a ride to work since it was her turn to open the kitchen with Nina and her car was in the shop. I tossed my tote across the console so it landed on the floor in the back, leaving the passenger seat clear for her.

The ride to the Bear Claw was a chance to get to know Rachel, the newest member of the staff, a little better. I'd been concerned that she felt like an outsider, especially since Victor and Nina were not only siblings, but both knew their way around the Bear Claw as veterans.

Rachel assured me she felt welcome, even when the sister-and-brother team tossed out diner lingo ad nauseam.

"Eventually, I want to go to law school," she told me.

It was all I could do not to pull over and give her a lecture. It wasn't only my calamitous relationship with Attorney Jamison that had soured me on the law — I never grasped the concept of contradictory arguments. I thought of the four-dog defense and felt relief that I'd never have to use it or define it again.

I let Rachel off the hook. "Good luck with that," I said, but in the nicest possible way.

We pulled up to the Bear Claw and were greeted by Annie and a long line waiting to enter. Apparently, the tour group was eager to get started, and the leader had sounded a wake-up call an hour earlier than agreed upon.

"I've got this. No problem, boss," Rachel said. She unbuckled her seat belt and turned to me. "Do you really want to be called 'boss'? Victor says that's what you prefer, but you don't seem like that kind of person."

A compliment? I couldn't tell. "That's Victor's preference. Victor and I go way back."

Of course, Victor, in his twenties, was too young to go way back with anyone but his parents.

" 'Charlie' is fine," I told Rachel.

I heard myself say, "Chahlie." Mrs. Johnson's influence, her accent more pronounced than her husband's.

Aha, came to my brain. I finally had a bead on what had been occupying my mind about Ethan's accent, as well as his mother's, as well as the groom's at the wedding Chris's sister had attended.

I needed to revisit the so-far unintelligible words Ethan had spoken as he was dying and evaluate them now that I could take his accent into consideration. I had the feeling Garrett and Kevin were factoring in the dialect incorrectly.

The tour group was impatient, shuffling their feet as if to ward off cold weather, which this morning manifested itself as a balmy fifty-nine degrees. I'd have to go back to the last utterances of Ethan Johnson a little later.

Rachel trotted ahead to pacify the tourists while I opened the rear area of my vehicle. I pulled out my tote, which was full of paperwork — forms, invoices, correspondence, ads I wanted to follow up on.

Stuck between the back seat and the edge of the door was a white business-size envelope, with no address or other writing on the exterior.

Not again. Was this another warning? I'd hardly gotten over the LAY OFF memo, though I hadn't laid off and nothing bad had happened. Except possibly an unwanted visitor on my property. I opened the car door and saw there was another such envelope that must have fallen out of the dry cleaning bag that Zoe had dragged away when I let her off at her dorm yesterday. But when I'd taken possession of her parka, I'd seen the plastic bag with the usual detritus, now strewn, or residually strewn, over my foyer. There had been no business-size envelopes in the mix. None that I had seen. These two might have fallen from a pocket that Millie had missed. Or maybe they fell from Garrett's jacket, also recently on my back seat.

First, no clues at all. Now, too many potential ones, from sheets of paper to notes to accents.

If Zoe hadn't been so fast on her feet when I had dropped her off, I might not have lost sight of her. I would have been able to call out and get the envelopes to her. If I'd gotten out and opened the door for her, both of us would have seen them.

But now what?

In her hasty exit, Zoe had disturbed the bulk that was Garrett's parka. Could she have released the envelopes from his parka and not hers?

The big question looming — should I open the envelopes? That they were not sealed was a factor, but so was Zoe's privacy. And what if the contents of the envelopes were important to the Ethan Johnson murder case? Surely, as a deputy of Trooper Cody Graham, I had an obligation to examine any possible lead.

Unless the envelopes weren't Zoe's, which was entirely possible given the number of people who'd been in my car.

Or what if they were Millie's, inadvertently shoved into the plastic bag that had held Zoe's parka? How many times had I done the same thing, sticking a sheet of paper that belonged in folder A into folder B with other B sheets? The envelopes could be important to Millie's business.

Finally, the envelopes could be mine, unearthed from a fold in my back seat, or they could belong to someone I'd driven in the car. I tried to remember whether Rachel, for example, had kept her belongings with her or tossed them in the back with mine.

I couldn't remember and I was out of guesses.

I walked to the front of the car and slipped into the driver's seat. I opened the first envelope. Inside was one sheet of paper, folded in thirds, that looked like it had been torn from a ledger. The pale green page was crammed with numbers, some circled in red. There was no heading to indicate what the numbers meant. The second envelope contained what was probably a page from a bank statement, barely legible, as if from a printer on its last drop of ink. It was hard to be sure, especially working from memory, but these could be the original pages from the copies Chris had found in my coat closet.

I put the sheets back into their respective envelopes and thought about my next step, if any. It was hard not to entertain the thought that someone, likely Ethan, had been about to challenge a financial transaction, or a series of them. But there was no sea-blue letterhead identifying J and M, for example, or any other business. Wouldn't it be neat and tidy if these pages incriminated someone for cooking the books and Ethan had found out? A more boring option: maybe someone was taking a bookkeeping class and this was their homework.

I knew it would be impossible for me to focus on bacon and eggs and hollandaise until I worked out the crisis of conscience brought about by opening the envelopes. I looked through the diner windows and told myself everything was under control.

Even though I had mouths to feed, I called Chris.

"Ready for some brainstorming?" I asked. I pretended I didn't notice the sleepiness of his answer.

Twenty-Five

Fortunately, Annie's tour bus people were the kind of travelers who came early, ate, and left right away. No extra desserts or to-go bags, except for the snack packs already prepared for them. No sitting around a diner chatting when they could be in their bus seats on their way to a park, a mountain, or a light show.

I sent texts to Trooper and Annie that we needed a meeting to follow up on a few things, by which Chris and I meant all the failures of the Ethan Johnson murder investigation so far. Annie had been missing meetings due to an overload of tour groups but now felt she could be more involved because of her connection, such as it was, to Irene Bloom and, by extension, to Noah.

I asked Victor and his women, as he liked to call them, to take care of any other patrons for the next hour or so, but promised that I'd be available in case of a rush.

The four of us, Trooper and his "favorite deputies," as he made sure to call us, took the back booth as usual, while Rachel directed all diner traffic to the front booths and stools. I noticed how patient she was when a toddler, who came in with parents who looked exhausted, spilled his milk. She gave him a Bear Claw towel that matched hers and made a game of wiping up together. *Wouldn't those talents be wasted in law school?* I asked myself.

Chris had cornered me as we were maneuvering toward the booth. I knew he wanted me to tell Trooper about my threat-like episodes, but I continued to downplay them, to him, at least.

"Too much else going on," I told him and made him promise to keep quiet about it. In turn I promised him I'd get to it soon, and certainly if one more incident reared its head. "I will show him the ledger sheets, however."

"Hallelujah."

"What does that mean?"

"In other words, about time."

Coffee was poured, bear claws were served, the meeting came to order, and I started by sharing the papers I'd found.

"What about the legalities of opening those envelopes, et cetera?" Annie said.

"Isn't there something about evidence being inadmissible if it's obtained in the wrong way?"

I knew we were a long way from needing the answer to that question, not to mention that it was too late to fix. I could always call on my personal lawyer, Willow, she to whom I owed my firstborn, when the time came, should that occur.

"We should be able to make a case for the fact that the sheets in the envelope and the folded-up pieces in Charlie's closet fell into her hands, so to speak. I can testify to the last event," said Chris.

"I didn't seek them out or break in anywhere to find them," I said, to Annie's relief, if a deep sigh meant relief.

"They're right," Trooper said, with a casual wave of his hand toward Chris and me. By now, I was used to Trooper waiting things out before offering up his opinion, though it was more valuable than any of ours. My turn for a sigh of relief.

"Question is —" he continued.

Uh-oh.

"— who's to say what they mean?"

No one ventured a guess. But Chris was ready to move on, and raised his hand. Back to fifth grade, but I thought it was cute. He launched into our plan of action, as worked out by phone the night before. "We're going to invade the dry cabin development where we think Noah has been hiding out. We think he knows what's going on and will be able to verify that what's on the pages Ethan extracted is proof of financial fraud. Or he may even have additional evidence of his own."

"Don't say 'invade,' " Trooper said.

"Right. Thanks, Trooper." Chris cleared his throat. "We're going to take my vehicle this time. Yes, the rattling pickup, and fill the bed with gardening implements, preferably old and used ones, and" — he looked at Trooper — "slip in."

"Great cover," Trooper said. "And 'slip in' is much better than 'invade.' I have some donations along the lines of rusty old rakes and wire brooms, as long as you promise never to bring them back."

Annie, who hadn't been seen in that part of town, would be the driver, and get as close as she could before the Doberman was dispatched, if it was. Neither Chris nor I was willing to risk riding with the tools in the open bed, since it was quite possible that the dog could jump into the back of the truck. I felt a little twinge of fear as the image returned — a huge, angry dog racing toward us. Just to be sure, I'd wear something different from the windbreaker I had worn that day.

"We'd better take a good supply of meat to use for diversionary tactics," I said, blowing out a breath to get rid of the image.

"Does that really work for guard dogs?" Annie asked. "I've only had cats. Like Yulie, who wouldn't fall for that."

"Yulie is a guard cat?" Chris asked.

Annie missed the humor and took off into stories of Yulie yowling at people who might be arguing with Annie over a broken window screen in their room or the lack of ice in their bucket.

"Interesting," Chris said, in that way that meant he didn't believe a word of it. For my part, I was sure Benny would come to my rescue should the occasion arise.

"Back to dogs — it depends," Chris continued. "Some people train their guard dogs not to fall for the meat trick; others don't do anything special about how the dog responds. They just count on the size and extreme loudness of the dog to keep people away. But not knowing the dog situation in this case, I think Charlie and I should squeeze into the passenger side of the cab. Keep down low, out of sight."

"Of both the dog and the residents," I added.

We hoped to gain access to the cabin we thought Noah had exited when we dropped in on Saturday or, failing that, convince a resident in a neighboring cabin to deliver him to us for a simple convo, promising protection from Trooper if he needed it.

"I assume this is based on the theory that Noah is a good guy and not the bad guy," Trooper said.

Chris, the former army MP, nodded. "He would have gone all the way home otherwise. And I suspect his mother would have arranged for a lawyer at the minimum. I'm betting he's just staying out of reach until whatever this is blows over."

"What was Irene's thing anyway?" Annie asked, still a little peeved, as I was, at Irene's behavior, excused only when I considered that she was trying to protect her son.

"My guess?" Chris started. "The PI she hired found Noah right away. Look at how easily Charlie and I found him." He turned to me and smiled. "After Charlie charmed a cat, that is. The PI determined that Noah was keeping out of harm's way until Ethan's killer was caught."

"You can see why Irene would be reluctant to share that," I said. "So she said that he was taking some R and R."

"She wouldn't want to give away his location," Annie said. "I guess I can forgive her. She did leave me her credit card information, which means she didn't stiff me. And believe me, it's happened."

"How do you account for the fact that Noah left his J and M job to go into hiding, if you will, long before Ethan died?" Trooper asked.

"It's very possible Noah was aware that Ethan was about to blow the whistle on whatever was going on at J and M," I said.

"And remember, Ethan started to get sick from the mercury before it actually got him," Chris said.

Just when we thought Trooper was with us, he folded his arms across his chest and asked, "You got any proof to go with these statements?"

Silence.

"I didn't think so," he said. "But go on. All we have are guesses."

"I suggest we check all our vehicles for a tracking chip," Chris said. *This is war* was the unspoken rallying cry.

"Isn't that a little extreme?" I asked. "Do you have reason to believe we're being followed?"

"You can't be too careful," Chris said. "And we need recon. We have to figure out the best time to approach."

"For instance, is there a time when everyone is at church, you mean?" Annie asked.

"Something like that," Chris said.

"Did you check for the water station, showers, things like that?" Trooper asked.

I personally felt I should hang my head in shame. Was I that much of a city dweller that I didn't know about life in communities so close to my home and business? I suspected people traveled great distances for dry cabin vacation rentals within a few miles of where I'd spent most of my life.

"I'll do that," Annie said. "I think I know just where to go. It's past that general store you guys stopped at. I'll buy a jug of water and pretend I'm visiting someone."

"A hostess gift," I said. "Bringing someone water. I like it."

The plan for Operation Dry Cabins was submitted and approved.

One item down.

The second plan, less worked out, involved determining where the J and M part-timers worked. We hoped to corner Garrett and Kevin outside the purview of supervisor Preston and, preferably, also of Attorney Jamison, contingent on inspecting and removing any tracking devices, if discovered. As the frequent deliverer of good food, I felt I had as good a chance as any of getting them to open up, perhaps even simply to nod at one or more theories.

"I may be able to help with that," Trooper said.

Finally, I said to myself.

"Or, rather, my one and only official deputy might. I'll have Josh call Preston to the station house for general questioning about the murder of one of his employees and suggest he might want to bring his lawyer."

"Wow," I said, then cleared my throat. I was afraid to overdo the gratitude, lest it increase suspicion in Trooper's mind that he shouldn't be participating this way.

Part two, where some or all members of the team headed for the working side of J and M, as opposed to the tourists' lobby, would get under way after the "slipping in" operation, as opposed to the invasion we'd first called it.

"Zoe?" Trooper asked now, almost a dare, challenging us to come up with a yes or a no for her involvement in Ethan's murder.

We were ready for him.

"What if Ethan didn't break up with Zoe because he no longer cared for her, but because he thought he needed to protect her from the bad guy or guys?" I asked.

"How do we find out?" Annie asked,

seeming despondent, then quickly rebounding. "We need to capture her, no matter how she tries to slip away. She may not know what she knows."

We all knew what Annie meant: No more coddling the delicate college girl.

"Maybe she doesn't know," I said. "Does anyone remember how the guys in the booth with Ethan claimed that in his last moments, Ethan fell on Zoe and wouldn't let go?"

"I remember." A voice from the kitchen. Nina, who had been on top of things that day last week, introducing me to everyone, and had been very aware of what transpired in the booth at the end. The end of Ethan, that is. "You think Ethan said something to Zoe while he was leaning on her?" she asked.

"That, too, but even the guys heard that," I said. "Those words he spoke that his friends thought were missing an 'R,' because of his Boston accent? There was no 'R' at the end; he was trying to say —"

"Parka!" Nina said, with a pump of her arm. "He put the proof in Zoe's parka."

"The first time," I said.

"Then he realized she was taking her parka to be dry-cleaned," Chris said.

"And the next chance he had, she was

wearing Garrett's parka," Nina added.

Meanwhile, Rachel was holding down the fort in the kitchen. She wasn't complaining about the overload, but apparently neither did she want to be left out of the fun completely.

"Tube steak," she called out to Nina, who was doubling as a waitress to a skiing couple at the moment.

"Who wants a hot dog at this hour?" Nina asked.

Rachel covered her mouth, red-faced, embarrassed. "I thought I was calling out 'steak fries.' "

The steak-fry orderer laughed with us. I wondered how much of the rest of our conversation he or other casual diners heard. I decided to lower my voice for the rest of our meeting, hoping my booth mates would do the same.

"Though he didn't live long enough to see for himself, Ethan probably figured the pages would end up steam cleaned," Chris said.

"When he realized that, he put the originals in the pocket of Garrett's parka, which was being worn by Zoe," I said.

"Does that mean he trusted this Garrett guy? He must have known it was Garrett's parka that Zoe was wearing, and he wouldn't have put them there if he thought Garrett was the one poisoning him." A good question from Annie.

All we could do was nod. Besides, by now I could hardly remember which theory was which and which one was only in my head, not shared with anyone.

In spite of myself, I smiled and thought of telling my mom we were investigating the Case of the Two Parkas. If I could ever smile with my mom again. I had to get this off my mind and ask her straight out what her plans for the rest of her life were. Or maybe I could approach my dad, where there was less baggage, of the good kind, between us.

Trooper stood. "I'm impressed with all you've come up with," he said. "I wish I didn't have to go."

What? No.

"We need you, Trooper," I said.

"Nah. You're on your own. You'll do fine. I have to pick up the Johnsons at J and M. They were pretty clear they didn't want me there while they talked. Preston and whatever other managers would be on hand. But they did promise to let me pick them up and to let me know what went on."

"And you'll tell us," I said, as if I had complete confidence that he would.

I thought of the trick Irene had played,

skipping town instead of waiting for me at Annie's, where she knew I'd want to know what she found out about Noah. I wondered if the Johnsons were as devious. I supposed if they were already on a plane back to Boston, we'd find out.

"After that, well, it's Monday, and I have to return to the public safety training project at Big Lake."

I didn't hear a promise to brief us on the Johnsons' interview at J and M.

I needed a credential.

I'd tried law school.

I wondered if I was too old to apply to the police academy. A badge would do.

Out in the Bear Claw parking lot, we prepared to prepare, so to speak. Chris was going to Trooper's house, where Trooper said his garage would be open and Chris would be free to pick off any old tools he needed for the covert operation at the dry cabin development.

"Who's in charge?" Annie asked, making it clear by her tone and her body language that it was not going to be her.

"We're in charge," Chris said, pointing to himself and then to me. "But you're driving."

Annie pointed out the window. "That? Me?"

"Yes, that, and yes, you," I said, a form of sentence I thought she'd relate to.

"It's the perfect cover, especially compared to the slick new Outback we showed up in the first time we went out there. I'll take the truck home and sweep for bugs, then head to Trooper's for the props," Chris said.

"You can do that?" Annie asked. "Sweep? Like spies?"

"I might know a little."

"Hmm," Annie said, glancing around, seeming to check the parking lot and herself for bugs.

"I'll round up some props, too. I know there are some old gardening tools in my garage," I said, having no special military skills.

"What about your neighbors? Every time I see them, they're out there gardening," Chris said.

"Too clean. I swear they give their rake and hoe a bath every night."

"Good point."

As long as I was going all in on the investigation, including wearing old coveralls and a flannel shirt — I stopped short of finding a piece of hay for my teeth — I thought I might as well throw all caution to the wind and call my parents. A non sequitur if I ever heard one, but who was counting?

I sat in my car and dug out my phone before I could change my mind.

Twenty-Six

But that's what I did.

I changed my mind.

Lost my nerve.

I was ready to take down a killer, but I couldn't face, even talk to or text, my own mother. When the investigation was over, I told myself, I'd have a heart-to-heart with her. When I had nothing else to do. Or when she and my dad came home, whichever came last.

Instead I called Benny, via the Bennycam. Even though he was sleeping in that perfect sunny place in the family room, I made my confession. I told him I was a coward, but I was his coward, and I was on my way home to play with him.

I wondered if the newest present I'd ordered had arrived. PREMIUM CARDBOARD, the ad said. One hundred percent nontoxic and extra thick. I could hear my mom laughing, if not scolding me about buying cardboard when boxes arrived at the diner or my home on a nearly daily basis. To help your cat get that extra-satisfying scratch and protect your furniture, the ad promised. Satisfy your cat's need to scratch while keeping their claws off your furniture. Never mind that I had no pricey scratchable furniture in my home, just wooden chairs and rockers, with a cushion here and there. Benny was welcome on all the pillows and already had a multistory scratching tree of his own.

When it came right down to it, I would gladly have Benny sharpen his claws on my furnishings.

Back in my house, I spent a few minutes with the colorful wand Benny seemed to like. Chasing a feather-and-bell combo seemed like a treat to him, especially when followed by an edible treat of what amounted to tuna jerky.

I went over the dry cabin plan again, hoping it would be more successful than the first plan had been. I searched for the denim overalls I had worn last Halloween for a "Wizard of Oz" party and finally found them at the bottom of a laundry basket, where they must have been since last October. How embarrassing. There was no time to wash and dry them before Chris would be picking me up in his truck. I spot-cleaned the bib of the garment, doing my best to scrape off the bit of chocolate from a fun-size piece of candy, shook them out, and hung them up to decrease the number of wrinkles. I could always say they got dirty when I was handling Trooper's old rakes and shovels.

Annie reported by text on her recon mission, with nothing helpful. She'd checked with various businesses in the strip mall that tiny home owners frequented, but there was apparently no regular patronage, whether of the post office, the water stations, the food services, or the showers. The dry cabin dwellers came in at random times, and almost never together. Neither could Annie find mention of a community meeting of any kind in the near future. Apparently, the residents really were focused on communing with nature individually. Or else, they just didn't advertise their get-togethers.

At the last minute, Annie said, she remembered the Doberman story from Chris and me and decided against walking up the path with a jug of water. No one could blame her.

Chris reported no bugs in his truck.

We were a go for the mission.

■ ■ ■ ■

Annie's outfit matched mine, except it smelled clean and looked freshly ironed. When this was over, I'd have to ask her on what other occasion she needed full-body denim. Chris had picked up Annie, then joined me in the passenger hole, back to back on the floor before we took off for the outskirts of Elkview. To accommodate our five-foot-two-inch driver, the seat had to be close to the steering wheel, and my legs were already cramped before we left the driveway.

It didn't help that we were sharing the space with a couple of pounds of raw meat: scraps of moose, elk, beef, and pork. We agreed that we needed to keep the packages close at hand, ready to fling out the windows. Chris's truck had no such luxury as windows that could be operated at the touch of a button. This meant we had to build in response time to account for rolling the window down, tossing the meat, then rolling the window up. Who knew how quickly that Doberman could be in the cab of the truck, coming at us?

Annie had taken the wheel graciously, though it was clear she had her doubts about whether the plan would work. "It's a good thing it's not me in that little well," she said, a reference to her chubbiness.

"Your short legs would be welcome," Chris said, earning an elbow from me.

Though we didn't need to start out in this uncomfortable configuration, we thought it better than trying to pull over on the way and calling attention to a roadside switch of personnel. The roads had no shoulder to speak of, and turning into the woods to rearrange our positions also seemed unwise in the unfamiliar territory.

In spite of the rattles and clanking noises Chris's pickup made, we tossed around possible scenarios. Maybe the residents had established regular patrols up and down the road, which would be in keeping with the impression Chris and I had gotten that Noah had landed in some kind of cult compound. Or maybe that first trip Chris and I had taken had alerted them that someone was onto them and they needed to muster their ammunition. I tried not to think the worst: that we'd be hearing rifle shots one after the other as we approached. I reminded myself that the instigation for living in a dry cabin outside of town was one of a peaceful existence, close to nature. That the rifles I'd seen in photos as I researched the lifestyle were merely for self-defense against large wild animals who unwittingly entered the area.

"We can't make a bathroom stop anywhere close. The staff in the general store are sure to recognize Chris and me," I said.

"At least the cat will," Chris said. "What's its name again?"

"His name is Cutaway, like the tuxedo jacket. He's a tuxedo cat," I explained.

"I've seen those," Annie said. "They're cool."

Any normal topic to calm our nerves, to help us forget we were on an extraction mission, without benefit of training except the occasional television show. And, possibly, except for Chris.

At one point, Annie swore she saw a bald eagle fly past, close to our windshield.

"They travel only in packs," Chris said.

"I heard they fly solo," Annie said.

"Nope. In packs."

"Did you say no bathroom stop, Chris?" Annie asked, in retaliation, perhaps. "Thanks for calling that to our attention."

In other words, the tension was high in the little cab.

We passed the general store, home of Cutaway the cat, and the moment of truth was closing in. It was all up to Annie right now to play it by ear as far as figuring out how close to the cabins she could safely get as Chris and I scrunched even farther down in the passenger well.

Annie turned into the development. She played it safe and moved only a few feet at a time toward the semicircle of tiny houses. The original idea of sauntering up the path with a jug of water or a few garden tools was scrapped as soon as we entered the compound, where the atmosphere seemed taut with possible armed lookouts. Chris and I waited for the onslaught of at least one Doberman.

A few more feet under Annie's accelerator foot. Nothing yet. Neither human nor animal.

Soon we were within about thirty feet of the nearest cabin, basing my estimate on the length of the Bear Claw.

Still nothing.

We got to within about twenty feet with no action.

Then the scene changed.

Déjà vu. First the Doberman coming straight at us, then the biker spinning out the side.

Chris, nearest the window, rolled down the window with one hand, grabbed a package of meat with the other, and tossed the meat through the opening. The wrapping was extra thin so the scent was obvious. He quickly closed us in again. I tore the wrapping off the second package, just to be sure, and handed it to Annie, who tossed it over on her side. We had no idea if Dobermans, like bald eagles, flew solo or in packs.

The biker, who we presumed to be Noah, kept going, just as last time, but now on a manual bicycle, not the motorized bike he'd used previously.

Annie backed down the path, drove out onto the road, and turned in the direction the biker had gone.

The biker was only a few feet ahead of us. He turned right into a clearing and waved his arm.

"Is he bothering to signal a right turn?" Annie asked.

"Maybe he's waving at us," I said, sitting up now, sharing the seat with Chris.

We turned in after him and found the rider sitting on a flat rock, the bike at his feet. His head was down, his hands on his knees, his breath somewhat labored.

I doubted he wanted to hire us for gardening work.

"Sorry about last time," he said.

"Hi, Noah," I said.

■ ■ ■ ■

We moved the vehicles farther into the clearing and made ourselves comfortable on a gathering of large rocks. After the long ride on the floor of Chris's pickup, the rock formation seemed cushy.

"How did you know it was us?" I asked Noah. With his flaming red hair cropped close and his wiry body, I had a hard time putting him physically in the Irene Bloom family.

"I wasn't sure. I hoped you would come back."

"Why are we hiding from your friends?" Chris pointed toward the tiny houses.

"They're not my friends, exactly. I just know one guy who's a friend of a friend who's working in Talkeetna, and he put in a good word, so I've been crashing here and there throughout the complex. They think I'm here to avoid my boss who's a workaholic and doesn't want to give us any time off. If they knew the real reason, they'd freak out."

"What is the real reason, Noah?" Annie asked. "Your mother is very worried."

"She's okay now. I got word through that PI she hired. She wants me to stay hidden now that she knows."

"Knows what?" Annie asked. Never one to give up when she wanted an answer.

"Uh, Ethan?" Noah said. "I figured we were going to get in trouble, but Ethan insisted we blow the whistle. Next thing I know, he started to get sick, but he wanted to hang around until he could get enough proof."

"Proof of what?" Annie asked. Maybe it was Annie who should go to law school.

"Why don't you start from the beginning, Noah?" Chris asked.

"Better yet, why don't you come back to town with us and talk to Trooper Graham about the case?" I suggested, swatting away a cottonwood blossom.

We were surrounded by the trees, famous for sending the white fluff into the air. Snow in June, some called it. Though I'd regret it in a couple of months, I wished we had some of the real variety now, instead of the hot, humid, and mosquito-laden weather we had at the moment.

Noah let out a heavy sigh. "Has Preston been caught? Is that why you came back? To get me? Is it safe now?"

Silence from the team.

But at least we were now each aware of

what the other needed to know to make any progress when we left the rocks.

Twenty-Seven

Noah accepted and made swift work of a chicken salad sandwich. Our time was limited, he told us, since his hosts and hostesses were already a little suspicious when he was gone too long. It seemed they knew almost exactly how much time a shower should take or how many minutes for a regular load of wash.

"What on earth are they suspicious of?" Annie asked.

"I have the feeling one or two of them might be skirting the law by being here, and what if I'm a spy for whatever they might be running away from? I drop in out of nowhere, without a job as far as they know, and don't apply for a place of my own."

"I never thought of that," Annie said.

"Don't get me wrong," Noah said. "Most of the people I've met are very nice and accommodating. They honestly just want to live in peace, save the planet, that kind of thing. And only one guy I ran across is here because he can't afford a regular apartment. The rest seem to like the minimalist thing, avoiding high-maintenance quarters."

"I'm not sure it's low maintenance to have to tote your own water from a station. It's like going back to walking to the river with a jug on your head," Annie said.

I thought back to twin girls I'd known in elementary school. At that age, no one seemed to care where anyone lived or what particular lifestyle had been adopted. We knew the twins came from far outside of town and that their house was very small, but no one was bothered by that, or even interested, let alone made a judgment. I wondered at what age that changed.

"I probably shouldn't have mentioned maintenance," Noah said. "They see their lifestyle as being back to nature. And if they think I'm taking a nap in some luxury hotel, they'll lose all respect for me."

Noah laughed at that, and so did we, except I wanted to move on.

"Let's speed it up, then," I said, eager to get all pertinent questions answered. I didn't look forward to another journey in what amounted to a wheel well.

I got us started with the printouts from my closet and the back seat of my car, all of which I'd taken to carrying in my tote, though Trooper now had his own copies. I wanted to use them as visual aids to jog Noah's memory. Or that of anyone else who might be able to assist us.

I handed the pages to Noah. "Do these numbers mean anything to you?"

"Oh, wow," he said. "Ethan actually got proof?"

Annie blew out a frustrated breath. "Like I asked before — proof of what?"

"Ethan and Kevin were the most senior of us and they were both good with numbers, so Preston let them work in the office occasionally, when things got busier there than out in the plant. They were sure Preston was cheating. Fudging numbers on the hauls. Reporting less catch than we actually brought in, then black-marketing the rest."

"Selling fish on the side?" I asked, having trouble picturing it.

"Actually, yes," Noah said.

"I thought Louis Preston was an HR person," Chris said. "How would he be involved in that end of the business?"

"J and M up here is small," Noah said. "Not like the main plant in San Francisco. And there are a ton of other companies up here, so it's not hard to fool around with numbers and find a buyer."

"Crooks are so creative," Annie said, and we all agreed to that.

"So Preston gets wind of the fact that Ethan and you are onto him, but you bug out before he can get to you," Chris said.

I knew that Chris was intending to summarize, not to criticize, but Noah turned sullen and defensive, a response we didn't need if we were going to win his cooperation.

"I tried to get Ethan to come with me. What power did we have to do anything about it? We didn't even live here. Who was going to listen to us summer hires over an established Alaska businessman? You think the guy didn't cover his tracks?"

I felt that Noah was arguing with the deceased Ethan all over again, maybe even feeling guilty for running off.

"What about Kevin and Garrett?" I asked.

"I don't know them as well. I just know Ethan, who was my buddy, was the one who wanted to tell the cops. Or the troopers or whatever."

Noah stood suddenly and made a turn around the rock pile, now and then kicking a small stone ahead of him. "Wait," he said. "This is what I was afraid of. Why I wanted to talk to you. You're telling me Ethan did not get the word out before he died."

"Hold on," Chris said. "We're not saying that. But we need you to corroborate. All we have is scraps of paper and a strong suspicion."

"You could help us build a case against Louis Preston," Chris said. "If you step up, maybe others will, too. Like Garrett and Kevin."

"You want me to testify, essentially. That's why you drove all the way here?"

"It may not come to that," I said, worried that we were at loggerheads before we'd gotten to other important questions that needed answering. "At the very least, you could verify that Ethan was looking into it and that these sheets are indeed from the ledgers."

"You're not here to tell me the case is all solved and everything?"

"The mercury compound," Chris said. "We need to know how it got into Ethan's system. Do you know who had access? How controlled it was?" Chris was moving ahead, worried, as I was, that we'd already lost Noah.

Noah took his seat again. "What if you were followed?" he asked.

"We weren't," Chris said.

I thought it best not to remind Chris that although he'd made sure we weren't tracked by electronics, we couldn't be certain we weren't followed the old-fashioned way. As far as I knew, we hadn't discussed the possibility with Annie, and I doubted she had been on the lookout in the rearview mirror.

"Okay, I don't know anything about mercury. Garrett's the chemist. I'm a history major. Is that what made Ethan sick? Mercury? Like what the research people are working on?"

Chris and I nodded.

"Does your mom know the whole story?" Annie asked, grabbing Noah's attention, still concerned about her former guest, delinquent though she'd been.

"Not exactly. I had the PI tell her that I was okay, so she wouldn't worry. I didn't exactly tell him there was a target on my back. What now?" Noah asked, but more to himself than to us, since he answered immediately. "I guess I just stay here until it's all cleared up. I don't feel safe going back. Or even going home. You never know how long a criminal's reach is."

I thought he was overreacting on that front. Wisconsin was almost four thousand miles away, after all. Unless every criminal knew every other one in the country — but who was I to declare otherwise?

I also felt skittish telling Noah that we

could protect him, even if the "we" included an Alaska State Trooper and his deputy in the mix. Besides, that never worked on television dramas. The bad guys always found a way to penetrate a wall of protection.

Nevertheless, we made another stab at getting Noah to come back to town, to talk to Trooper and generally be available as the case developed, if it ever did significantly. Annie offered him a room at the inn, not without laughing softly. "They wouldn't think of looking for you there."

"At least you could follow the investigation, and maybe even help," Chris said. "You can tell the whole crew at J and M that you were just exhausted by coming up here to Alaska so soon after school ended and you needed some breathing room. Tell everyone you really did need R and R and you're ready to take your place again."

"Tell them you were off climbing Denali," Annie said. This time I gave her a poke.

"How well do you know Garrett Marsh?" I asked. "And the mercury research?"

When I saw Noah's reaction to all these questions and suggestions, I was sorry I'd pushed him for information. He looked overwhelmed. I thought I heard him whisper Ethan's name. For a minute, I thought he was going to cry, but he blinked a few times, then recovered.

He picked up his bike. “I have to go.”

“Wait,” Chris said. He reached over to Noah, now straddling his bike, and handed him a phone. “At least take this. It’s is a burner phone. That way you can reach us and vice versa without worrying about a trace. If you change your mind about coming back to town, just call and we can pick you up.”

Annie and I looked at Chris. Who just happened to have a burner phone handy? It wasn’t the time for wisecracking about Chris’s military past, but once we were on our way, Chris had some explaining to do.

“Or if you think of anything else that would help,” I said, but Noah was pedaling on his way.

Annie looped her thumbs around the straps of her overalls. “I guess we didn’t need these costumes after all.”

“And we’re going home first class,” I said. “Sitting straight up on the seat of the pickup.”

The trip home was an executive summary of our meeting with Noah Bloom, or “Irene’s son,” as Annie chose to call him.

Chris was in the driver’s seat and Annie

took notes while I doled out the contents of the snack packs I'd brought along. As usual, the elk jerky went first. I didn't know why we bothered with the variety of nuts and other goodies. We ought to just bundle up sticks of jerky. When Chris was nearby, the second-favorite Bear Claw menu item was a bear claw. I'd cut up a couple that were imperfect, unsuitable for paying customers, but still delicious, into bite-size chunks. Annie was easy to please. She reached her hand into the container and took potluck.

Confirmed: Ethan had been working to expose financial fraud on the part of human resources manager Louis Preston. Follow-up: Get Trooper to officially request the books for J and M Fish Processing.

Confirmed: Zoe had more than likely told us all she knew. If she wasn't even aware of how the pockets of two parkas she'd worn had been trifled with while she was wearing them, she was likely oblivious of everything else. Follow-up: One more chat with her, perhaps to hear Ethan's method of breaking up with her. Had he said anything that sounded off?

Confirmed: Chris Doucette was looking and sounding more like an intelligence agent every day. The clean-shaven reporter with a broken-down pickup was his cover.

His explanation: He'd had a last-minute thought about the burner phone and wasn't sure we were going to meet Noah, but had bought it just in case. No, he owned no other spy or criminal equipment. Not that he could think of.

Confirmed: We needed to come up with a way into the research area of J and M. Possible follow-up: Chris could ask for a tour for a feature article. Research in our very own Elkview. I would consider, possibly, maybe, hesitantly, cozying up to my ex, Attorney Ryan Jamison, to assist with the request. Follow-up part two: Fake it with Preston and maybe also Garrett and Kevin, telling them we saw Noah and he spilled everything. No costumes needed for that operation, except a straight face while lying. That plan was on hold, needing further elaboration.

Confirmed: It was easier to communicate when we were all sitting on the seat of Chris's pickup and not directly breathing in the dust of the floor mat.

Twenty-Eight

The team of four — trooper, Chris, Annie, and I — set a meeting for three o'clock to give us all time to change into our normal clothes as well as figure out the next step each of us might take.

We sat around my dining room table, but we might as well have been at the Bear Claw, given the variety of snacks available, courtesy of my staff. Rachel had been sent with the food since she'd never been to my home.

"I was told I had to meet Benny," she said. "I hope he's home."

"He's always home," Annie said.

Rachel dropped the containers on the table. See-through boxes of cookies, jerky, stuffed celery, and a whole cream pie. The final container was for Benny — plain, grilled salmon pieces. The smell brought Benny around, but I could tell there were entirely too many people to suit him, especially since the crowd included someone he'd never met. He sniffed Rachel's feet but ducked and backed away when she bent to pet him. He didn't growl or hiss or otherwise make a negative sound, which was a good sign.

"Next time he'll be more friendly," I assured her as Benny sat out of reach, his bright green gaze pinned on the salmon. "He'll eat this treat and remember who brought it."

After Rachel left, Benny ate his salmon and settled down to groom himself, and we got down to business.

"Trooper first," Chris said. "Before his antique pager goes off and he has to get in the saddle and ride off into —"

"That's enough," Trooper said. "Do you want a report or not?" A hint of a smile.

We were all ready to hear what Trooper had learned from the Johnsons. How were they greeted? Did they get past the lobby? Was J and M's attorney present? I grimaced at the last question.

Trooper had picked up Ethan's parents after their meeting at J and M and taken them to Doc Sherman's. Doc's assistant would accompany them and the body of their son to the Anchorage airport for the long trip home to Boston. My heart went out to them.

At the moment, the whole case of who had murdered Ethan Johnson seemed to be on Trooper's shoulders, since it would be up to him to officially ask for J and M's financials. The question was whether Noah's testimony, formal or informal, was required or whether, even if he swore under oath, it would be enough to connect Preston to Ethan's murder.

I started to think it was hopeless. *One thing at a time,* I had to tell myself. Trooper embarked on his report, secondhand though it was — how the meeting had gone between the Johnsons and Preston on the promised laboratory tour.

"Mr. Johnson was something else. He gave me the same lecture he said he gave Preston. Johnson had read an article in some fish magazine, or maybe a fish*ing* magazine, that said how metals like mercury and some others are a cause for concern. He had this food chain chart showing how salmon get mercury from impure water, say from an industrial plant, then the tuna eats the salmon, sort of doubling the mercury, then the halibut eats the tuna and, wow." Trooper gave out a wildish gesture of mercury levels rising, ending with "halibut."

"But halibut can be so bland," Annie said.

I pondered whether there was a taste to mercury, then Chris cut into my thoughts with another question to Trooper.

"How did Preston react?"

"He was supposed to be giving them a tour of the research facility, trying to present it as safe and certainly not related to their son's death. But it was clear he knew nothing beyond what was in the brochure. Less, even. He couldn't comment at all on Johnson's mercury chart. All he did was pivot to 'Here are some chemicals' or 'Over there's where they experiment.' That's according to Mr. Johnson."

"Maybe Preston was playing dumb?" Chris suggested.

"According to Mr. Johnson, he was really dumb. He kept going back to his prepared talk, how some work can be very strenuous, like stacking fifty-pound cases of frozen fish, how working conditions are wet and cold and very noisy."

"Boilerplate stuff," Chris said.

"Exactly. But I saved the best for last. I can see where young Ethan got his spunk, though it turned out badly for him in the end."

"What's the best part?" Annie wanted to know.

I didn't know what her hurry was, except

to get to the part where we talked about our denim-clad mission.

"When we left the facility, Mr. Johnson asked for my phone. He wanted to transfer some photos, he said. Harmless, I thought, but to be safe, I gave him my personal phone, which, as you know, I hardly ever use."

Trooper took out his phone to show us. I held it while Chris and Annie looked over my shoulders.

"You have to swipe," Trooper told us, using his index finger to demonstrate. We kept our faces straight, letting him think he'd taught us something.

But we didn't laugh at the selection of photos.

I scrolled through photo after photo of a laboratory, the J and M laboratory, I presumed. Opaque brown bottles with red caps, some with black caps, lined up on shelves, the images clear enough to read the labels. Scales, vats, experimental setups with cables and wires attached. Cabinets with glass doors. I focused on sample tubes like the kind technicians use when they draw blood. The labels read MERCURY TEST.

"How did he get these photos? All from different angles? Wasn't Preston with them the whole time?" I asked.

"Absolutely. Beats me how he did it. Maybe Preston was just not paying attention to him. Johnson said how every now and then he stretched or sort of bent over, as if to get some kinks out of his arms and legs. No one saw that he was holding his phone and taking photos. Never heard a click or saw a flash or anything like that."

One photo pictured a sign that looked like it was tacked to a corkboard. I could make out certain warnings about mercury.

- NEVER use a mercury thermometer in a laboratory oven. This is a hazmat situation!
- Do not leave open containers of mercury in the laboratory.
- Do not keep excess mercury around if you do not need it.
- Clean up spills promptly.
- Put mercury waste in the special container designated for that purpose.
- Read the Safety Sheet for mercury before using it.

This alone was enough to make me glad I was not a chemistry major. Although when I thought about it, I realized there had been plenty of rules posted in my cooking classes. If I were to make up my own poster, it would include:

- Store knives in a block or drawer.
- Never cook in loose clothes.
- Keep dry towels and pot holders nearby.
- Turn pot handles away from the stove front.

And more!

"And by the way," Trooper said, "according to Johnson, the room itself was locked, but not the cabinets."

"Bottom line here," Chris said, "anyone in the lab can take a sample and take pictures." He shook his head.

There was one question I kept hoping someone else would ask or Trooper would answer on his own. It wasn't happening, however, so I took a deep breath and tried to bring my voice down an octave from the nervous squeak it would be otherwise.

"Did Mr. Johnson mention anything about J and M's attorney being there? Ryan Jamison from San Francisco?"

"Oh, yeah," Trooper said. "Apparently he was there but hardly said a word. Mr. Johnson figured he was hanging around in case the word 'lawsuit' came up. And since it didn't, the guy was silent."

"Makes sense," Chris said, since my throat was too dry to respond. He shot a glance at me. "Maybe the guy will go back to his fancy offices now."

I felt he'd read my mind.

Our turn came to brief Trooper on our trip to the land of Oz. Except it was not as conclusive as his report, and we had no photos.

Maybe that's why Trooper left before we were finished.

"Did anyone else notice that Trooper spoke more during this hour than in a normal week?" I asked.

"I was going to say 'than in a year,' " Chris said.

"He was certainly impressed with Mr. Johnson," Annie said. "Maybe because he made Trooper's job easy. He didn't have to deal with uncontrollable parents. He just had to listen and then report to us."

"Are we so hard to deal with otherwise?" I asked.

I wasn't surprised that neither of them answered.

Having snacked all day, I had no need for dinner. And I didn't need to go into the Bear Claw except for the couple of hours between ten and midnight.

While I was still awake, I grabbed one of Benny's wands, the one with the loudest bell, and shook it until he appeared. He came out of the bedroom, his tail swaying slowly from side to side, his eyes focused on his wand.

If I didn't know better, I'd have thought that Benny was sneaking dance lessons on the side. He seemed to travel farther and farther on his hind legs with every lift of the wand. I was glad I could help him get some exercise, especially after the major helping of salmon he'd had this afternoon.

It was fun while it lasted, but then my cell phone rang.

Chris sounded excited. I couldn't tell whether it was a good excited or a bad excited. I hoped for the former. It would be such a nice change for all of us.

"Are you dressed for travel?" he asked.

"As much as I was when you saw me last."

"Good. I'll be there in ten."

"Where are we going?"

"Rather not say."

Just to be sure, in case Chris wanted to elope to the Yukon Territory, I called Tammy and asked if she and Bert could cover for me this evening.

"Of course we can," she said.

Now that they were a couple, it made my

life so much easier. I wondered if their homework was suffering.

I checked Benny's feeder — all okay — and wished him good night. I was glad I'd exercised him enough to guarantee him a deep sleep.

As for me, I guessed it was my turn for exercise.

TWENTY-NINE

I was ready with the keys to my outback as Chris pulled into my driveway. We wouldn't need my heated steering wheel this evening, but one trip a day in Chris's old pickup was more than enough for me.

I handed him the keys and buckled myself into the passenger seat. "Where are we going?" I asked him.

Chris pulled a phone out of his jacket pocket and handed it to me. "Click to hear the message," he said.

I clicked, and it took only a few seconds to recognize Noah's voice.

"Can you come and get me?" Noah sounded more excited than either Chris or me. And, again, I wasn't sure if it was the good or the bad kind. "I'll write down everything you guys want to know if you'll take me to the airport afterward. I want to go home. I've had enough of this."

"Wow."

"Yes, wow. We got through to him, apparently. That's what I'm hearing."

"He's trying to do the right thing, but not hang around for any potential consequences," I said.

"Best of both worlds? Can't blame him."

"Where do we take him before the airport? He'll need a place to write. Not the Bear Claw. Too open," I said. "Even with the windows crummed up from the last rain."

"Someplace where he'll feel safe."

We sailed along with no traffic to speak of. Was it only this morning, Monday, that Chris and I had been scrunched into the passenger well of his pickup? We enjoyed a grove of cottonwoods on both sides, their blossoms hitting the car's windows like enormous flakes of snow. It was as if Alaska just couldn't be without some form of white stuff swirling around the sky, no matter the season.

We ran through the options for where we could take Noah. My house? His house? Annie's house? All with disadvantages, more negatives than positives.

"You know the best place?" Chris asked. "Though he won't like it."

"Trooper's place. We can try to convince him. We're doing okay so far."

"The question is whether he'll trust

Trooper to let him leave town when he's finished writing his statement."

"We can't risk having Trooper keep him," I said. "It wouldn't be fair."

"Maybe we should go right to the airport. Find that diner where we ate when we picked up your mom that time."

"Wright's Classic Diner. I remember. I guess that would work. Then we'd be right there and can check flights and get him on a plane as soon as he's done."

"We should have it notarized. Whatever Noah writes. I'll bet there's a place at the airport."

"I'll check," I said, then asked my phone the question.

A computer voice answered immediately. "The ten best notary publics at the Ted Stevens —"

I tapped off. "I guess we'll run into one. I'll bet Fran herself is a notary."

"Fran?"

"The waitress at Wright's."

"You remember her name?"

"Professional courtesy," I said.

Chris laughed, just before he uttered a panicked "Uh-oh."

We'd turned onto the main road leading to the Elkview Brothers General Store, home of Cutaway the tuxedo cat. Chris was looking into the rearview, frowning.

"What?" I joined his panic. "Does the car feel funny? Something rattling that I don't hear?"

He slammed his fist on the steering wheel. "Stupid!" he cried out. "I didn't check your vehicle for bugs. Since we weren't taking it this morning, I didn't think to clear it. Stupid!"

"We're being followed?"

"He's staying pretty far back. An older silver Taurus. But he's been there since the middle of town, I'm pretty sure now."

I turned in my seat as far as the seat belt would take me. I looked over at the speedometer. Chris was well within the speed limit. Not a cop. Or even a civilian volunteer who might have forgotten his portable siren.

"Hang on. I'm going to make a quick turn."

In seconds, we were in a clearing, on the other side of the road from the one where we'd had our meeting-on-the-rocks this morning. Chris put the car in park and got out of the vehicle faster than I'd ever seen anyone do outside of an action movie. *The name's Doucette. Chris Doucette,* I thought.

He disappeared momentarily. Then, seconds later, I saw him stamping his foot over and over, presumably killing the bug.

I wouldn't have been surprised if he'd taken out a gun and shot it.

Back in the driver's seat, Chris drove farther into the clearing and turned around, the car now facing the road, free of bugs.

Compared to the live action sequence that preceded it, the wait seemed forever, until the follower, if there was one, passed.

"There he goes," Chris said.

I barely saw the flash of silver.

In the time we'd spent in the clearing, we'd accumulated enough cottonwood blossoms to build a snowman, but apparently we hadn't stalled long enough to satisfy ex-MP Doucette.

Finally, Chris called Noah and asked him to ride his bike to the spot where we'd convened this morning. Then Chris sped out of clearing number two and headed for clearing number one. That was fine with me. A Doberman-free trip was always welcome.

Noah was understandably jumpy. His carrot red hair was almost completely hidden by a khaki cap with a logo that said GRAND TETON NATIONAL PARK WYOMING and had an embroidered moose in the background. It was nice to be reminded that there was more than one state where moose were revered, but I was surprised Noah would call attention to his homeland. Then I remembered he was from Wisconsin, a different W state, and that made more sense.

He'd secured a large duffel to the back of the bike with a bungee cord. Surely not all of the belongings he'd brought to Alaska, but he'd be going home.

"Is everything okay?" he asked. "You're a little late and then you wanted me to come out here."

"Avoiding that Doberman," I said.

"But now I have this bike with me, and it isn't mine."

I sensed annoyance in Chris's expression and thought I'd save him the need to answer.

"We'll pull over and maybe you can leave it at the edge of the driveway to the development and call in to its owner to retrieve it. Can you do that?" I asked.

"Yeah, I can do that."

That maneuver went smoothly, and we were on our way down the road to the main part of town.

"Here's what we're going to do," Chris said. "There's nothing to worry about, but I like to cover all the bases anyway. We'll drive to this friend of mine in Elkview and switch cars, then drive to the airport in Anchorage in Bo's car."

"Bo?" I asked.

"Short for Beauregard, but don't tell him I told you. It made middle school difficult for him. He's a big-time software developer now, but that still haunts him."

Chris outlined the rest of the plan for Noah, from writing out his statement to catching a flight to the Midwest of the lower forty-eight.

Meanwhile I kept a lookout for a silver Taurus. No sign of one, I reported.

The car switch also went smoothly. We commandeered Bo's newish blue Honda, and he seemed happy to take my car wherever he pleased, as long as it wasn't to Ted Stevens International Airport. Maybe the day's drama had peaked and we'd have it easy from now on.

Two hours later, we found Wright's classic Diner where I remembered it, at the airport between a chain coffee shop and a bar. I was glad to see Fran on duty today. We hugged like old friends. I explained that we needed a table for an indeterminate amount of time, if she could arrange it, and of course, she could. And, by the way, this box of chocolates from Alaska's best chocolatier that I'd picked up as we walked through the airport shopping area, this was for her.

I still wasn't very hungry from the heavy-duty snacks of the afternoon, but I was confident that Noah would make up for it on our tab with his order.

Sure enough.

"I'm starving," Noah said.

We couldn't expect him to pour out his knowledge on an empty stomach, so Chris and I gave Noah all the time he needed to eat. He polished off a bacon cheeseburger — an item no longer on the Bear Claw menu, in deference to the hearts of our diners — a side of fries, and a diet soda.

I was left making small talk with our witness as he consumed the hundreds of calories on his plate. I liked the design on his paper place mat, with sketches of Wilbur and Orville and the first flyers. I tucked a clean mat into my tote for further study, and perhaps inspiration. The design included ten fun facts about flight. I wondered if I could come up with ten fun facts about bears for the Bear Claw place mats.

While I was musing about redecorating my diner and watching over Noah, Chris had taken on the mission of finding a large notepad, a notary office, and the schedule of flights to the Midwest.

"Success all around," Chris said when he

returned. He even managed to carry in a couple of cappuccinos from the coffee shop next door, invoking the permission Fran had given us on our first trip months ago.

"Okay," Noah said, pushing aside his empty tableware and used napkins. "I guess I'm ready. How do you want me to start?"

Chris rolled his eyes.

"You'll have to use your own words," I said. "But try to think back to the first time you or Ethan became suspicious or aware that something illegal was going on at J and M. What did you see or hear? It would help if you could give us the approximate date also."

Noah closed his eyes, heaved a big sigh, and started writing.

On the way to picking up Noah, Chris and I had had a serious talk about whether this plan had a chance of working in terms of bringing Preston to justice for fraud and murder. Whether something not sworn to under oath in a court of law would carry any weight anywhere. We decided it was worth a try. Noah had made it clear that he would not testify in court. A notarized statement would at least get us halfway there with Trooper, who might then use it as probable cause to obtain J and M's books. The notary would verify Noah's ID, if not the contents of his statement, and attest to the facts that there had been no coercion and that he was of sound mind. Chris rolled his eyes at that also.

If Noah was then forced to come back, presumably he'd be afforded some protection. It wasn't our problem at that point. I hoped it wasn't our fault, either.

Once Noah finished his statement, we said goodbye to Fran, with the suggestion that I might be back tomorrow to pick up my parents. We made our way to have Noah's account notarized.

This lap of our trip was easier than we had expected, since Chris had found a mobile notary service within the airport, where they came to us. We went to a seating area just outside the security checkpoint, and a professionally dressed woman, about my age, introduced herself as Lydia. She arrived with a kit and did the deed, so to speak. She had a hand scanner and gave us copies plus stamped envelopes in case we wanted to mail copies immediately. For an extra fee, she'd pass it through a special air service.

"You mean a bush plane?" Chris asked.

"It'll get there before you do, guaranteed," Lydia promised.

We chose the special service and handed

her the envelope, addressed to Alaska State Trooper Cody Graham at the Matanuska-Susitna Borough Station House in Elkview. We paid her and settled into a short row of seats, Noah between us. Not that we were concerned he might split. Not at all.

Noah sat back and promptly fell asleep, not surprising, even on the hard plastic chair, given the meal he'd put away plus the stress of the pseudo testimony. When he woke up, we handed him his boarding pass. It took him a couple of minutes to realize what we'd done.

He stood abruptly. "Hey, this has the wrong info on it. This is going to O'Hare." He drew in a loud breath. "Chicago? I'm going to Milwaukee. I know there are direct flights from here."

"Here's the plan," Chris said, not for the first time this evening. "It's better that you not go directly to the Milwaukee airport. You can get a bus or train from Chicago. Go into a big hotel, go out the back door, and hail a cab to the train or bus station." He handed Noah what looked like a credit card. "This looks like a credit card, but it's actually a gift card. It has enough money on it for train or bus fare between Chicago and Milwaukee, plus some snacks. It does not have your name on it, and it expires in fourteen days."

"None of this is absolutely necessary, Noah," I said. "Don't let it freak you out. Chris is trying to cover your tracks, which never hurts."

"One more thing," Chris said. "Don't call your mom ahead of time."

"Just show up?"

Chris nodded. "Just show up. Act normal. We'll let you know what's going on up here as soon as we can. Then you'll be rid of us and can get on with your life."

"You should have told me all this before," Noah said, his voice cracking.

I couldn't disagree with him.

"Think of it like insurance," Chris said. "Like for your car. You'll probably never use it, but you don't want to be without it, either."

Noah frowned but apparently knew he'd lost this round. We walked with him as far as we could go without a boarding pass.

"Here's a copy of your statement," Chris said, handing it to him along with a new burner phone.

Noah turned and headed for the line through security.

No thank-yous, no goodbyes, on either side.

"Not very satisfying," I said.

"At least the day's over," Chris said. "No more stressful interactions."

"Except I'll need the story of your life between high school and now," I said. "Sweeping for bugs, burner phones, car-switching tactics, spare credit cards. Not even allowing a direct domestic flight."

"You go first and tell me more about you and that lawyer I've been saving you from."

"Never mind," I said, and quickly added, "and don't roll your eyes."

Thirty

We stopped for a quick pizza in the town of South Willow, then reversed the car drop-offs, ending up, amazingly, with Bo's Honda at Bo's and the two of us at my house in my vehicle, Chris's pickup waiting in my driveway.

Also waiting in my driveway was Trooper. At first I thought he was napping in the patrol car, but if he was, he certainly snapped awake when we pulled in.

And I'd thought the hard part of the day was over.

Trooper stepped out of his car as Chris and I stepped out of my car. He was holding the large envelope we'd entrusted to our notary.

"Lydia wasn't kidding," I said.

"People tend to fast-track priority mail addressed to a state trooper," he said.

"Even from the airport?" I asked.

"Especially from the airport. This is some

maneuvering you two undertook. I'm assuming Mr. Bloom is on his way back to Wisconsin at the moment?"

"Can we go inside and talk?" I asked, with a fake shiver that fooled no one.

"It's probably above fifty degrees out here," Trooper said.

"We want to check on Benny," Chris said.

"I already did," said Trooper, who had a key, of course. "He's fine."

I was glad to hear it, and also happy to hear Chris add himself to those who wanted to check on Benny.

We continued the conversation inside.

"I should take your badges away," Trooper said. The threat was weak since it was spoken around a mouthful of rhubarb pie. Pie made by and distributed by me. And there weren't any badges to take away, but it didn't seem the time or place to mention that. "You should have told me you knew where the boy was."

"It wouldn't have done any good. He was afraid."

"And he thought you two could protect him better than the state of Alaska?"

He had a point.

Chris shrugged. I grimaced. And I kept myself busy giving Benny treats. He refused to sit on my lap, but hung out around my feet, possibly because he thought he might need a quick getaway if Trooper turned enemy tonight.

"Can you use that to haul Preston in?" Chris asked, pointing to the legal-size envelope.

"Sure going to try," Trooper said. "It's more than we had yesterday."

I supposed we shouldn't push our luck and expect gratitude.

"When are you going to arrest him?" I asked.

As soon as I asked, I expected a version of "none of your business," but Trooper had had time and enough pie to mellow out.

"We'll ask him to cooperate, to show us the books. You know the drill, Charlie, or didn't they teach you anything in law school?"

I had another question, a comment really, that I hesitated to bring up. I thought about my LAY OFF note and the guy walking around my property. Neither of those antics fit the Louis Preston I'd observed. For one thing, that guy had a lawyer, so why would he need to make his own case, take the chance that someone would see him? The note seemed juvenile; Preston did not.

Was this the time to talk to Trooper about my unwelcome guests? I glanced at Chris, also enjoying pie and coffee, like Trooper, not looking like he had any loose ends to wonder about.

I decided I'd go over notes I'd jotted down right after I talked to the Tuckers about the guy circling my house. See if they remembered anything else since then.

For now, I'd let it go.

I wanted to check my messages before I succumbed to sleep. First there was my mom, who'd called to say they'd be heading home, arriving at Anchorage tomorrow, Tuesday, around seven thirty in the evening.

It was almost eleven in Elkview. Why couldn't I remember the time change for San Diego, California? I'd had little difficulty converting when Mom and Dad were cruising the Danube earlier in the year. And I'd actually lived in the San Francisco time zone, so what was the trouble?

I thought it best not to consult Freud or any living analyst about that. I checked my browser and learned that SoCal, like NorCal, was an hour later.

I clicked on their number before I lost my nerve.

"Hi, honey," Dad answered. "How come you're up so late? Everything okay?"

"Sure. Just checking that you're coming

home tomorrow?"

"That's right. And have we got a surprise for you."

My heart did a flip and slammed back down. "Oh? What's up?"

"Uh-oh, I shouldn't have said anything. Your mom will kill me. Just pretend I didn't say anything."

"Is she there?"

"No, she's having a girls' night with some of her new friends."

"Nice," I said, not really meaning it.

Why did my mom need new friends? She had plenty of friends right here in Elkview. Then, of course, I thought, *No, not really.* She'd worked so hard for so many years. Unlike me, she hardly ever took even a half day off, and then only for a doctor's appointment or to hear me plunk a few notes in a school recital. Selfish beyond redemption, that was me.

"I'm planning to pick you up," I told my dad, since it was the least I could do. "Do you have your flight info handy?"

I heard some shuffling and a muffled, "Be right back."

I knew I shouldn't have called. Big surprise coming, huh? Not nearly. But better to have warning.

"Here it is," Dad said, and I did my best

to concentrate on writing down the information. Flight 483, at seven thirty p.m.

"I'll be there." Then, an afterthought. "Did you have a good time with the Russells?"

"The best. You need to come down sometime."

We said good night and I prepared myself for hearing the surprise. I also parsed every word Dad had said. I needed "to come down sometime," for example. Why wouldn't he say, "after we move"? Maybe he didn't want to give away the surprise. Then there was "the best" to describe the time he'd had. Why wouldn't he want to live where it was the best?

When my phone rang, it was a relief. Otherwise I'd have been questioning Dad's prepositions by now.

"Hi, Annie," I said.

And another worry presented itself. I hadn't talked to her since Chris's summons had taken me around the narrow roads to tiny houses and then down the highway to Ted Stevens airport.

"I left a message earlier. Was your cell off?"

Now what? I could never lie to my friend. Neither could I tell her what I'd been doing this evening. Chris and I hadn't deliberately excluded Annie from the escapade. Chris had received the message from Noah out of the blue, and we'd responded as quickly as possible, lest we lose the opportunity to talk to him.

I could brief Annie now, after the fact, and she would be perfectly satisfied with what might be considered progress and not feel left out. But it would also be like Annie to call Irene, Noah's mother, immediately. She wouldn't even intend to; it would just happen and no one would be able to blame her. I didn't want to take that chance before we knew Noah was safely home.

I did have one trick that worked with Annie more often than not, which was to wait her out. Annie would forget her question and launch into another topic of her own. It might be a Yulie anecdote, a tour group tale, a funny story from a guest, or an Annie's Inn spiel. Tonight it was a combination, in a way, as she introduced the topic of a woman who had checked into the inn.

"She's a pet photographer. Have you ever heard of that?" she asked.

"Can't say that I have."

"She does photo shoots for pets. Families hire her for greeting cards or just to have as nice a picture of your cat, you know, as you have of a wedding or something. Isn't that cool?"

"Very. So did you arrange a photoshoot for Yulie?"

Of course she did.

"She came up with a great album. For example, in one photo, Yulie is hitting that tall skinny plant in my lobby, and it keeps springing back at him, so he doesn't stop. It's a riot. Of course it's not a video, which I might end up doing sometime, but you can tell what's happening."

What luck. This was the perfect way to keep Annie talking so I wouldn't have to. "Did you try to pose Yulie, or did she just take candids?"

"Both. In some of them, he's looking right into the camera," she said. "In others, you'd swear he was posing like some movie star, looking over his shoulder at you. Oh, and I think my favorite is where he's under the bed and stretched out like he's yawning."

"Is she very expensive?" This time I really did want the answer, on the off chance I'd want to sign Benny up for a session. I imagined his getting a movie contract.

"I'm not sure exactly," Annie said. "We're going to make a deal, trading the photos for the room fee. It depends how many copies I'd want, how many nights she wants, and so on, but I'll tell you as soon as we figure it out."

"I can't wait to see the album," I said.

"I know. It's very exciting."

We signed off without my ever having to answer the question of where I'd been all evening.

It was close to midnight when Chris called. I'd started to get ready for bed, which was always tricky when it wasn't fully dark outside.

"Sounds like you're still awake," he said. "I can't sleep until I hear from Noah that he's home. What's keeping you up?"

"Noah also. Plus, I'm wondering when the full results are coming in about the poison."

"The mercury compound? Me, too. You don't suppose Trooper is holding back?" Chris asked.

"I hope not."

"By the way, did I hear you tell Fran you'd be back at Wright's tomorrow?"

"Not necessarily back at the diner. Just that I'd be picking my parents up at the airport tomorrow evening. They'll be coming back from San Diego."

"I don't suppose you've asked them yet what their plans are?"

"I figured I might as well wait until we're face-to-face." I squeezed my eyes shut. "Pretty lame, huh?"

"Yup. Do you want some company?"
"Company?"
"To the airport. I'd be glad to drive. Your car, of course, so you wouldn't be scrunching into a two-by-four space."
I laughed. "Another trip to Ted Stevens," I said. "We have to stop meeting this way."
"I agree."
"I was kidding," I said.
"I wasn't." He cleared his throat. "I was thinking maybe we should plan a nonworking trip sometime. Not to Ted Stevens. But" — another throat-clearing. What was up? — "How long since you've been fishing? Or kayaking? We could do something in Talkeetna. It means 'the place of three rivers,' you know. A tourist destination right in our backyard."
I knew what it meant, as did every Alaskan teen who'd been a docent and recited the phrase several times a day. "That sounds great."
Was this a date? I wasn't sure.
"We should probably hang around here until we see how it goes with Preston."
"I agree. And with Noah, too."
"Maybe the weekend will work?"
"That sounds good."
"Okay, night."
"Night."

Neither of us could hang up fast enough. That told me it was definitely a date.

I drew a deep breath, then headed to the guest bedroom, a wide smile on my face.

"Wait till you hear this, Benny," I said.

THIRTY-ONE

Tuesday morning was looking good.

While my coffee was brewing, I moved my front curtains aside and waved off Buzz, an eager young guy and the last of the civilian volunteers who'd stood watch for me during the night. He'd slipped a note, half under my door but stuck in the gasket, reporting that there had been no activity at my mailbox and no one approaching my property.

Before turning in last night, I'd made a trip outside with a few snack packs for the crew. I figured three or four of the volunteers would spell each other during the night. Their shifts were short, as well they should have been, given the pittance of compensation they received.

I wasn't due at the Bear Claw for a few hours, which would give me time to review updates to regulations and payroll taxes involving tipped employees. This was not the fun part of the business, and I always made sure I surrounded the task with the pleasurable parts of what was known as the quick dining industry, like cooking.

This morning, I planned to try a new recipe for a no-bake breakfast bar that involved peanut butter and maple syrup. If it was as easy as claimed, the bar would make a nice addition to our snack pack.

Benny trotted around the house, looking pleased with his automatic feeder, newly replenished; the fresh catnip mouse I'd unwrapped; and the assortment of toys within his reach. Plus, I'd scrolled to the laser dot app on my phone, something I'd neglected lately, and my cat got exercise chasing the little red light up and down the walls and furniture and all across the floor. I'd learned to rig the game in Benny's favor by having the dot linger on a specific item — a colored ball, for instance — and letting Benny land on it. *Success!* I'd yell for him.

For me, it was great distraction and a good finger workout.

The local news reported that a male in his early fifties had been taken in for questioning in connection with a financial crime related to the local fishing industry. The books had not yet been fully released, but allegedly, batches of fish were being rerouted in a black-market scheme to benefit the accused. I sent virtual thanks to Trooper and whatever magistrate cooperated with his request for further documentation.

I was surprised there was no mention of a lawyer trying to block the release of the company's documents. And, of course, there was no mention of a connection between the man's financial misdeeds and the murder of a young summer employee, because we informal deputies couldn't make the case. I felt like we should start from the beginning, as if we'd just met Preston, Garrett, and the rest of Ethan's buddies, including Zoe. Maybe the clue was in plain sight. I could hardly wait until all the details were filled in and someone could write CLOSED on the Ethan Johnson file.

Was it possible my good mood also had to do with two pending meet-ups with Chris Doucette? I didn't want to build up hope for anything more than a fun day kayaking or canoeing. I wouldn't tell my mom until after the fact, or she'd set up an emergency shopping trip for a new outfit, which would probably entail looking for the latest in paddling jackets and neoprene paddling booties.

In the back of my mind was always the possibility that the date might fall through.

That it might never happen, since we hadn't chosen an exact time and place. Maybe Chris had felt pressured to suggest a non-working get-together for some reason. He might have been to a seminar on teamwork, and this was a setup for work colleagues reviewing their interactions and productivity.

I blamed my experience with Ryan for my slightly paranoid and very negative attitude toward dating and relationships.

Benny, however, had been very receptive to my sharing the news with him after Chris's call. I told him I was counting on him for support whichever way things went, by which I meant if this was only a one-time event. He snuggled closer to me, the better for me to reach his back for a scratch, then retreated to his own quarters next to my bed.

On the bright side, the proposed dateless date did help lessen the dread of picking up my parents at the airport. The parents who had a big surprise, according to one of them.

Annie, who was always up before me, texted that she'd heard from Irene, who wanted to thank her for sending Noah home safely.

Uh-oh. How did that happen?

It took a few seconds, but I managed to

sound sincere when I said, "I'm glad to hear everything went well."

"I assume the story got mixed up somewhere and Noah forgot your name?"

I tried to remember if I'd ever given Noah my email address or phone number, and couldn't recall. Maybe I hadn't even identified myself by name. Our meeting didn't fit into "normal" in any way. It would be understandable if Irene assumed Annie was the nice lady who helped him escape the fishing industry in Elkview, Alaska.

"First, let me explain how this came about," I said.

"It must have been last-minute," Annie said, letting me off the hook.

What are BFFs for? Annie's friendship was prize-winning. She put me to shame as I recalled more than one occasion when I was peeved at Chris because he did something or went somewhere that had to do with an investigation we were working on and he didn't give me a heads-up. I needed to take a lesson from Annie on how not to jump to conclusions.

I gave Annie as complete a report as I could, starting with the late-night call from Noah.

"No overalls this time?" she asked.

"And no raw meat."

I ended with a request for her to taste test my new breakfast bars. She seemed willing.

Trooper called for a meeting at the station house. There was no way to tell whether this would increase or decrease the ease with which Tuesday was rolling along. Everyone else had tried a breakfast bar, which I'd packed into impromptu lunch bags. Rave reviews all around, which made me want to go home and quit while I was ahead.

The three of us had ridden together in my car, which made conversation much smoother than if Chris and I had made the drive alone. How do you chat, make small talk, when a date is pending? Shouldn't you save some topics for the date itself?

Had it been that long since I'd had such a problem?

Apparently so.

Trooper opened the meeting without chitchat. "He says he didn't do it," Trooper said, a healthy sandwich, furnished by the Bear Claw, in front of him. "The murder, I mean. Preston is opening up about siphoning off part of the catches, but says he didn't murder Ethan over it. He says he had no reason to. And I'm inclined to believe him."

"How come?" Chris asked. "It's not a case

of alibi or no alibi. The poisoning was administered over time. Isn't that what Doc Sherman said?"

"Yes, and speaking of him, we have a full report now. Or fuller, I guess you'd say. I'll do my best to explain, but I'm no chemist."

"Neither are we," Annie said. Always the comforter.

"The mercury compound was slightly different from the one that killed the famous actress years ago, which Doc initially thought might be the case."

"Olive Thomas and mercury dichloride," Chris said. When we all looked at him, he explained. "I looked it up when Trooper said Doc Sherman cited it as the possible murder weapon. Fascinating story from a hundred years ago. This really beautiful silent film actress, who married into the Pickford family, and —"

Trooper held up his palm. "Sorry I mentioned it. Maybe we can write that down and anyone interested in further details can look it up?"

Annie raised her hand, then pulled it down quickly.

"Ruled accidental," I heard Chris whisper to her.

Annie smiled and mouthed a thank-you.

"There was another, more recent, incident

— the death of a lab researcher about twenty-five years ago." Chris spoke this in fast forward, as if he had to get it out there no matter how much Trooper wanted to squash offshoots to his report. "Let me know if you want more information," Chris finished.

"As I was saying," Trooper continued, as best he could, "you'd think we'd have understood everything there is to know about mercury compounds by now, but there's still research going on." He pulled an envelope from a folio he'd carried into the meeting room and treated us again to the photos Mr. Johnson, Ethan's father, had taken surreptitiously in the J and M lab. "Our guys in Anchorage worked on these so you can read the labels better."

This time he pointed out enlargements of the bottles of mercury on the cabinet shelf. In some instances, I thought I saw tablets; in others it looked like liquid stored in small bottles.

"Doc says it was impossible to tell exactly what went on with Ethan, since he'd been sick a long time and there were not that many traces."

"In that researcher's case, it was almost a year between getting a couple of drops of the mercury compound on her rubber glove, and dying from it." Chris again, but Trooper had given up control of the situation. And, also, it seemed he'd told us all he knew.

"Now what?" Annie asked.

"Now we figure out who managed to find just the right amount of whatever was here" — he pointed to the photos of the chemicals in the J and M research wing — "to kill Ethan in such a way that we wouldn't be able to figure out exactly when and where the poison was administered."

"Didn't you say the Johnsons were not impressed at Preston's knowledge of what went on in the lab there? And they didn't think he was faking it?" I asked.

"That's what they told me," Trooper said. "And when Preston told me he didn't have the slightest idea how to use those chemicals, I was tempted to believe him. He seemed almost afraid to look at the photos, like he thought he could be killed just by being near such toxic stuff."

I added, "Also, Preston said, or implied, that there was only loose control of the chemicals, so it wouldn't have been hard to get into the lab and find the stuff and sneak it out."

"What are you getting at?" Trooper asked me.

"I'm trying to narrow down the number of things we have to figure out. If we know there was easy access to the chemicals, that's one less thing we need to worry about. I think Preston was sorry he told me that."

"What if word got out to the funding agency for the research that the safety and security measures in place were sloppy?" Chris asked.

"Exactly what I mean," Trooper said. "I'm sure the paperwork for the money included testimonials to the great safeguards put in place."

"Bottom line, Trooper," I said. "Are you saying you believe Preston is innocent of the murder?" I asked.

Trooper shrugged and blew out a breath. "Maybe. It's a gut reaction, but usually gut reactions have something behind them, and that's been coloring my thinking. I'm not drawing any firm conclusions either way right now. We have him on the money, and that's all we need to hold him here."

He stood abruptly. Didn't he always, as a sign the meeting was over? "Sorry to bring you all the way out here for this, but I'm pressed for time today. I need to get back to the training project they drafted me for. Hopefully, this is the last day I have to make that trip."

We got the message and agreed to reconvene at Aly's.

No one ever wanted to stay in the station house a minute longer than necessary.

We took a table at Aly's, where I was not surprised to see Ryan fill the doorway again. I felt my jaw tighten as I lowered my eyes to half-mast.

Ryan came to our table and stood with his hand on his hips, an unpleasant grin on his face.

"Anyone would think you liked Aly's food better than what you serve in your own diner."

I found something to be grateful for — he spoke too softly for anyone in the crowded restaurant to hear. Otherwise, I was steaming inside. Annie came to my rescue.

"Or she's just trying to hide from you."

She surprised me, and Chris, also, it seemed, although he recovered quickly with, "That's what I was thinking."

Then, not to be too serious, Chris picked up the oversize menu and held it in front of my face. Both he and Annie chuckled. Since all my emotions were being taken care of, I chose to stay quiet and enjoy the drama.

Ryan frowned. "I just came to say goodbye, which seems like a very good idea now."

He walked out.

Silence.

I wasn't sure whether to be embarrassed at what might have been labeled rudeness or grateful for the protective shield that rose up when I was challenged.

"I wonder why they're not using him for Preston's defense," Chris said, as if he couldn't have asked him a minute ago.

"They probably need someone closer to home," Annie said.

"And embezzlement cases are not Ryan's expertise," I said. "His specialty is labor law, which he's been working on for his entire career. He's done all he can here, so he's off."

"Works for me," Chris said. "Back to our case."

"I'm glad we don't have to go knee-deep in fish and catch Preston in the act of selling off batches," Chris said.

"I wonder who did," I said. "Someone had to do the hands-on work, so to speak."

"Isn't that person just as guilty?" Annie asked.

"I'm sure that will all come out from Preston as his lawyer tries to make a deal," Chris said.

At that moment, a woman at the table

next to ours returned from picking up four coffees at the counter, a common practice when the place was crowded and the wait-staff was overloaded. There was always a stack of molded pulp fiber cup carriers on the counter, mainly for to-go orders.

Annie gestured to the woman, who smiled back. "That's a good idea," she said, moving her chair back. "I'll get us fresh coffees."

"I'll go," Chris said. "I think it's my turn."

Something clicked in my brain. "That's how Ethan was poisoned," I said.

Thirty-Two

"What are you talking about?" Annie asked. She'd been about to head for the counter in Aly's to get us all fresh coffees.

I tried to remember the exact time I'd heard the key point from Garrett, but it was fuzzy. "Here's what I recall," I said, hoping to drag the details out of my brain in real time. "I was talking to Garrett about the coffee in the dorm, which was bad — stale, either too weak or burnt. He said he and his buddies took turns getting good coffee from a shop down the road. There were five of them, I think, and they rotated the job of getting up early and delivering decent morning coffees, to the bedsides, as he put it."

"So one of them could have put mercury, in whatever form, into Ethan's coffee," Chris said. "Every five days."

"Wow," Annie said.

"According to Garrett, the five are, or

were, himself, Kevin, Noah, Zoe, and Ethan," I said.

"So we eliminate Ethan, unless we think he killed himself," Chris said.

We all agreed on that point.

"It's hard for me to believe Garrett would have told me this little story about life in the dorms — and I'm pretty sure he brought it up, in the context of them all being buddies — if he used the routine to murder Ethan."

"I hope it wasn't Noah," Annie said. "And I don't think so, because why would he go and hide?"

I didn't follow Annie's reasoning, but I also didn't think Noah undertook to murder Ethan. After spending time with him yesterday, I was willing to believe he was an unwitting victim.

"Are we down to Kevin and Zoe?" Annie asked.

"Zoe has been duplicitous about several things," Chris said. "And she had at least a possible motive if he broke up with her."

"And Kevin is a bit creepy, like the time he came into the diner after hours," I said.

"What?" Annie asked.

"Never mind. What would Kevin's motive be?"

"What was he doing in the diner? Harassing you about something?" Annie asked.

"No, really," I said. "Sometimes I get creeped out when I'm by myself late at night. Kevin had gotten off a late shift and wanted food, that's all."

Now that we had the how of Ethan's murder, we parted with two pieces of homework. Who was first? Short of a coin toss, no one came to mind as definitive. And the why we probably wouldn't know until the who.

Why did I feel like I was back writing essays for English class?

I had Chris drop Annie and then himself off, and I took my Subaru back on the road to the Bear Claw.

Victor had texted me that our new slow cooker had arrived, and I wanted to show my enthusiasm and approval of Victor's initiative in requesting the appliance. When I entered the diner through the back door, close to where I'd parked my car, I got a whiff of a warm, spicy scent that was clearly a perk of putting the new equipment through its paces.

"Chili," Victor said, but I already knew. "I started it this morning, and it just gets better through the day."

"Want a taste?" Rachel asked.

I was full from snacks all morning and lunch at Aly's, but I didn't want to insult my cooks. "Of course I do."

I wasn't exaggerating when I called it a triumph. It may have sounded that way to the several tables full of customers, but that didn't keep them from ordering a cup.

Nina pointed out the multiple uses for stews, chowders, and soups. I was aware that the shiny new stainless steel pot made all our other kitchenware look shabby.

Maybe that had been the point all along.

Maybe my staff missed me being here full days with them and were trying to lure me back with upgrades. I noticed a new photo on the wall also, one of a Denali climbing group that had passed through the Bear Claw. This particular group had included a celebrity, a pop singer I supposed I should have known. I wondered which photo had been replaced. I was willing to believe it was one of Franklin Delano Roosevelt, who visited Alaska in nineteen forty-four. Yes, upgrades needed on all fronts.

I missed my diner and could hardly wait to turn in my almost-deputy papers.

Not wanting to deplete the Bear Claw's inventory, I made a grocery run, picking up staples to stock my parents' fridge. I also used up some of the ingredients to make a batch of chocolate chip cookies, which were my mom's favorite, and a batch of lemon cookies, my dad's favorite. I did the baking in their kitchen deliberately so the house would smell welcoming.

I straightened the house up a bit, fluffing pillows, running a small load of laundry so everything would be clean and ready to wear. I'd added a group of sunflowers to the groceries and arranged them now in a tall green vase for the table in the entryway.

I couldn't help feeling I was staging the house for sale. *Better get used to it,* I told myself, with a lump in my throat.

At least this time there was no parka to deal with.

It took a lot longer than I expected for me to finish with the batches of cookies. I'd inadvertently used the recipe amounts appropriate for the diner. Worse mistakes had been made in that department, and I packaged the extras for Trooper, Chris, and Annie.

I resigned myself to wearing the clothes I'd been in all day and texted Chris, who was due to pick me up for our airport run.

Running late. Pick me up at parents?

I got a thumbs-up emoji in return and settled for removing my apron and running a brush through my hair. I found a shoe-shine kit in my dad's closet and brushed the flour and sugar from my shoes.

It was a good thing this wasn't a date.

We were on track, leaving Elkview at about four thirty to meet a seven thirty flight. The trip to Ted Stevens was so routine now, we didn't need my Outback's GPS. We talked about making this trip another time and stopping to enjoy the sights on the way.

"Thunderbird Falls," Chris said. "I haven't hiked that in eons."

I hadn't hiked anywhere in eons, probably not since I lived in San Francisco, ironically. Or maybe it wasn't unusual to ignore the wonders of your hometown but not miss a sight when you were away from home.

Fortunately the hiking expedition didn't come up until we were almost at the door to the airport. I wouldn't want to have two dates-without-a-date scheduled.

Chris dropped me off at the front door of the airport nearest the main concourse. By now, we had a routine that seemed quite natural.

I found a table in Wright's Classic Diner, disappointed that Fran wouldn't be in until the late shift at seven. By then we'd be making our way to Baggage Claim to meet my parents.

When Chris arrived, I was scribbling a note to tell Fran I was sorry we missed her. I'd brought a Bear Claw place mat with me so she'd be able to see the cartoon bear I'd talked about replacing.

"I wonder how many people passing through this airport bother to make a connection with their diner server?" Chris asked.

"They all should," I said. "You know, diners go back to the nineteenth century when —"

"A guy turned a horse and wagon into what we'd now call a food truck, but in between was the stationary diner."

"Right, and there's a diner museum —"

"In Rhode Island. You've told me about it."

"Sorry. I forget not everybody is into diner history."

"No, I'd love to see that museum sometime."

We weren't going there, five thousand miles away, together, either physically or verbally, at the moment.

"We should probably head for Baggage," I said. Only about one mile away.

■ ■ ■ ■

We followed the trail of escalators and elevators to the ground floor, where we took seats in uncomfortable chairs, facing the arriving passengers. I was jittery, somewhat relieved that Chris knew why — I never had confronted my parents with my suspicion that they'd been looking for retirement living in San Diego. I kept second-guessing when I thought they'd tell me. Right away, before they claimed their luggage from the carousel? In the car on the way home? After we were settled with coffee and cookies in their Elkview home?

At one point, Chris leaned over to me and patted my arm.

"We'll know soon," he said.

"Know what?"

And we laughed.

When we heard the plane was delayed a few minutes because it had arrived early and, therefore, had to wait for an open runway, we laughed again.

Finally, the plane landed and we started to see passengers dribble in. My dad was almost as tall as I was, so it was easy to spot him. Mom, being about the height of an eighth grader, though not me as an eighth grader, was hidden as usual among other adults.

Excited hugs all around as the travelers told us about turbulence, horrible coffee, and no peanuts since someone was allergic.

Chris moved himself to the edge of the carousel armed with descriptions of the luggage he was looking for. Mom suggested he get a cart, even though it seemed like not a lot of bags for four people to carry to the car. Mom stood back, giving a thumbs-up to Chris when he pointed, with a questioning look, to a familiar roll-on.

"Where'd Dad go?" I asked, unaware that he'd disappeared right after our initial hug.

"He'll be here. He had to collect something from the special luggage area."

I laughed. "What did you buy now? Vintage diner stools? I hope not a slow cooker, because we have a brand-new one. In fact, Victor made —"

Mom interrupted with an elaborate wave of her arm. Something was more interesting than slow cookers.

"Here he is. He's carrying Midway."

Chris had hurried forward to relieve my dad of his package. Thus, he was the first to get it. "You mean you named that puppy after the USS *Midway*?"

"Surprise!" Dad said, holding up a carrier

of a different kind with the cutest puppy I'd ever seen. "Told you," he whispered to me. "Hope I didn't give it away."

If Mom thought I was overreacting to the puppy, she didn't mention it. How could she know I was comparing surprises. The "We have a puppy!" surprise weighed against the "We bought a house thousands of miles away from our only daughter!" surprise.

Midway was almost all we talked about on the way home. He was a Chihuahua, only ten weeks old, mostly white but with adorable brown and black markings. Dad had always wanted a puppy, and now that Eggs Benedict was established and happy in a new home, Dad's wish could be indulged.

"The Russells have just adopted a Jack Russell terrier, of course, and named him Junior. He has the same general coloring as Midway here." Dad tapped the carrier and looked at me. "Did I ever tell you your grandfather served on the USS *Midway* after she was commissioned in forty-five?"

"Once or twice," I said.

"That would be nineteen forty-five," Mom said.

I'd had little more than a peek at Midway since we didn't want to wake him up.

"Poor guy had to go in the cargo hold

because someone was allergic," Dad said.

Mom shrugged. "Peanuts. Pets. I guess people are allergic to all kinds of things."

"Why didn't they send the guy to cargo?" my dad asked, and I knew he'd lost it over this little dog. "But one thing for sure," he continued. "Midway here isn't getting on a plane ever again."

"That's the best thing I've heard all day," I said.

Only Chris laughed, barely able to keep his hands on the wheel.

Thirty-Three

We women were stronger than the men in terms of our ability to stay up late chatting, especially since there were endless cookies. So what if none made it to the Bear Claw tomorrow morning?

Chris's pickup was at my parents' house, so he took off soon after accepting a bag of half chocolate chip, half lemon. My dad pleaded jet lag, though we tried to convince him he'd actually gained an hour.

"He just wants to play with Midway," Mom said. "Your father is nuts over this puppy. Do you believe he went to a dog-treat-making class at the rec center in San Diego? I'm happy for him."

"So am I."

I looked around the kitchen I'd grown up in, stumbling out to breakfast before school, Mom letting me help her bake for school functions, and so many birthday parties around this same table. I was glad it wasn't all going away too soon.

I'd thought of taking Mom to visit Benny at my house, but figured one pet was enough for tonight. And since she wasn't moving to Southern California, there was no rush.

"Now, I want to hear all about the case you've been working on." Mom was back on duty, refilling our mugs of coffee and adding a notepad and pen to the table decor.

I did my best to cover all the who, what, where, when, and why of Ethan Johnson's unfortunate demise.

"All that remains is to figure out who did it, and you're down to only three suspects?" she asked.

"Maybe four, if we're wrong in eliminating Louis Preston, the human resources manager for J and M. Or maybe a few billion if we think a random citizen of earth wandered by and chose Ethan as his target for murder."

"Hmm." My mom tapped her pen against the palm of her hand, meaning she was thinking hard.

She'd already said she was sorry to have been away and unable to join Trooper's special deputy force. She told me she was also considering sending a sympathy note to the Johnsons in Boston, but I managed to talk her out of it, at least for the rest of this century.

"What are you thinking now?" I asked.

"Hmm," she said again.

It was hardly possible for my mom to know who killed Ethan. She didn't know anyone involved, except Ryan, and even I didn't think my ex was capable of murder. Well, maybe I did, a little, but he'd been nowhere near Alaska when it all went down.

"I'm thinking of this last mystery I read on the plane and how the detective solved the murder."

"Mom, you don't seriously think —"

"Hear me out, sweetie. You would do well to read a few of them if you're going to keep serving on Trooper's team."

"Okay. I'm listening," I said. *What do I have to lose?* crossed my mind.

"You find a way to get all the suspects together. It's going to be easy with only three or four. And you let it slip that there's evidence somewhere, say at that research laboratory or somewhere guaranteed to be empty after hours, and the evidence is going to be taken to the station house the next day. And you lie in wait. Not you, of course. The cops. And you see who comes to pick it up." She spread her palms in an easy-peasy gesture.

"What kind of evidence?" Not that I was going to do anything about it.

"It could be specific, like you could say you found fingerprints. Or, if you're not sure there would be fingerprints anywhere, you could make it general, like 'a key piece of evidence was found.' "

"I have to wonder — would a real killer fall for such a ploy?"

"You know what they say. If criminals were smart, there wouldn't be any jails. Or something."

When such a smart saying was followed by a long, loud yawn from Mom, I knew it was time for me to go. I knew Trooper would be pushing hard, now that he'd told the Johnsons he was close to finding their son's killer. I wouldn't have been surprised if he called another meeting in the morning to see if there had been any progress. I didn't relish the idea of another early morning at the station house.

There was only so far a batch of cookies could go.

I kissed both parents good night and drove home. I skipped kissing Midway for the time being.

A dog could take only so many Cookes at once.

THIRTY-FOUR

I couldn't get Mom's idea out of my head. Probably because there was no other idea competing with it. I thought of my team, whether I should call them and see if they considered the ploy a viable one. But it was late and none of those three had been drinking coffee and downing sugar for the last hour.

I pulled up to my house, sorry in a way there was no patrol car out front. I climbed the steps, and as I approached my door, I noticed a piece of paper half inside and half outside, stuck under the gasket. A fairly regular occurrence. Someone tries to shove a flyer or pamphlet into my house and they're stopped by the strip of rubber at the bottom of the door. I entered the foyer expecting to see a flyer for pizza or an offer from a realtor to sell my house.

Best would be a notice of the Fourth of July celebration along Main Street, which was always fun. I'd already planned to donate mini bear claws to the cause.

Worst would be what I saw once I got inside and closed the door. Benny sitting on a target practice sheet depicting a human shape.

My heart did a flip as I dropped my tote and scooped Benny up, as if any minute I'd hear a gunshot and a hole would appear in the black paper. The white rings around the torso had been clawed by Benny, but otherwise there were no markings.

I dug out my phone and texted for a volunteer to come and check things out, but I was sure the threat was over. My alarm system had been armed and, most certain of all, Benny wouldn't be sitting there calmly if a stranger were in the house. He'd be hiding. I considered taking him and retreating to my car, but the would-be intruder was as likely outside as inside, and I chose to stay in with Benny until help arrived.

When did I become such a wimp? I could tell myself it was understandable after two threatening notes and a potential prowler wandering my property. But I didn't like the role of victim.

Benny cooperated and let me carry him around. I tried to breathe as normally as possible as I walked casually around. He seemed calm as I returned to the family room.

I picked up an old book on cat-friendly homes and went through the photos now, with Benny on my lap. I couldn't tell which if any appealed to him, but one that caught my eye was a family room/living room combo that stretched across an entire wall of the home. At each end was a stairway, with short steps and short risers, floor to ceiling. Connecting the stairways at the top was a ledge, giving new meaning to the word "catwalk."

"Maybe someday, Benny," I said. "For now, please listen. I might be about to do something stupid."

Instead of running for cover, my cat stayed with me, ready as needed.

What if I took things into my own hands? What if, instead of waiting for the next arrogant note from a killer, the next person casing my home — what if instead of that, I went on the offensive?

A sensible option would be to follow Mom's advice and gather the suspects with all of the team present. Chris could pretend to be writing a feature article and let it slip that we had evidence. But did I really want

Chris to save me, to restore my peace of mind?

Or I could simply wait it out — take Chris up on his offer to stay here at night until the case was solved. Or have Trooper's crew sit in a car in my driveway all night. Or both.

But enough of that.

I needed to be proactive. I was the one to whom they wrote the LAY OFF note. I was the one whose property was invaded. And now I was the recipient of a target practice sheet.

I thought of writing notes to each of the suspects to test Mom's trick. I wouldn't have to sign it, any more than LAY OFF or this nasty torso paper was signed. I could just wait for a reaction.

I tried to picture the barracks where Kevin and Garrett lived. I assumed Zoe's in the women's quarters had a similar layout. There had to be a way for them to get mail. There was no lobby, as such, on the inside of the males' housing, only the few pieces of tile that marked a barebones kitchenette of sorts with a coffee station and a vending machine where I'd talked to Garrett. I pictured the thin carpeting that was under the row of beds.

The outside was equally minimal, with no shrubbery that I remembered. There was a wooden stand, however, with the address of the residence in crude white paint. Were there also mail slots? I had to take a chance that there was at least one.

By the time Buzz and Fergie, two of my regulars, arrived at my house, I'd crafted my notes. I'd gone back and forth with options, from I'M NO QUITTER to SAME TO YOU, BUDDY, both of which gave me a laugh, but were not my intention. I settled on WE HAVE THE EVIDENCE IN A COFFEE CUP, SAFELY LOCKED UP UNTIL LAB PEOPLE COLLECT IT, typed in a large font. I was going out on a limb thinking that the mercury killer hadn't found it necessary to collect the used paper cups. Who would think of protecting those?

I made copies of the note and waited for the patrol car.

"Does Trooper know about this?" Buzz asked me, signing in.

I shook my head in a way that could be interpreted as "of course" or the truth — "no."

"I'll be out for about forty-five minutes. Benny's inside."

Buzz saluted. "Okay, we're on it."

"Me, too," I said.

It was easier than I thought.

Darkness had set in. I parked in a stand of birches on the side of the road and walked in toward the dorms, dressed appropriately in black jeans and black windbreaker, my light brown hair tucked into a black cap. The wooden sign turned out to be on top of a cabinet-like box with a large slot labeled MAIL and another one, larger, labeled NEWSPAPERS.

I had to rethink my strategy. If I put all three envelopes, labeled GARRETT, KEVIN, and ZOE, each one would know that the others had also been targeted and brush off the accusation.

I didn't have time to waste, so I chose KEVIN and walked away.

It was hard not to second-guess what I'd just done. But I focused on getting home to Benny and sleeping well while Buzz and Fergie kept watch.

Or, more likely, I'd get a start on the mini bear claws for the holiday and knead out my stress while I waited for the mail to be delivered.

THIRTY-FIVE

For me, cooking and baking were the perfect answer for relieving stress. This late at night, real food was not appealing, so I got out an old recipe book I hadn't used in a while and found one for cinnamon roll cookies that might be good for the Fourth of July fair. I'd have to make the sacrifice and do a taste test.

Benny was milling around as usual, hoping for some scraps. Nothing was appealing, so he walked back to where there were many choices for a comfy place to curl up.

When the doorbell rang, I thought it might be Buzz or Fergie needing to use the facilities. I looked outside and saw their car still there. It was too dark to see which one had left, which one was at my door. I opened it.

My blood froze.

"Kevin?" I tried to sound casually surprised, maybe pleased, even. "What are you doing here?" *And how did you get past my guards?*

He grabbed me in an embrace and whispered close to my ear. "Wave to the goons down there in the car, smile, and move inside quickly. I'm your new boyfriend."

I started to object, to scream, but the hard object poking my ribs stopped me. Kevin moved my arm in a wave as if I were his puppet. He was taller than me, and a whole lot stronger. I remembered thinking *NFL* the first time I saw him. He closed the door behind him, and I heard the patrol car start up.

My long "No" was muffled, falling on Kevin's fishy-smelling hand.

Kevin took his hand off my mouth. I stepped back and saw that his other hand held a gun, and that gun was pointed at me.

"No use screaming now," he said with a sneer. "No one will hear you. Did you think you could just goad me with that note and I wouldn't respond?"

Somehow, I found my voice and croaked out, "How did you —"

"You really need to hire some better goons to protect you. Dumb and Dumber out there were too easy. I just told them, wink, wink, I'd be taking over for the rest of the night." He waved the gun around as if it were a cheerleader's baton. "Oh, to be fair, I did have to show them ID, which I happened to have. Tomorrow, when they find your body, they'll be looking for one Arthur Mitchell."

Kevin pushed me onto the rocker where I'd been reading to Benny. I thought if I ever came out of this alive, I'd have to wash the pillows and anything else he'd touched.

Kevin's laugh was what you would expect from someone who'd already killed once. That we were aware of. I knew I should be talking to him, using psychology the way people on TV dramas did when they were held at gunpoint. But the words were stuck in my throat. I focused on looking for something I could use as a weapon. The only things within reach were Benny's napping blanket and the book I'd been reading to him. What was that saying about bringing a knife to a gun fight? If I lived, I'd create a new one about bringing a book and a blanket.

"I've been watching you," he said. "I knew you were trouble. I'm surprised you haven't been following me, in fact, instead of the other way around. In case, you know, you got too close to figuring things out. Which you did."

Kevin paced, talking to himself as much

as to me. "It was going so well until Ethan got it in his head that we were doing something wrong."

"If you weren't, you could have just explained to Trooper, and —"

"Turned ourselves in? Right."

Apparently, I was destined to have my sentences cut short. Like Kevin intended to cut my life short.

"It was a sweet deal," Kevin continued. "Ethan and I were just the messengers, delivering the extra fish a few nights a week. We got paid for our time, that's all. Maybe a little bonus now and then from poor Louis, who's now going to take the fall for Ethan's murder. We weren't becoming millionaires. We weren't hurting anyone."

All crime hurts someone, I thought. I didn't share my insight, however. I was too busy trying to figure a way out of this mess. Kevin hadn't tied me up, but his pacing in front of me left no room for me to jump up and run away, not even to the next room, much less out of the house. Besides, I would never leave Benny.

Benny!

Where was he? He'd left before Kevin arrived, and I hadn't seen him since.

In a minute I knew exactly where he was.

I heard a marching band coming by way

of my bedroom. An early Fourth of July medley of John Philip Sousa songs with "Semper Fidelis" just ending, and "The Stars and Stripes Forever" beginning. I'd never heard them played so loud, and they were never so welcome.

The music threw Kevin completely off-balance.

I propelled myself out of the rocker and launched my body at Kevin with a loud yell. His eyes widened and his mouth gaped in surprise. His gun hand jerked down, and I knocked the weapon out of his grasp.

Benny came running out, either pleased with himself for hitting those clock radio buttons or scared by the high volume.

I was so glad I hadn't been able to train him out of that old clock radio habit.

As Kevin went for the gun, I grabbed Benny's oversize blanket, threw it over Kevin, momentarily blinding him, and kicked the gun as far as I could toward the door. I grabbed Benny and ran toward the door, picking up the gun on the way out.

"So sorry, Benny," I panted as he struggled. "I know you don't like to be outside, but this is necessary and I'll make it up to you."

In less than a minute I was down the steps and into my car with the doors locked, texting everyone I knew to show up, starting with Trooper.

Kevin came roaring out the door. He pounded on my windshield. I hit the horn and kept my left hand on it and held the gun with my right. He didn't have to know that I had no idea how to shoot. I did know enough to point the weapon straight at him.

Kevin had ridden his bike. What luck. I drove forward, pinning him and his bike to my fence until I heard the siren and saw the patrol car, Benny howling in my ear.

If Benny wondered later in the evening why he was being given extra love, he didn't show it.

THIRTY-SIX

It was the perfect day for a picnic, and who knew how to do a picnic better than the Bear Claw staff? My dad thought we should wait until the Fourth, but everyone else voted for now, some with arm pumps that left no doubt.

The vote was unanimous also that we have the event on the deck at my house, in spite of the plethora of parks in our neighborhood. We all felt that Benny, the hero of the day, should be there celebrating with us, even if a lot of the food was unappetizing to him. I made sure he had his own buffet in his usual kitchen dining area.

For the rest of us, Victor and his staff outdid themselves, using my stovetop to grill mushrooms, corn on the cob, eggplant slices, and marinated chicken.

Chris and Annie had come early to help set up.

"Before I forget," Chris said, handing me

a package. "You can look at them later. I just didn't want to forget to give them to you."

I tucked them in my tote, empty now of all the snack packs and extra cookies.

With Sousa marches in the background, partygoers took turns apologizing to me.

Mom went first, because it was her idea, she said, to put the trick to lure out the killer into play. I reminded her that it was my own spin on it that got me into trouble, and I assured her that her mayo-less pasta salad made up for possible bad advice.

Chris was sorry he was so selfish, just too tired to offer to stay over. Not his job, I reminded him.

Trooper apologized for Buzz and Fergie. "They never should have let Kevin go up those steps. They should have either turned him away or walked to the door with him."

"They couldn't know his ID was fake or that he was a suspect," I responded.

"What about Noah?" Annie asked, ever vigilant for Irene, one of her many guests, even if she hardly knew her. Annie's perpetual care and attention were part of the inn's service, whether you liked it or not.

Trooper knew the answer to this one. "Kevin claims he didn't know Ethan had confided in Noah, so all Noah's running and hiding turned out to be unnecessary."

I had thought eventually it would have come out that Noah was privy to the scheme and he would also have been a target.

Trooper also reported that Louis Preston's fate was still unclear, though the murder charge was no longer an issue.

Garrett and Zoe accepted my invitation and asked that we have a toast to the memory of Ethan Johnson. We were happy to arrange it, along with a moment of silence to honor his absence.

I couldn't have asked for a nicer day, and the night had its own pleasant surprise.

Just before I turned out the light, I reached down to the tote leaning against my night table. I opened the package from Chris. Papers fell out all over my quilt. A dozen or more flyers and newspaper clippings with information and reviews of driving highlights between Talkeetna and Anchorage.

Benny was thrilled, stepping on them over and over, enjoying the crunching sounds.

When I could extract one or two pieces from under Benny's paws, I noticed Chris had circled dates and hours of operation for events and activities.

I smiled.

We now had a date date.

BEAR CLAW DINER FAVORITE RECIPES

SPICY ELK JERKY

Preparation

3 lbs lean meat (partially frozen is easier to cut)

Cut strips to desired size (aim for about 1/4-inch thick; about 3/4-inch wide)

Count on 5 or 6 servings per pound.

Marinade

1/2 cup soy sauce

1/4 cup sesame-seed oil

2 T Worcestershire sauce

1 tsp brown sugar

1 tsp onion powder

1 tsp cayenne pepper

1 tsp crushed red pepper

Directions

Place all marinade ingredients in a bowl and whisk until combined.

Place meat and marinade in sealed bag and chill in refrigerator at least 8 hours.

Stir occasionally.

Place in dehydrator on jerky setting for about 8 hours.

Cool before storing.

Or

Place the strips on a baking sheet lined with foil and place in oven at 200°F. With the oven door propped open, let the strips dry for 5 to 7 hours until they are pliable.

Salmon Patties

Ingredients

1/2 red or yellow bell pepper, diced
4 T olive oil, divided
3 T butter, divided
1 lb boneless cooked salmon, flaked
black pepper to taste
1 cup plain or seasoned bread crumbs
2 eggs, lightly beaten
3 T mayonnaise
1/4 cup fresh parsley, minced

Directions

Sauté bell pepper with half the olive oil and half the butter.

In large bowl, combine salmon, sautéed

bell pepper mixture, and all other ingredients.

Mix well and form patties: about 1 heaping tablespoon each, molded into 1/2-inch patties.

In a skillet, heat the other half of the olive oil and butter.

Add to skillet salmon patties in a single layer.

Sauté 3 to 4 minutes per side or until golden brown and heated through.

Remove finished patties to a paper towel–lined plate and repeat with remaining salmon cakes.

Makes 12 to 14 patties.

THE FOUR-DOG DEFENSE (FROM CHAPTER 24)

A Classic Legal Strategy!

SAY YOU'RE THE OWNER OF A DOG THAT'S BEEN ACCUSED OF BITING SOMEONE. YOU DENY IT USING THE FOUR-DOG DEFENSE:

First of all, I don't have a dog.

And if I had a dog, it doesn't bite.

And if I had a dog and it did bite, it didn't bite you.

And if I had a dog and it did bite, and it bit you, then you provoked the dog.

Clear?

ACKNOWLEDGMENTS

Thanks as always to my critiquers: Gail Abbate, Sara Bly, Nannette Rundle Carroll, Ann Parker, Sue Stephenson, and Karen Streich. They are ideally knowledgeable, thorough, and supportive.

A special word of thanks to friends who also provided advice and photos throughout the project: Alaska resident Kris Hutchin; Nina Balassone, Ann Damaschino, Heather Haven, Ellen Kirschman, Nancy Kors, Susan Lawson, Jo Mele, Gail Meyers, Judith Overmier, Lyn Roberts, Priscilla Royal, and Sheryl Ruzek.

Special thanks also to expert ice climber and frequent Talkeetna visitor William McConachie, who showered me with information and outstanding photographs of the Last Frontier. Thanks to professional embalmer Robert Durkin, and retired Inspector Chris Lux for expert advice.

My deep gratitude goes to my husband,

Dick Rufer. I can't imagine working without his support. He's my dedicated webmaster (www.minichino.com) and personal on-call IT department.

Thanks to my agent, Lois Winston, for her hard work and welcome attention, and to the copyeditors, artists, and staff at Berkley Prime Crime for all their work on my behalf.

Finally, my gratitude to Jennifer Snyder, my dedicated, talented, and my newest Berkley editor, and to all the Berkley Prime Crime staff. I hope we have many projects together!

ABOUT THE AUTHOR

Elizabeth Logan is the pseudonym for a long time mystery writer who has published series with Berkley and Minotaur. The first book in her Alaskan Diner Mystery series was *Mousse and Murder.*

The employees of Thorndike Press hope you have enjoyed this Large Print book. All our Thorndike, Wheeler, and Kennebec Large Print titles are designed for easy reading, and all our books are made to last. Other Thorndike Press Large Print books are available at your library, through selected bookstores, or directly from us.

For information about titles, please call:
(800) 223-1244

or visit our website at:
gale.com/thorndike

To share your comments, please write:

Publisher
Thorndike Press
10 Water St., Suite 310
Waterville, ME 04901